"I would never do anything to hurt you," Caleb said softly.

"If I hadn't pulled away, something might have happened that would be all wrong. I can't want you!" But Megan did want him, right or wrong. "You can't care for me!"

"I already do."

"No! We're enemies!"

"You know we aren't. The war doesn't have anything to do with us. Or with how we feel." Tears glazed Megan's eyes and he wanted to hold her and kiss them away.

"I can't love you," she whispered. Then she pulled away and hurried from the room.

For a moment Caleb stood there. He slowly lowered himself back onto the bed, his leg hurting like demons were playing in it. Love? Until she had said the word it hadn't occurred to him. Now it refused to leave his mind. Love. He was falling in love with her—the one woman in the world he couldn't have...!

Dear Reader,

The award-winning author of close to three dozen books that range from mainstream to contemporary and historical romance, Lynda Trent has written another stirring tale with this month's *The Fire Within*. Don't miss this story of a young woman whose plan to trade a wounded Union captain for her Confederate fiancé is threatened when she falls in love with her prisoner.

In her third historical for Harlequin, *Man of the Mist*, Elizabeth Mayne tells the heartwarming story of childhood sweethearts who, as adults, must unravel their feelings of hurt and betrayal and learn to accept that their love was meant to be.

Our other titles include a new Medieval from Margaret Moore, *The Norman's Heart,* the delightful story of a staid nobleman and his willful bride. And *Birdie*, by Taylor Ryan, the Regency Era story of a young woman who must battle countless odds on her journey to happiness.

Whatever your taste in reading, we hope Harlequin Historicals will keep you coming back for more. Please keep a lookout for all four titles, available wherever books are sold.

Sincerely,

Tracy Farrell
Senior Editor

Please address questions and book requests to:
Harlequin Reader Service
U.S.: 3010 Walden Ave., P.O. Box 1325, Buffalo, NY 14269
Canadian: P.O. Box 609, Fort Erie, Ont. L2A 5X3

LYNDA TRENT

The FIRE WITHIN

Harlequin Books

TORONTO • NEW YORK • LONDON
AMSTERDAM • PARIS • SYDNEY • HAMBURG
STOCKHOLM • ATHENS • TOKYO • MILAN
MADRID • WARSAW • BUDAPEST • AUCKLAND

ISBN 0-373-28914-6

THE FIRE WITHIN

Books by Lynda Trent

Harlequin Historicals

Heaven's Embrace #59
The Black Hawk #75
Rachel #119
Beloved Wife #154
Thornbeck #232
The Fire Within #314

Harlequin Books

Historical Christmas Stories 1991
"Christmas Yet to Come"

LYNDA TRENT

started writing romances at the insistence of a friend, but it was her husband who provided moral support whenever her resolve flagged. Now husband and wife are both full-time writers of contemporary and historical novels, and despite the ups and downs of this demanding career, they love every—well, *almost* every—minute of it. The author is always glad to hear from her readers.

To Clark and Sharon and love everlasting

Chapter One

Caleb Morgan leaned close to his horse's neck as the animal reared and plunged. His long sword gleamed in the sunlight, red streaks running from its tip. He was exhausted from the battle but he couldn't sound retreat. Not when there was still a chance they could defeat the Rebels. His dark blue uniform was stained with gunpowder and enemies' blood, and his horse was lathered with sweat.

With a shout, Caleb encouraged his men to greater effort. As their captain he had their loyalty and their respect. He never sent a man into territory too dangerous for him to go as well. Caleb turned the horse into the fight and kicked him into a charge. The horse had seen many battles and plunged forward, his ears flattened viciously. When it came to a heated battle, this mount was priceless.

All around him Caleb saw men, some in blue, others in gray or butternut, slashing at one another and shouting in pain or battle fury. In the midst of a battle, they looked curiously the same. The acrid odor of gunpowder filled Caleb's nose and he shoved his sword at the nearest Rebel. It made contact and the man shouted as he grabbed at the wound on his arm. Caleb took him down with the next thrust.

His horse reared again, pawing at a man who had run too close. The animal liked battle more than Caleb did. In quieter times Caleb wondered if the animal would ever be docile again—assuming the cursed war would ever end. At times it seemed as if the fighting and ceaseless marching would go on forever. To a man like Caleb who loved his home and family, it was as if hell had broken out on earth. Caleb was gentle by nature and a soldier by necessity. He was good at both.

"Captain Morgan! The flag!" a voice shouted beside him.

Caleb looked up to see the flag bearer stagger and fall. He spurred his horse forward and caught the flag before it could hit the ground. He wouldn't allow the enemy to capture it. His men shouted approval and one grabbed at the wooden pole. Caleb released it and went back into the thick of the battle.

He had no idea how long he fought. He was beyond tired. His arms and legs were numb from exhaustion and his breath came in short gasps. Suddenly he felt his horse tremble and stumble. He looked down to see a wound gaping in the animal's shoulder. The horse tried to lunge, but Caleb could tell he was finished. He looked up to see a Rebel soldier aiming another shot at him. Although the horse tried to dodge at his command, Caleb felt the thud of the bullet into his own leg. At first there was no pain and he watched the spreading blood as if it had nothing to do with him.

A Rebel ran toward him, sword raised and Caleb slashed at him, but not before the enemy's blade sank into his arm. Caleb shouted in anger as much as in pain. The bullet wound started throbbing at the same time. Caleb reeled in the saddle, marveling that his horse was still on his feet and that he was in the saddle. A curious lightness was making his head spin. Caleb shook it to clear it, this was no time for weakness.

"Captain! Should I sound retreat?" The bugler was a young boy. Too young in Caleb's opinion.

"Sound retreat!" he commanded. The day was lost. He wondered why he couldn't hear the sound of the bugle as the boy put it to his mouth. A glance at his leg told him he was losing blood fast, but somehow it didn't seem to matter to him. "Retreat!" he shouted to his men. He reined his horse aside to let the men pass before him.

At the edge of the woods his horse stumbled again and Caleb knew he would never be able to carry him to safety. He roared his anger at losing such a precious fighting mate. He had no love for this particular animal, but he respected his strength of heart. Another bullet sang past his ear and he felt the horse stagger. He was shot again.

The animal traveled several yards into the woods, then fell heavily to one side. Caleb felt himself falling with the horse, but it was as if it were happening to someone else. In slow motion, the floor of the forest came to meet him and he tasted dry leaves. Then nothing.

The autumn air felt crisp on Megan's face as she bent to hoe up the last of the year's potatoes. Her garden was small but filled most of the level space between her house and the slope of the mountain. She had spent all her life in Black Hollow, Tennessee and she felt as much a part of the tan earth as were the potatoes she was digging for the root cellar.

Far in the distance she heard the sound of a rifle, then another. Megan straightened and listened. It was too late in the day for her father to be hunting. Besides, he rarely took two shots to bring down game. As she listened, several more shots rang out. These seemed closer than the others. The next were closer still. Megan gathered the potatoes into her apron and ran toward the house.

For four years the Civil War had raged. Her mountain had been taken first by one side, then by the other, back and forth. It all meant little to Megan as long as she and the ones she loved were safe.

She closed the door behind her and crossed the room to put the potatoes on the table. Even with the shutters closed she could hear the sounds of the battle. It was taking place in the clearing where her father had shot the bear the summer before. That was too close for safety. Megan went around her small cabin, barring the shutters and doors with the iron straps her brother-in-law had made for the purpose.

The cabin was dim with the door and windows closed but she didn't waste lamp oil by making a light. Oil was too precious, as was everything else, to be used by day.

She sat in the rocker Seth's uncle had made for a wedding gift and rocked slowly. The chair's rockers were slightly uneven so its gait was jerky and it edged across the floor if she rocked for long. Still, it was a rocking chair and it was her own so she didn't mind. The Brennans had never been much at making furniture.

The cabin was snug and strong. Anything less than a direct strike from a cannonball would bounce off its sides. She told herself that as she listened to the battle, the sounds muffled now by the thick logs. Her father had made the cabin, and Samuel Llewellyn was thorough in everything he did. Once he set his mind to a thing, he didn't rest until it was accomplished.

At times like this, Megan disliked being up here in her cabin and away from the rest of her family and the small settlement nearer the bottom of Black Hollow. It wasn't a town and likely never would be. They built their own cabins and the furniture to go in them and planted the food they needed. Patrick Cassidy knew enough about blacksmith work to keep the horses and mules in good shape, but that was as far as they were willing to go. If Black Hollow became a town, strangers would eventually move there, and no one in the settlement welcomed change.

The last stranger to move to Black Hollow had been Megan's mother, Jane. She had come there as Samuel's bride, her language still filled with the lilt from her native Ireland. Bridget had taken her bright red hair from Mama's side of the family. In Megan and Owen it was a darker red, like mahogany.

Samuel had met Jane, courted her and won her during one of his brief visits to his cousins who lived in Oak Ridge. That had been more than twenty-two years ago. Megan knew because her older brother, Owen, was twenty-one and he had been born within a year of their marriage. For a forbidden moment she thought about Owen and wondered if he was well. Since Papa had disowned him, Owen wasn't to be discussed or even thought of.

Next had come her own birth when Owen was two, then two years later, their sister Bridget. Bridget was a duplicate of their mother and their father's favorite, just as Owen had been their mother's. No one had favored Megan, but she understood why. She was much too outspoken and rebellious to suit the settlement. The only boy who ever showed interest in her was Seth Brennan.

She sighed and wondered when Seth would come home. He was impetuous. That was the word her father used, at least. In her opinion, he was simply bullheaded. More than a year ago, Seth had drunk too much whiskey from the still at the bottom of the Hollow and had enlisted in the Confederate army. Unlike Owen, he had chosen the side the settlement favored, but he had chosen to do this the week before they were to be married. Megan had spent the next few months being angry, but her temper had had ample time to cool and now she was just lonely.

Samuel had built the cabin in a pretty spot up the mountain from the others, on the only place flat enough to build one. In some ways Megan enjoyed the privacy. Or at least she did when army troops weren't passing by or fighting in the clearings. The cabin's remote location gave her a chance to do the one thing that her family disapproved of most— read.

Books were Megan's passion, and she had loved them ever since one of her aunts had taught her to read. It had been during a hard winter when there was nothing else to do. Her aunt had meant to teach only Owen, but Megan and Bridget learned as well, by looking over Owen's shoulder and borrowing his book. Bridget rarely read anything but Megan read everything she could find. When she had a rare bit of money of her own, she would walk to the nearest town, Raintree, and buy a book.

Since she moved to the cabin, she had brought her books out of their hiding place in the barn and had hidden them in the cabin. Seth was no fonder of her reading than was her father, so she didn't plan to let him know she was still doing it.

That Megan had moved into the cabin at all had been a matter of convenience. It was expected that the war would end soon, and it had been time to put in the garden that would see her and Seth through their first winter together. The cabin was remote enough from her parents' house for it to be inconvenient for Megan to live at home and walk there. Besides, her parents' house was crowded with two grown daughters, and it was time for Megan to move on.

Bridget was married now. When Patrick heard Seth had enlisted, he signed up, as well. Before he left, he married Bridget. They had been in love ever since they were children so it was no surprise to anyone, nor was it a question of ensuring that Bridget would wait for him. Bridget was like their mother—once she fell in love, she would follow her man, even to a place like Black Hollow, and be faithful forever.

Although she never told anyone, Megan was disappointed that Seth hadn't loved her enough to marry her before he went away. Especially since they had made love one night in the clearing where the battle was now being fought. For several long, agonizing weeks Megan had prayed she wasn't pregnant from her lapse of discretion. Fortunately she hadn't been and no one knew what she and Seth had done. But Seth knew and he hadn't married her before he left. That was one reason Megan had been so angry over his rash enlistment. Their wedding had been set for the following week! Why had he chosen to leave at a time like that?

There was no use wondering about it, Megan told herself. Seth did as he pleased, when he pleased. Usually this didn't bother her and it was unreasonable to mind it one time and not another. At least this was what she told herself during the long, dark nights when she was alone in the cabin with only the calls of night birds for company. At least now she could read or draw when she pleased, for there was no one to hide it from.

Megan also loved to draw. No one had taught her: it came as naturally to her as breathing. With a sliver of charcoal from the hearth she could draw an owl or a raccoon that looked real. Brother Benjamin Grady, the man who was Black Hollow's self-styled preacher, disliked her drawing even more than he did her reading. He maintained it wasn't natural to draw a thing on paper, that it wasn't much different from making graven images, which was clearly against God's law. But drawing didn't feel wrong to Megan so she simply hid that, too.

She closed her eyes and tried to block out the sound of the battle by remembering what Seth's voice sounded like. Lately that had been difficult, though she would never have admitted it.

The sounds of battle had lasted for hours. Megan stopped rocking as the reports from the guns moved farther down the mountain. She could tell one side had overpowered the other. It didn't really matter to her which had won. Unlike her family, she wasn't a staunch supporter of either side. The issues that had caused the war didn't touch her. Tariffs and central banking had no part in Black Hollow, and Megan had never seen a slave in her life.

She cautiously opened the door and stepped out onto the porch. She could still hear the guns but they were too far away now to be accompanied by the soldiers' shouts or the shriek of the horses. Once again her cabin had been spared.

Megan went inside and got the knife she used for dressing out meat and as many tow sacks as she owned. Horse meat wasn't something she enjoyed, but she had learned to eat almost anything. There were too many soldiers and stragglers on the road to keep food safe. Her smokehouse had been emptied only the week before when she was visiting her family, and she wasn't eager to spend the winter without meat on the table.

She made her way through the familiar woods, stopping every few feet and listening to be certain the soldiers weren't doubling back. When soldiers were around, the only safe place was indoors with the door firmly bolted and barred.

Soon she was in the clearing. Megan stopped and stared at the once familiar meadow. Horses' hooves had churned the late grasses into the dirt and there was blood everywhere. Horses lay dead on the ground, their saddles still strapped to their backs. There were no men. While part of the conquering troop chased the retreating one down the mountain, the rest of the soldiers had stayed behind to gather the dead and wounded of both sides into wagons and haul them to their headquarters.

The silence was menacing. Megan stepped farther into the clearing and for a moment wondered if she was in the place she remembered. Could this be where she had played as a child and where she had given herself to Seth just before he joined the army? It was no longer a peaceful woodland meadow, but a place of death and destruction. She knew she would never enjoy coming here again.

Eager to do what she had come to do and be away from the place, Megan went to the nearest horse. Kneeling on the ground, she began the task of dressing it out for her smoke-house.

As she worked, she heard a sound. Megan froze, her eyes darting about. Were the soldiers coming back?

The sound came again. She stared into the woods, trying to pierce the shadows and saplings to see who was there. It was no animal sound, but rather that of a man. Apparently he was in pain.

Holding the knife close to her side as Owen had once taught her, she went nearer. Every time she heard the moan she paused, deciding whether to go on or to flee. Not too far inside the woods she saw the body of a horse. A man lay beside it.

As quietly as she could, Megan went closer. He had been thrown clear when the horse fell. Judging by the sluggish way he moved, he had been unconscious when the other dead and wounded were taken away and no one had found him. She edged nearer. She could tell by his uniform he was an officer. His right leg and left arm were covered in blood. If it was all his, it was a miracle he was alive at all, let alone able to move and call out.

Megan lost her fear as she went to him. He was young and handsome with black hair that was matted to his head with sweat. His skin was pale from loss of blood. He wore a Yankee uniform, but so did her brother, Owen.

She knelt beside him. "Lie still. Let me see how badly you're hurt."

He tried to focus on her face but the effort was too much for him. "My men . . ." he said in a hoarse voice.

"Your men are gone. They left you behind." She looked around, wondering what to do with him. He might be the enemy, but he was also a human and she couldn't leave him to die. "You sure picked a bad place to get wounded. I don't know if I can get you to the house or not." She was speaking as much to herself as to him. She pulled his leg straight and examined the worst of the wounds. "You might recover with some help."

He tried to sit up but fell back.

"Stop moving around before you bleed to death." She took her skinning knife and slit his pant leg so she could tie one of the tow sacks around the wound. She made it as tight as she could to stop the bleeding. Then she did the same to his arm.

"Can you hear me?" she asked. He was so pale and so still she wasn't sure he was conscious. He nodded. "I'm going to try to get you to my cabin but you're too big for me to carry so you're going to have to help me."

This time when he struggled to sit up, she pulled him upright. The bandages seemed to be holding against the loss of any more blood. She braced herself and pulled him to his feet. Before he could fall, she slipped his good arm around her neck and balanced him. "Can you walk? It's not too far. Just past these woods."

Leaning heavily on her, he managed to limp at her side. "Too bad they didn't leave me a short, skinny man," she complained good-naturedly to boost his spirits. She wasn't tall and he towered over her by several inches. If he were standing straight, she didn't think the top of her head would reach past his shoulder. Most of the other men in the Hollow were short or medium in height, including Seth, and this man seemed huge in comparison.

Her determination was finally paying off. Like her father, Megan was too stubborn to give up once she decided to get the soldier safely into her cabin. By the time they went up the sloping grade and across her small yard, she was breathing heavily and aching from supporting his weight. "Steps," she gasped. "You have to go up three steps now."

He doggedly lifted his feet. She held to him firmly. They had come this far; she wasn't going to drop him now. She kicked the door open with the toe of her shoe and took him into the house. He hesitated and blinked, as if he was only now aware of his surroundings.

"Don't stop now. We have a few more feet to go." She took him into the tiny bedroom she was to have shared with Seth and let him drop onto the bed. Thank goodness she had covered it with an old quilt. She went to the trunk where she kept her outdoor slicker and carried it to the bed. After some pulling and prodding she managed to get it between him and the quilt.

"Now let me see what you have wrong with you," she said in the gentling voice she used with hurt animals. She peeled off his uniform and tossed it into the corner. His chest was thick with muscles but his waist was lean. Under his pants he wore white cotton underlinen, now soaked with blood. She cut it away above the wound and studied it for a moment. "Gunshot," she informed him. Gently she reached beneath his leg. "Thank goodness it went all the way through. I wouldn't want to have to dig for it."

She examined the long cut on his upper left arm. "Must have been a sword. That's my guess. It looks too long for a knife wound as hard as you must have been fighting." He gave no sign of having heard her at all, but she was talking as much for herself as for him. "You know? I think you really might live after all." Until now she hadn't been all that sure.

Going to the pump in the kitchen, she drew water in a pail, then went back to him. "I need to get you cleaned up. I've seen small cuts go bad if they're not tended properly. I guess large ones would be worse." She dipped a soft rag into the water and began to sponge the wound. "At least you've stopped bleeding."

She glanced at his face. His eyes were closed and he seemed to be unconscious again. "It seems to me they should have looked harder for you since you're the captain. I guess that means your side lost. My family would be glad about that. Papa is about as Confederate as they come."

She paused. "Papa. What on earth am I going to tell my papa?" She went back to cleaning battle grime from the soldier. "I just won't tell him," she said to assure the wounded man as much as herself. She just hoped Mama or Bridget didn't decide to pay her a visit any time soon.

As she washed him, she couldn't help but notice how well built he was. Even relaxed, his muscles were strong and firm, and his hands were large and capable. There was a virility about him that reminded her of the pumas that occasionally wandered near the settlement. He might be equally dangerous. Megan wondered if her father would shoot a man in his condition, and decided it wasn't worth taking a chance. After working this hard to save him, she wasn't going to lose him now.

After hesitating, she cut off the other leg of his underlinen. Short pants on such a large man looked odd, but she couldn't get him clean with them on and she was reluctant to cut them off completely. She tore up a sheet to make fresh bandages and went into the kitchen to make a poultice of herbs to place on the wounds. Then she bandaged him again. By shoving and pulling, she managed to get the soiled slicker out from under him. The quilt hadn't fared badly so she left him lying on it and pulled another one over him.

"I'll be back," she said in case he could hear her. "I have some butchering to do."

Although she was already tired, she went back to the clearing and finished the job she had gone there to do. She beat her family to the scene by minutes.

"I was hoping you'd know to come get some meat," Jane Llewellyn called from one of the other carcasses. "This will taste just like beef once it's cured."

"Not to me it won't. I hate doing this." Megan wondered what her mother would say if she had any idea what she had been doing only minutes before.

"We won," Bridget said as she helped Jane with the horse. "Papa saw the Yankees running for all they were worth and our boys chasing after them. I wonder if Patrick was one of them."

"If our Patrick, or Seth for that matter, were within a mile of here, he'd come see us all," Jane said. "He's likely in the next state."

"I sure hope he's safe." Bridget looked over at the stained grass. "You think he's safe, Megan?"

"Sure he is. We would have heard if he wasn't." Megan tried to sound positive for her sister's benefit. There was no one to send word to her prisoner's family that he was alive. It was odd to think she had a Yankee prisoner at her house. At the time she hadn't thought of it that way.

"Be sure and wash this meat before you hang it up to dry," Jane reminded Megan. "It's not like butchering a hog where we hang it off the ground to dress it out. You can't keep it clean like this."

"I know, Mama." She glanced around the clearing. Some of the other women from the settlement were arriving and gathering meat for themselves. Megan hoped they would be able to get enough to feed them through the winter. "Once mine is fully smoked, I'm going to hide it in the woods. I'm not taking any chances on losing this, too."

"Those Yankees will take anything," Bridget said angrily. "Can you imagine our soldiers stealing from people that don't have enough to eat as it is? They wouldn't ever!"

Megan wasn't sure this was true so she didn't comment. She had been hungry often since the war started and she didn't think a soldier would be all that particular if there was food for the taking. Bridget just couldn't bear to think Patrick would do such a thing. And, knowing Patrick as well as she did, Megan wasn't sure that he would. Patrick was as good a man as the Hollow had ever produced.

"Hurry and get through, Bridget. The soldiers might come back and we don't want trouble from them."

"They're long gone from here," Megan said quickly. "There's no reason for them to come back." She wondered if that was true. She didn't know all that much about soldiers, but wouldn't someone come looking for a missing officer? But, she reasoned, their side wouldn't know he was missing and the other would assume he had been killed or captured. Maybe no one would come looking for him at all.

When she had all her tow sacks full, Megan started carrying them to the smokehouse. On each trip the grade seemed steeper. The other women had finished, by the time she made the last trip, and a few of their husbands or sons had come to help them carry the bounty home.

As her mother had taught her, Megan washed the meat, then packed it in salt. Fortunately they still had salt in the settlement. She had heard of a family beyond Raintree that ran out of salt and had to scoop dirt off the smokehouse floor to pack around the meat. The dirt had salt in it from other curings but she couldn't see how the meat would ever lose its gritty flavor.

She hung the meat onto the iron hooks that were suspended from the ceiling, then brought some hickory wood from the woodpile. Taking care not to make the fire too large, she started one burning in the pit in the center of the tall building. Stepping out into the fresh air, she saw the room fill with silver smoke, then she shut the door and latched it against marauding animals.

When she went into the house, she stripped off her clothes and bathed by the cabinet. Putting on a wrapper, she went in to see about the soldier.

He lay just as she had left him, but she could see the gentle rise and fall of his chest. He wasn't dead. Every hour he lived through put him that much closer to his recovery, assuming the wounds didn't turn septic. His skin was hot to the touch so Megan got a bowl of water and a cloth and sponged his forehead. A fever wasn't unlikely in such a situation and she wasn't worried. All the same, she sponged him until he was cool to her touch.

She sat in the ladder-back chair and studied him. He was a big man and almost filled the bed. What would he be like when he awoke? It suddenly occurred to her that she was quite isolated from the others and that he might be dangerous if he wasn't unconscious. She shook her head in her own answer. He had lost too much blood. It would be a while before he would give anyone much trouble.

After a while she went into the kitchen and lit a lamp. The glow filled the cabin and turned the log walls to warm gold. She started a fire in the fireplace and soon the chill was gone. Since she had left the bedroom door open, she knew the man would be warm enough even if he kicked off the cover. The cabin wasn't that large.

Megan frowned slightly. The cabin wasn't large at all. Where was she going to sleep? The soldier was on the only bed. She went to the back room and opened the door. It was used to store the things she didn't need every day. The mattress from Seth's bedroom was tied into a roll in one corner. He had brought it to the cabin before he knew her family was stuffing them a mattress as a wedding gift. His family hadn't needed it back so it was still here.

Going to it, Megan hauled it into the middle of the room and untied the cords that bound it. The mattress unrolled at her feet. The ticking was stained from rain that had blown in Seth's window years before and it was old, but it was a bed of sorts. Certainly it would be more comfortable than the floor.

Megan got her gown from the hook in the bedroom and took it to the back room. Closing the door, she put on the gown and blew out the lamp before opening the door and sitting on the mattress. Unconscious or not, she didn't trust the soldier and she kept her skinning knife close beside her. She pulled one of the extra quilts onto the mattress and listened to see if the soldier was stirring. There was no sound.

She unpinned her hair and let it tumble around her as she sat there in the gloom. Still listening, she braided it into a thick dark-red plait before lying on the bed.

From the main room, the fireplace sent dancing light over the walls and floors. This was the first time since she had moved here that Megan hadn't slept alone in the cabin. She wished it were Seth in the next room and not some stranger. Although she tried not to worry about Seth, she couldn't help but worry at night when she had nothing else to occupy her mind. Was he safe? It was probably too much to hope that he was warm and comfortable. She had seen too many tattered Confederate uniforms to believe Seth's was in better shape. Living outside was too hard on clothes.

At least she had a smokehouse full of meat. She gazed up at the shadowy rafters above her and planned where to hide it once it was cured.

Chapter Two

Megan knew it was important to keep her prisoner clean if he were to heal without complications. Why this was so, she couldn't have said, but she had observed from cuts and scrapes she had received herself that cleanliness was important. If it was true for an everyday scrape, it should be doubly true for bullet and sword wounds.

She took a pan of hot water into the bedroom and stared down at the man. She had never in her life seen a naked man. The night she and Seth had made love in the clearing hardly counted, since the moon had given no light to speak of and he had kept his unbuttoned shirt on the entire time. She stepped nearer the soldier. She had to do what was necessary.

Not giving herself time to think, Megan pulled the covers back and sat on the side of the bed. He looked powerful even in repose and he was more handsome than she remembered from the day before. A day's growth of beard darkened his jaw but did nothing to impair his looks. His hair was black and thick. She remembered his eyes had been a silvery gray.

Megan drew in a deep breath to give herself courage and bent to cut the underlinen down the side seams. Once they were washed, she could resew them, but she wasn't sure how she would manage to put them back on him. As she pulled the cloth away, she couldn't help but look at him. He was beautifully made, like the Greek statues she had seen in books. As she looked, he stirred and she hurriedly dipped the cloth in the wash water.

She washed him as well as she could without moving him. Beneath her fingers his skin was warm and supple, his muscles strong. She had also never seen a man with tanned skin all the way to his waist. Her father and the other men in the settlement never removed their shirts outside so only their hands and faces tanned. The brown of his skin for some reason made the man seem even more virile. She found herself imagining him chopping wood without his shirt, his muscles bunching and releasing. The thought made her blush and she tried to put it out of her mind. She wasn't entirely successful.

Carefully, she removed the soiled bandages and dropped them on the floor with the underlinen. After they were boiled clean, she could use them again. She was glad to see neither of the wounds bled, though the edges were puffed and reddened. Was that normal in a severe wound? There was no one she dared to ask.

After she had cleaned the wounds as well as she could, she put fresh bandages on them, tied them into place and covered him with the quilt. To her surprise, she found her hands shaking. He affected her more than she thought possible. There was an element of danger about him even as he lay unconscious. She wondered what would happen when he finally woke up.

Megan lifted her head. Someone was coming. She could hear them running through the brush and into the yard. Hastily she left the room, pulling the door shut behind her. By the time she reached the main room, Bridget had run into the cabin and stopped in the middle of the room. She was out of breath and the freckles stood out on her pale skin. Her bright red hair was in a tangle all about her face.

Megan glanced at the door to her bedroom. It was closed and the soldier still hadn't gained consciousness. Nevertheless, she ushered Bridget back onto the porch. "What's wrong? Is Papa having one of those spells with his heart?"

Her sister shook her head. "It's Seth!"

"Seth is at the settlement? He's home?" Megan was a bit surprised that the news didn't lift her spirits any more than it did. "I'll get my shawl."

"No, no, Megan. Listen to me for a minute." Bridget put her hand on Megan's arm to stop her. "It's a letter, not Seth in person. He's in a Yankee prison."

Megan's heart plummeted. "A prison?"

"He was captured last month. The letter only arrived today. He's not injured or sick. Just scared."

Megan sat on the ladder-back chair on the porch. A cold wind was blowing but she didn't feel it. "Seth has always been afraid of being locked up. Remember how he was that time he was locked up in Raintree for getting drunk and breaking the chairs in that saloon? He hates being locked up." Now that the news was sinking in, she was near tears.

"I think you should come to the house with me. Seth's parents are there and you can read the letter yourself."

"Yes. I'll do that. Let me get my shawl." She left Bridget on the porch and ran back inside.

In the bedroom she frowned at the soldier lying on her bed. It wasn't fair that he was being carefully tended and doctored and Seth was in some prison. It made no difference that Seth wasn't wounded or sick. She had heard about Yankee prisons and they were infamous for brutality and bad living conditions. She tried not to think about that. Throwing her heavy wool shawl about her shoulders, she hurried back to Bridget.

They ran most of the way to the settlement and were out of breath when they entered the house. The old, familiar smells enveloped Megan. Jane's house always smelled of cooking and the strong lye soap she made every summer.

The main room was crowded with the Brennans there. As usual, Aaron Brennan was pacing furiously and Sarah Ann Brennan sat stoically silent.

"Those damn Yankees have my oldest boy," Aaron was saying in a loud voice. "There's no telling what they're doing to him."

"Now don't get so riled up," Samuel Llewellyn said in a calming voice. "We don't know Seth is being mistreated. He doesn't say anything about it in his letter."

"Those Yankees are capable of anything! Anything at all!"

Sarah Ann bent her head and sobbed as silently as possible. Jane went to her and put her arm around the woman. Sarah Ann leaned her head on Jane's shoulder. Megan knew that the woman would get no comforting from her husband. It was well-known around the settlement that Aaron wasn't kind to her. Megan also went to the crying woman and touched her other shoulder. Sarah Ann looked up, her small eyes red and swollen already. She patted Megan's hand with the pudgy fist that held her soggy handkerchief.

"May I see the letter?" Megan asked. Aaron handed it to her with only a glance in her direction. He had always maintained that girls shouldn't be allowed to read.

Megan managed to interpret Seth's scrawling hand. He had never learned to spell properly but she could make out the words. "He's being held just outside Corbin in Kentucky. Where is that?"

"It's in the southern part, not far from the state line." Samuel was watching her. "I'm real sorry, Megan."

She managed a weak smile. "At least he's out of the fighting. Had you thought of that, Mrs. Brennan? Seth can't get shot in a prison."

Sarah Ann looked up at her hopefully and the cane-bottomed chair creaked as she shifted her weight to sit straighter. "That's true, ain't it? He won't be in no more battles if he's fastened up in prison. I hadn't thought of that."

Aaron continued pacing, though there was barely enough room to move about. "We got to get him out!"

"Now be reasonable, Aaron. How are we supposed to get Seth out of a Yankee prison in Kentucky? Neither one of us even knows how to get there."

"We could ask along the way. We know it's north of here."

Megan became thoughtful. They couldn't hope to break him out of prison, but couldn't they trade for him? Trade a Union captain, for instance?

"I wish I had me a Yankee here now," Aaron growled. "I'd kill him before he knew which end was up."

"So would I," Samuel said. "They're no good, the lot of them. Shoot first and ask questions later, that's what I'd do."

"Had you thought that our Seth is safer in prison?" Sarah Ann asked, still clinging to her only hope. "Had you, Aaron?"

"Shut up and let me think." Aaron stomped to the other side of the room and Bridget shifted out of his way.

"Seth *is* safer in prison, ain't he, Jane?" Sarah Ann persisted.

Jane glanced at Megan. "Yes, I'm sure he is."

Megan looked across the room at Bridget. Her sister stood in the shadows, twisting her narrow gold wedding band. She knew Bridget was worrying about Patrick. Bridget worried about him almost constantly, even when there wasn't bad news pertaining to the war. Their eyes met and Megan said, "Patrick's all right."

Bridget nodded but her eyes still looked haunted. Megan knew what she was thinking. If this could happen to Seth, it could happen to Patrick, and if Seth had been captured in battle that meant Patrick had been fighting, too. He could be dead or wounded and word just hadn't reached them yet.

"Patrick ain't got nothing to do with this!" Aaron said angrily to Megan. "This here's about your man! You'd think you'd at least shed a tear for him!"

"She's never cried easy," Jane said quickly. "You know that, Aaron. Megan almost never cries."

"I'm as worried about him as you are," Megan told Aaron. "You have all had time to think about it, and it's still sinking in to me."

"I can't leave my oldest to rot in some stinking Yankee prison," Aaron repeated to Samuel.

Megan opened her mouth to tell them about the Yankee captain at her house, but she remembered what both men had said about shooting a Yankee on sight. Even if they didn't shoot him, they certainly wouldn't let her give him any degree of comfort or medicine. In the settlement, they lived by an eye for an eye. If the soldier wasn't tended, he might die and she wouldn't have any bargaining power. Megan kept quiet.

For the next hour the Brennans sat in the close quarters of the Llewellyn cabin and poured out their anger and grief. Sarah Ann cried until her eyes were mere slits in the puffiness of her face, and Aaron roared until he was hoarse. As word spread through the settlement, others came to offer their sympathy or righteous anger. Brother Grady, along with his mousy wife, Elvira, and their herd of children, arrived with a plate of steaming food for Sarah Ann and Aaron's supper, as though Seth were dead and not merely imprisoned. Sarah Ann accepted it gratefully.

As soon as she gracefully could, Megan escaped to the peace and quiet of her own cabin. She was glad it was up the mountain and less accessible to the others. She had her own way of grieving and it didn't involve a public display of tears.

For a long time she sat in the main room of her house, rocking in the uneven chair and thinking what this could mean. It was common knowledge that sickness ran rampant in prisons and that the food the men ate was no better than slop. Seth might never get out. The war had been expected to be of short duration, but it had already lasted four years and could go on until there were no men left to fight. She couldn't depend on it ending quickly and Seth being released.

Her eyes drifted toward the closed door to her bedroom. She heard a small sound in there, as if the soldier were regaining consciousness. He would be her best bet for getting Seth back. Wouldn't the Union army prefer to have one of their officers back than keep a Confederate private who would rather be home instead of fighting? Surely by now all the fight had gone out of Seth. It took whiskey to make him really cantankerous.

She heard the sound again. She stood and crossed the room to get the squirrel gun she kept behind the door in case of intruders. She was going to nurse the soldier back to health, no matter what it took.

When Caleb opened his eyes, he was looking at the barrel of a shotgun. He blinked, trying to make sense of it. A glance told him he was lying in a strange cabin. Holding the gun unwaveringly was one of the prettiest women he had seen since leaving Pollard's Crossing, Ohio.

"How do you feel?" she asked, not lowering the gun.

"I hurt like... I hurt." Caleb had been brought up from birth not to use strong language in front of ladies and he automatically censored what he had been about to say. "Where am I?"

"You're in my cabin, Mr...."

"My name is Captain Caleb Morgan." Speaking made him hurt from head to toe. "Who are you?"

"I'm Megan Llewellyn." She lifted her chin defiantly. "Where do you hurt worse?"

"Everywhere. Could you put that gun down? I'm not going anywhere."

She lowered the barrel. He tried to focus his eyes in spite of the pain. She was a small woman, not much taller than the rifle she carried. The light coming from the only window gave red highlights to her dark hair, and her skin was milky white. Her brown eyes glared at him as if she had a personal vendetta against him. Under different circumstances he would have found her extremely attractive.

Caleb lifted the quilt and looked down. He was naked under the covers and there were bandages on his right thigh and upper left arm. Reflexively he pulled the quilt up to cover himself. She didn't seem to care that he was showing more skin than was decent. "How did I get here?" He was having trouble remembering what happened before he lost consciousness. Hadn't he been in a battle?

"I brought you. You were shot in the leg and there's a cut on your arm. I guess they didn't find you when they came after the dead and wounded. You were in the woods by your horse."

"Surely you didn't carry me here all by yourself."

"Yes, I did. You helped some."

"I don't remember it at all." He tried to shift to a more comfortable position and she quickly raised the rifle again. "Will you calm down? I couldn't hurt you if I wanted to." He pulled himself up to a half-sitting position, ignoring the pain that racked him. "Where's your husband?"

"I'm not married."

"Your parents, then. Surely you don't live here alone."

"Yes, I do. My parents and sister live downhill from here in the settlement."

"Why would you live here all alone, as young as you are? Are you a widow?"

"I was promised to marry Seth Brennan, but he enlisted before the wedding. I'm living here to take care of our house until he comes home."

"I see." Caleb couldn't have cared less about these details; he only wanted to put her at her ease so she would stop pointing the rifle at him. At this range, she would kill him with one shot.

"No, sir, I don't believe you do. Seth was captured and is in a Yankee prison. I plan to trade you for him and get him back."

"I see."

"Stop saying that. I figure they would rather have you back than keep Seth. You're a captain and he's just a private."

"That makes sense. Could you put that rifle away before it goes off? There won't be much to trade if you pull that trigger." He touched the bandage on his arm. "How badly am I wounded?"

"Bad enough to be unconscious since yesterday. Don't pull on that bandage."

"I don't suppose this settlement of yours has a doctor, does it?"

"No, we take care of our own. I know how to make poultices and change bandages. Just don't try running away. You wouldn't get far on that leg."

"I'm not in the mood to run anywhere. Where is my uniform?"

"I've got it soaking. You can't wear it like it is. And I hid your boots so you may as well decide to stay put."

"Why would I want to leave? You've already said that you'll trade me for your fiancé." He watched her carefully. If he could get her to let her guard down, he might be able to escape. His boots wouldn't be that hard to find in a cabin no larger than this one must be. As for his uniform being wet, he had worn it wet every time it rained.

"I guess that makes sense." She put her head to one side as if she were trying to decide if she should believe him. "Are you hungry?"

He nodded. He wasn't, but he knew he would need to get his strength back if he was going to escape.

"I'll be back after I fix you something to eat." She turned and left the room.

Caleb waited until she was out of sight, then tried to swing his legs out of bed. Pain shot through him and he suppressed a groan. Carefully he pushed the quilt aside and probed the bandage on his leg. He was hurt more than he had thought. There was no way he could walk on his leg. He couldn't even get out of bed. He refused to think that the bullet might have shattered the bone. If it had, he might never walk again. He lay back and closed his eyes.

Megan put the rifle in easy reach against the cabinet and reached in the water where the uniform was soaking. It was heavy and almost black in the water. She held it up to drain, then squeezed as much water as she could from the fabric. Did Seth have such a warm coat? She tried not to think about that.

When she had it as dry as possible, she took the uniform to the fire and hung it over the rocker to dry. She didn't dare risk putting it on the line outside. To ensure it would dry quickly, she added another log to the fire. Although she had no intention of returning the uniform to him until he was well enough to travel, she couldn't risk having Bridget or her mother come in and see it drying.

While she waited, she washed the long underlinen and bandages, then put the bandages in a pot to boil by the fire. She hung the underlinen on the chair with the uniform.

"Miss Llewellyn?" Caleb called from the other room.

"What is it?"

"Who won the battle?"

"I'd say we did. Mama said your side was in retreat when they were seen going down the mountain. I couldn't tell from what I saw in the clearing. There was nothing left but dead horses."

"Did you say my horse was dead?"

Megan went to the bedroom door. "If you were riding a big bay with a blaze face, he was. There was such a horse lying beside you. You're lucky he didn't pin you underneath him. I might not have been able to get you out."

"I probably owe you my life. Thank you."

Her eyes met his and she found it difficult to turn away. His silvery eyes were hypnotic and seemed able to look into her soul. "You're welcome. I would have done as much for your horse, but he was already dead."

"Thanks," he said wryly.

"I didn't mean it like that. I only meant that I love animals and would have taken care of him. Were you fond of him?"

"Not very. He was a good animal, but I didn't have him that long."

Megan leaned against the doorjamb and folded her arms. "That just goes to show how different we are. I could love an animal at first sight. Especially if it was one I considered to be a 'good animal.'"

"You learn not to be attached to horses in a war. I've had several shot out from under me. I stayed detached on purpose."

"Can you do that? Remain detached? I've never learned how to turn my feelings on and off like that." She knew she was goading him, turning his own words against him, but she was upset. "You take Seth, for instance. He's fond of drink, and if the truth were told, of loose women as well. But I don't stop loving him. I can't. If I could, I might be less human."

"Or you might be simply discerning. Why do you want to marry a man who drinks and runs after loose women?"

Megan frowned and straightened. "I don't know why I told you that. I don't want you talking about Seth." His words echoed thoughts she had had in the past. More than once she had wondered why she loved Seth. Could it be merely habit? Or the fact that no other man in the settlement cared about her? "Get some rest," she said sharply, and left the room.

Caleb didn't close his eyes. She had a number of weaknesses. He was certain to be able to use one of them to escape. He had no intention of remaining here until she got around to trading him, even if such a thing were feasible. She was too quick at pointing a gun at him. What if she got word that Seth had died or escaped? She might shoot him just to be rid of him.

He looked around the room. It was small and the chinking between the logs seemed new. The floor was made of broad pine planks instead of dirt or split logs, so someone had gone to a great deal of effort to build it for her. What had she said? It was meant to be the house she and Seth would share. He wondered if Seth had built it himself. It was unusual for a new cabin to have more than one room. Rooms were usually added later as children arrived. In many cabins the children just slept in the loft until they were grown and had places of their own. For a cabin, this was quite grand.

It was also clean. After living in tents or on the open ground for the past four years, Caleb didn't take cleanliness for granted. Once the war was over, he planned to bathe three times a day.

Megan's clothing hung on pegs in one corner. There were three changes of dress, an everyday poke bonnet, a Sunday bonnet, a lightweight shawl. Beneath was a pair of polished black shoes with a pair of white cotton stockings rolled neatly in them.

Caleb turned his head and studied the wall beside him. Unlike the outer walls, this one was of pine planking. A drawing of a raccoon beside a stream was nailed to it. The drawing was unusually good and he wondered who had done it.

A color caught his eye and he reached into the crack between the bed and wall and brought out a red book. Beneath it was a green one. Caleb was educated, as were his mother and sister, but he knew it wasn't common to find mountain women who could read enough to enjoy a book. "Is this yours?" he called out.

"What now?" Megan came back to the doorway. When she saw the books in his hand, she froze.

"These books. Are you reading them?" He read the titles. "*The Mysteries of Udolpho*? You're reading Mrs. Radcliffe? And this other one is on Greek mythology. Are they yours?"

"Give them to me." She came to the bed and held out her hand. He noticed she was trembling.

Slowly he handed them over. "I've read both. Are you enjoying them?"

She glared at him. "There's no need for you to tease me, Captain Morgan. I assure you I can read—probably as well as you can. And yes, I *am* enjoying them."

"I wasn't trying to make you angry."

Megan turned on him, her books tucked protectively under her arm. "Why should I believe anything you say? I wasn't born yesterday. I know men don't like to know women can read. That's why I hid them. How was I to know you'd come along and end up in my bed?" She realized what she had said and blushed.

Caleb smiled at her choice of words. "Can't we talk like civilized people? We've found a common ground. We both read and we apparently like the same books. Have you read the others by Mrs. Radcliffe?"

Megan came a step nearer although her movements were reluctant. "Has she written others?"

"Three others. My favorite is *Mysteries of Udolpho* but I also enjoyed *The Romance of the Forest*."

"I've read *Udolpho* three times. I bought it because it was the thickest one on the shelf." She looked away. "I shouldn't be telling you all this. You're my prisoner. I couldn't care less what books you read, or if you read at all."

"Why were you hiding them?"

"That's none of your business!" She turned and stalked from the room.

Caleb watched her go. In spite of himself he was intrigued by her. He had never known anyone to be so defensive about reading a book. Who had forbidden her to read? It was obvious someone had. Why else would she be hiding them in her own house? Caleb's family were all voracious readers and he couldn't imagine his sister reading in secret or hiding a book. Most of the girls he had known in Pollard's Crossing read to some extent, some more than others. It wouldn't have occurred to any of them to defend their right to read.

He moved his body lower in the bed. She was a mystery, his jailer. Under different circumstances, he would have enjoyed solving that mystery a great deal. Now, he only wanted to get out of here and either join his regiment or be sent home.

Home. It was like thinking of heaven. The war hadn't reached Pollard's Crossing, according to his parents' letters, so it would be waiting for him just as he left it. He was determined to survive this hell of a war and go back home again. Just now survival meant rest. He could smell Megan cooking food in the other room and his stomach rumbled expectantly. He had to get his strength back and heal quickly so he could be on his way.

Chapter Three

Caleb watched as Megan sat on the side of the bed and started untying the bandage on his arm. She was trying to ignore the fact he was looking at her. "Tell me about yourself," he said.

She glanced at him in surprise. "There's nothing more to tell. You already know I'm promised to Seth Brennan and that I'm going to use you to get him back."

"There's more to you than that. Have you lived in the settlement all your life?"

"Of course. I was born there. So were my brother and sister."

"You didn't mention a brother yesterday. I gather he's off fighting on the Confederate side?"

For a long time she was silent. "We don't talk about Owen. And no, he's fighting for the North." She closed her mouth as if she had said too much.

Caleb was intrigued. "He's on my side? Then why are your parents Confederate?"

"When Owen joined up Papa disowned him. As far as the settlement is concerned, Owen is dead."

His voice softened. "Are those tears in your eyes?"

"No." She turned away abruptly and reached for the pan of clean water.

"I can do this for myself," he said.

"I don't want to take a chance on you pulling the wound open. You've lost too much blood as it is." She gently washed the wound clean and put another bandage around it.

Caleb automatically caught the quilt as she tried to pull it away. Her dark eyes met his. "I have to keep you clean. As for modesty, I've seen you already."

Caleb surrendered the quilt. When she removed the bandage, he caught his breath at the pain. This wound was far more severe than the one on his arm. For a moment his senses reeled as if he were about to pass out.

"You're still weak," she said. "That's why I'm doing this for you." She kept the covers over as much of him as possible as she probed the swollen flesh circling the wound. "This one doesn't look so good."

He raised himself on his elbows and looked. Again his head spun. "Is the bullet still in it?" He dreaded her answer. If it was, she would have to cut it out.

She shook her head. "The bullet went clean through. I don't think it even nicked the bone, at least not as far as I can tell. I had hoped it would mend as quickly as the other one. Of course it's still fresh. It's too soon to know if it's going bad."

Caleb had seen many wounds and he knew this one could be a problem. He had also seen too many amputations in field hospitals. "Promise me something. Don't cut off my leg. If it goes bad, I might pass out and not know what you're doing. Promise me."

"I don't plan to cut off your leg, Captain Morgan. I wouldn't know the first thing about how to do that."

"Neither do most army doctors. If I'm going to die, I'd rather do it with all my parts intact. Promise me."

Her eyes met his. "I promise."

He lay back with relief. "During the first part of the war I was assigned to oversee the wounded and be certain they received medical treatment. I saw things in the hospital tent that will give me nightmares for the rest of my life."

Megan lifted his leg enough to slide the fresh bandage beneath and tied it into place. Caleb bit back his pain. "I know that hurts," she said, "but we have to keep it clean or it will go bad."

"How do you know that?"

"I don't know it for sure, but cleanliness can't hurt. When I cut myself, it seems to heal quicker if I keep the place clean."

"I know some army doctors who should take lessons from you." He tried to shift himself into a more comfortable position. There wasn't one.

"Besides, I want you to heal fast so I can get Seth back sooner."

"Tell me about him."

"Why do you want to know?"

"You don't seem eager to talk about yourself and I'm trying to have a conversation." Caleb needed to know all he could find out about his captor if he was going to escape.

"There's not much to say about him, either. We grew up together. Everybody has assumed all my life that we would marry."

"Is that why you're marrying him?"

"Of course not. I love him." She frowned slightly, as if she were considering the question. "What about you? Are you married?" She ducked her head. "I was thinking that if you are, I could get word to her somehow that you're alive. I'd want someone to do the same for me."

"No, I'm not married."

She looked at him with her level gaze. "Why not?"

He smiled at her straightforwardness. "I never met a woman I wanted to talk to all my life."

Megan put her head to one side. "That's a funny way to put it. Talking is really important to you, isn't it?"

"Isn't it to you?"

"The men in my family rarely talk to their wives and daughters. They talk to each other, I guess, but only about crops and hunting. Things like that. What would you have to tell a woman that would take the rest of your life to say?"

"That I love her, for one thing. I wouldn't marry her unless I did and that's something that needs to be said often, assuming it's true."

Megan frowned and let her hands drop into her lap. "I never in my life heard Papa tell Mama he loves her."

"Most likely that takes place at night when they're alone."

She laughed. "You never lived in a cabin, did you? There's not much privacy." She caught herself and stood. "I have things to do."

"I like talking to you. Can't they wait?"

She went to the door, the soiled bandages soaking in the pan of water. "I'm not used to talking so much. I have work to do." She paused as if she were considering coming back into the room, then left, pulling the door shut behind her.

Caleb lay back on the pillows. She intrigued him. Certainly she was nothing like anyone he had ever known before. "Doesn't Seth talk to you?" he called out.

She opened the door again. She had already put the bandages to soak in clean water and was drying her hands. "What?"

"I said, doesn't Seth talk to you?"

"He talks to me when he has something to say. What sort of a question is that?"

"But does he talk just to hear what you think or feel?"

Megan laughed, then saw that he was serious. "Captain Morgan, we have a lot more work to do here in Black Hollow than you seem to realize. We don't have time to stand around talking about nothing in particular. Who would wash the clothes and mend the fences and repair the shutters if we spent the day in conversation?"

"It seems to me Seth would want to know about your thoughts and feelings if he's in love with you."

"Seth loves me," she said with a stubborn lift of her chin. "You don't even know him. Why would you ask such a thing?"

"You don't seem to be accustomed to talking to a man."

"Maybe it's just that I don't want to talk to the enemy. Have you thought about that, Captain Morgan?" she retorted.

"Call me Caleb. It seems only right since I'm sleeping in your bed." A thought suddenly struck him. "There is another bed, isn't there? For you?"

"I'm quite comfortable in the back room on a pallet."

"I'm sorry. I thought you had two bedrooms—with beds."

Megan gave him an exasperated look. "Does this look like a palace to you? I have one good feather bed and you're on it. When I have children and they grow old enough to need a bed, Mama and I will stuff another ticking. Until then, it would just go to waste."

"Why didn't you put me on the pallet instead of in here?"

"I guess I just didn't have time to think about it. You were hurt so bad and this was the closest bed."

"But you left me on it, even after I started getting better."

"Captain Morgan..."

"Caleb."

"If you want to sleep on the floor, I'd be glad to oblige. But right now, I have a wash to do and a fire to tend in the smokehouse. I can't stand around here all day and do nothing but talk." She turned and pulled the door firmly shut behind her.

Caleb sighed and opened *The Mysteries of Udolpho*. He started on the first page. The familiar words greeted him. His convalescence would be long if there was no one willing to talk to him. Until now he had never realized how much he enjoyed conversation. "On the pleasant banks of the Garonne, in the province of Gascony..." he began reading.

"Here are your things," Megan said, holding out a handful of the objects Caleb had carried in his pocket. There was a pocket watch, the money left from his last pay-check, a locket. "She's very pretty." Megan had the grace to blush. "I looked inside. Normally I wouldn't have pried, but under the circumstances..."

"If I can share your bed, you can examine the content of my pockets. I think she's beautiful."

"Is she your intended?"

"No, she's my sister."

Megan found herself smiling. "Your sister?"

"Her name is Felicity, but that's a contradiction. She's full of mischief. Since she's the youngest, we've all spoiled her shamelessly." His expression told Megan he loved his sister and didn't regret the spoiling in the least.

Megan wondered what it would be like to be pampered. Also, this talk about brother and sister made her miss Owen a great deal.

"Were you spoiled as a child, Miss Llewellyn?"

"Certainly not. And you may call me Megan. After all, you gave me permission to call you by your first name so it's only proper."

"And after all, I'm sharing your bed."

"Will you stop saying that?" She frowned at him in exasperation. It put too many ideas into her head. In the few days he had been here, she had started to find him far too interesting. "In the Hollow we don't believe in spoiling children. It only leads to trouble later."

"I don't believe that it does. How can it hurt to love a child?" His gray eyes gazed into hers and she had the uncanny impression that he could see her thoughts.

She turned away. "I was loved. Just not spoiled."

"I would think Seth would pamper you a great deal."

Megan didn't want to talk about Seth to Caleb. He always came off in a bad light. "I'll remind him to do that as soon as he comes home again," she said tersely.

"If you were my fiancée, I would treat you as if you were the most beautiful and the most cherished woman in the world."

She looked at him in surprise.

Caleb looked away this time. "Sorry. I guess I overstepped the bounds. It's none of my business how Seth or anyone else treats you."

"That's all right." She was dismayed at the surge of warmth his words had caused. Had he been able to tell? She was afraid to meet his eyes. Reluctantly she came farther into the room. "Seth means well. He really does. I'm a plain person, Capt—Caleb. I'm not used to frills, nor was I brought up to want them. Seth is the sort of man I've known all my life. He's like my father and my uncles and my cousins. He fits into my life. It's not natural for men like Seth to pamper their women."

"I think all women bloom when it's obvious that they're loved. I couldn't love a woman and not treat her as if she were a fragile treasure."

Megan laughed. "Fragile treasures don't haul water from wells and hoe gardens. I wouldn't know the first thing about being a woman like that. There aren't any fine ladies in the Hollow."

He smiled at her as if he disagreed with her. For a moment Megan wondered if he were trying to sweet-talk her in order to get her to free him. But that made no sense. He couldn't walk as far as the road, let alone all the way to a Union camp. Besides, she had already told him she would return him to his people in exchange for Seth as soon as possible. No, she must have misunderstood him altogether.

"What's wrong?"

"Nothing. Tell me about your sister. Does she like to sew?"

"Yes, but she prefers to read. Felicity has loved reading all her life. Even before she learned to make out words, she had me read her stories. Mama would have been appalled if she knew half of what we read. Felicity's head was so filled with pirates and sunken treasures, she had trouble sleeping."

Against her will, Megan was intrigued. She went to the straight-backed chair and picked up her darning. "Your parents didn't object to her reading?"

"Of course not. They encouraged it."

She shook her head. "I don't see how that can be. I know Bridget and I are busy all day with chores and have been ever since I can remember. Mama would never have the time to sit down and read. Neither would Papa, for that matter. How is it that your family has all this spare time?" She expertly dropped the darning egg into the sock and started making the tiny stitches to repair the heel.

"I suppose we just live differently."

"I suppose. Do you live in a city?"

"Yes. Pollard's Crossing isn't as large as, say, Chicago by any means, but it's still a city."

"You've seen Chicago?" Megan's fingers stopped momentarily.

"Several times. Have you?"

"No," she said with a laugh at the idea. "I've never been beyond Raintree." She glanced at him to see if that lowered her in his estimation. He was only looking at the locket he still held in his hand.

"I think you and Felicity would be friends."

"We have so much in common," she said wryly.

"Actually you do. She loves Mrs. Radcliffe's books above all else. She can even quote complete passages from *Udolpho*."

"How old is she?"

"Nineteen."

"We're almost the same age."

"I thought you must be."

"I'm quite close to my sister, Bridget. She doesn't like to read but she knows I do and she's helped me hide my books from time to time. She *can* read," Megan added quickly, "but she prefers not to."

"Does she have red hair, too?" he asked with a smile.

Megan automatically reached up and touched her hair. Red hair wasn't considered a beauty trait in the Hollow. "Yes. Hers is even more red than mine. We get it from Mama."

"And does Owen also have red hair?"

She shifted uncomfortably. "I've told you I'm not supposed to talk about him. He's dead to the family. But his hair is the same color as mine. Dark red."

"Auburn," Caleb said. "That's what I'd call it. It's beautiful."

"You shouldn't say such personal things. We're stuck here together until you get well. I can't allow you to be so intimate."

"We're only talking about your brother's and sister's hair coloring. That's not too intimate, surely." He sounded innocent but she caught the teasing sparkle in his eyes. If she were a different person in a different place, she would think he was actually flirting with her.

"Are you forgetting I'm promised to Seth?"

"Not for a single minute."

She laid her darning in her lap and looked at him. "You confuse me. You're not like any man I know. Not at all."

"Yes, I'm certain that's true. In my family we don't believe in working a woman from sunup to sundown."

With a frown she said, "That's not fair. You don't know my family or what we're like."

"That's true. I apologize." But he was smiling as if he were enjoying teasing her.

Megan put her darning back into her workbasket. "I have other chores to do while it's daylight. You'll have to amuse yourself. Memorize *Udolpho* while I'm gone."

He opened it to the back. "All seven hundred pages?" he asked with a grin.

"I have a lot of chores. You'll have time." She left him and went into the other room.

For a minute she leaned against the wall, feeling its bumpy sturdiness and trying to remember who she was and, more important, who he was. This was her enemy. She couldn't indulge in a flirtation with him even if she wasn't engaged to Seth. She felt unfaithful as it was. What had she been thinking of to sit in the bedroom with him and do her needlework, just as if he were a family member? Megan pressed her fingers to her forehead and closed her eyes. After this she would be more careful.

She went out onto the porch. A cold wind had blown in the night before and the air had a snap of winter in it. She pulled her knitted shawl closer about her shoulders. There was kindling to chop and corn to be shelled. A shutter had worked loose during the night's wind and she tried to put it back into place. It dropped at an angle again. She would have to go out to the shed beside the smokehouse and find a hammer and one of the square nails Patrick made for the settlement. It was hard for one person to keep up a house.

She frowned at the window set in the bedroom wall. How had she believed even for a moment that Caleb's womenfolk had time to sit around and read? Even in a city there must be shutters to mend and fire to be fed and corn to be shelled. These things didn't tend to themselves. He must have been teasing, thinking she was as green as grass in the spring. With an angry movement, Megan knotted her shawl more securely and went down the steps.

The woodpile was at the side of the house nearest the settlement. She bent and put a pine log on the large stump she used as a chopping block. With her hatchet, she slivered the pine into long splinters that would easily catch fire and ig-nite the heavy oak logs in the fireplace. The pine was from an old tree that had been felled during a storm the winter before and had rotted to the point of exposing its core. Heart of pine was the best kindling to be found.

As she chopped, she noticed a flash of yellow coming through the woods and looked up to see Bridget crossing the clearing. Megan waved to keep her sister from going into the house. Bridget veered to join her.

"Mama wants to know if you need any of the meat we're smoking? She put by a sizable amount and you can have some if you want it."

"No, but tell her I appreciate the offer. I brought up all my smokehouse can hold so I have plenty to see me through the winter. Assuming the soldiers don't find it."

Bridget nodded. "I can't help but think of Patrick when I see them passing. Our boys look so hungry and so poorly clothed. It's all I can do not to send them off with all our food and extra wraps. Patrick must look just like them."

"I know. I share stew with them whenever I can. But we don't know that all the states are like this. Maybe in Geor-gia things are better. News never reaches us until it's old. Patrick may have plenty to eat and warm clothes as well." They both knew this wasn't the case, but Bridget needed to hear it.

"This is true. I pray for him every night. Maybe some Confederate mother or sister is taking care of him for me."

"I'm sure that's true."

"We've hidden our smoked meat. Have you done that? If you haven't, Papa says he'll come over tomorrow and help you."

"I'm doing it today. I wanted to smoke it as long as pos-sible." Megan stacked the irregular sticks of kindling in the box she stored them in. "It's so different from curing hogs. I hope it tastes all right. There was no time to let it age in salt. I just rubbed it with black pepper and borax to keep the skippers out and hung it up."

"So did we. It might be tough, but we can boil it tender, I guess. Nobody ever handed down a recipe for horse meat that I know of."

"I sure never thought I'd be reduced to eating a horse." Megan picked up the kindling box and paused. She couldn't take it into the house and risk Bridget finding Caleb. Bridget would try to keep the secret, but her mouth sometimes outraced her mind. Megan put the box back down on the ground and started splitting more kindling.

"How much kindling do you need?" Bridget asked.

"If I don't do it now, I'll just have to do it later. Kindling will keep."

"I almost forgot. Papa said he saw a Union patrol down the mountain yesterday. He says for you to be real careful. They may be coming this way."

"I'll watch out for them." Megan wondered if they could be looking for Caleb. By now he would have been missed and someone might have a way of knowing he wasn't captured or buried.

"I've got to be going now. Mama says she'll be expecting you for dinner on Sunday."

"I always eat there on Sunday. Why would she have you remind me?"

"I don't know. You know how Mama is. She has the sight just like her grandmother did. Maybe she saw something keeping you from coming down."

"Tell her I'll be there." From time to time Megan had also experienced the family phenomenon. She always became uneasy whenever a death was about to occur. She had never told Bridget because her sister would only have worried.

"Anyway, she said to tell you she expects you for dinner."

"Tell her not to fret." Megan frowned slightly. Did her mother somehow suspect that Caleb was in Megan's cabin?

Frequently Jane knew things no one had told her, and on occasion Megan had experienced this herself. As far as she knew, Bridget had no glimmerings of the sight at all and was as uninformed as their father in that respect.

When Bridget was gone, Megan took the brimming box of kindling into the house. Since she rarely allowed her fire to go out, there was enough kindling to last her a year. She dropped it beside the hearth and put another log on the fire.

A glance at the window told her that evening was only a couple of hours away. She shouldn't have wasted the precious minutes of daylight talking with Caleb earlier.

She went back outside and to the shed where she kept the tools and ropes needed around the farm. Taking several lengths of rope, she went into the woods. After tying a chunk of wood to the end of a rope, Megan tossed it over the highest limb possible. Then she went back to the smokehouse and brought out the first of the smoked meat, tied carefully in a tow sack.

She tied the sack of meat to the end of the rope and hauled it up into the top of the tree, being careful not to leave it suspended too close to other limbs. She didn't want to go to all the trouble of hiding it from soldiers and have some predator eat it.

When the end of the rope was tied to the trunk of the tree, she looked up. If a person didn't know where to look, it was as good as invisible.

For the next two hours she repeated the process until every spare roast was tied in the treetops and hidden as well as she could manage. She ached from the unaccustomed effort and was glad to fasten the smokehouse door and go back to the cabin.

As she approached, she heard voices. Fear congealed in her veins as she rounded the corner and saw three Union soldiers entering her yard. The sun hung low over the treetops and night would soon be falling. What did they want at her house?

"Yes?" she asked in a cold tone. Had they heard Caleb inside? They could have been in there with him for all she knew.

"We're looking for food, ma'am," one said. None of them were smiling.

She kept her distance. "So am I. Your army already cleaned me out." She jerked her head in the direction of the smokehouse. "See for yourselves."

The man in charge motioned for one of the men to go look. "We're also looking for a man named Captain Caleb Morgan. Have you seen him around here?"

"I don't know of any Morgan family living in these parts." She deliberately made herself sound a bit slow of wit. That had worked in the past. "You could ask over to Raintree. The Morgans might live there."

"No, this was a Union soldier, not a family," the other man said impatiently. "We're trying to see if he was killed or captured."

"I haven't killed anybody." Megan crossed her arms over her chest. "If you find any food, I'd appreciate it if you'd share it with me."

"Not much chance of that," the second man said again.

His superior frowned at him. To Megan he said, "I apologize for my men. These are hard times for all of us."

Especially those of us who don't get to ride around on horses and steal from women who are trying to keep body and soul together. She frowned at them in the fading light.

The other man returned. "The smokehouse is empty. It smells like smoke though. Maybe she heard us coming and is hiding the meat."

Megan held her arms out. "Do you think I could hide much under this shawl? Maybe it's in my shoe?"

Behind her, she heard a voice call out. Caleb had heard the men. She stepped up on the porch, blocking their way. "Since there's nothing to steal, I won't object to you riding away."

"Is that a man in there?" the second soldier asked. "Who do I hear?"

"You hear my brother. He's a bit slow in the mind and the army doesn't want him. He's been on a three-day drinking binge. If you'll take him off my hands, you can have him." She held her breath.

The officer grinned. "No, we aren't recruiting drunken brothers today. We'll be on our way."

"Wait!" she could hear Caleb shouting. "I'm Captain Morgan!"

To cover his words, Megan bumped against the washtub that hung on the porch and it fell with a deafening clatter. The soldiers' horses shied away. "Sorry," she said. "I've always been clumsy." She made more noise as she wrestled the tub back onto its peg.

When she turned around the men were riding away. Megan hurried into the house and sighed with relief as she shoved the bolt in place on the door. She leaned her forehead against the wood and closed her eyes. That had been too close. If she had been a bit slower, they would have found her precious cache of meat and it was only luck that they hadn't discovered Caleb.

"You can quit shouting. They've gone," she called to him as she went to the pump to wash her hands.

"Get in here!" he commanded. "You kept them from hearing me on purpose!"

"Of course I did! Do you take me for a fool?" She pushed open the bedroom door and frowned back at him. "You're my prisoner. I'm not giving you up until I can trade you for Seth."

"They might have known where to find a doctor! Not one of those army sawbones, but a real doctor."

"More likely they would have put you on one of their horses and you'd have bled to death before they reached Raintree. You couldn't travel if you tried!"

"At least I would be with my own army!"

She glared at him. "Is it better to die with your army, with strangers, than to stay here and be doctored back to health and traded? I think not. Certainly it wouldn't serve me as well."

"What about me?" he demanded.

"You're my prisoner," she said loudly and slowly so it would sink in. "I'm not giving you up until it suits me."

He was still arguing but she closed the door. This was turning out to be more difficult than she had originally supposed.

She put a bit of the horse meat on to boil for supper, then went to the back room. This was farther from the road and had a door that could be latched. She had wondered at the time why her father had fitted a latch on it, but now she was glad he had. He had said it might come in handy. She hoped he would never guess in what way. Not until she had Seth home safely.

Her pallet lay in the middle of the floor, its covers neatly in place. What would it take to make a proper bed out of it?

With a great deal of difficulty, Megan managed to maneuver four kegs from the barn into the back room. Then she went out to the smokehouse. Taking a hammer, she knocked the pins from the hinges and dragged the door back to the house. It was long past dark by the time she finished. With all her muscles aching, she pulled the pallet up onto the door and braced all of it in the corner. It was pretty sturdy. Would it be strong enough to hold a man Caleb's size? There was only one way to find out.

She went back into the bedroom and caught the wrist of his good arm.

"What are you doing?" he asked suspiciously.

"You're moving. I'm not sharing my bed with you any more." She pulled him up and helped him swing his feet over the side. "Wrap the quilt around you," she said as she drew his good arm over her shoulders. "Stand up."

Caleb did as she told him, though she knew he must have questions. He was as heavy as she remembered, but he at least tried to hop on his good leg. It was no easy job getting him into the back room, but at last he was leaning against the makeshift bed. "This is your room."

"Why?"

"Because I can lock this door." She helped him sit on the bed and was glad to see that it remained in place. She looked up at his face and saw he was sweating from the pain but he hadn't cried out. "I'll soon have you some stew to eat."

As she was about to leave, he caught her wrist. "You should have given me to the soldiers."

She looked into his eyes. In the dimness of the room they were almost as black as his hair. He seemed so male and so large when she had to look up to see his face. "Lie down," she said as she hastily moved away.

As she scooped stew into her gourd dipper, she reflected that he was right. It might have been better to let the soldiers find him. She was almost afraid of what she was already thinking about him and feeling for him, and he had only been there a few days. How would he affect her by the time he had been there long enough to heal?

Chapter Four

Megan was peeling potatoes when she heard the bell be
ing rung at her parents' place. She dropped the potato into
cold water so it wouldn't turn dark and dried her hands on
her apron. A small frown creased her forehead. Why would
someone be ringing the bell?

"What's that sound?" Caleb called out.

"It's the alarm bell. Something is wrong." She untied her
apron and hung it on its peg. "I have to go. They wouldn't
risk letting strangers know the settlement is there unless they
were calling everyone together for a reason."

She left the cabin and hurried down the road into the
Hollow. As she neared, she could see others converging on
her parents' cabin. They all seemed as mystified as she was.
Had there been an attack by the Union army? If that was the
emergency, why ring the bell in such a way as to bring the
women as well as the men? The settlement had long ago
worked out a system of ringing the bell in a certain pattern
to call only the men.

Megan hurried up the steps and through the crowd into
the cabin. The Brennans were seated at the table with her
parents. When she came in, they all looked at her.

For a moment she thought they had somehow found out
about her prisoner and were gathering to kill him and call

ꜟer to task. She stopped and stared back at them. "What is ꜟt?" she asked.

Samuel held out a sheet of paper. It was torn and badly ꜱmudged but she recognized Seth's almost illegible handꜤriting. She took the letter and sat in the closest chair.

Conditions are real bad here. Folks are dying right and left of me. Mostly it's prison fever, but lately some have come down with the measles. It might not be much of nothing for a child, but in a grown-up, it's a killer.

The guards here are no better than animals. Men get beaten regularly and they leave us to lie in rags. When it rains, which it does more than I thought possible, water stays on the floor, seems like forever. We have to lie in it or stand. It's real cold, too. No fires here to speak of because there's no way to get wood. I don't rightly know what's going to happen when we get the first freeze.

I sure wish I was home. Signing up was the worst thing I ever done. When I get back to the Hollow, I'm not ever going to leave. Tell Ma I said hello and that I'll be home as soon as they let me go.

Megan looked up and met Sarah Ann's eyes. Seth's ꞃnother was crying softly and his father stood behind her, a ꞇowl on his face. "My boy's in the cold and wet," Sarah Ꞁnn said in a broken voice. "They's treating him worse than ꞇe would an animal."

"Yankees aren't as good as animals," her husband ꞔrowled. "That's a fact everybody knows."

"Maybe we could send him some warm clothes and fireꞄood," Megan suggested. She was feeling sick from picꞇuring the conditions Seth was living in. Why had Seth sent ꜱuch a letter, when he must know there was nothing they ꞉ould do but worry about him? Didn't he care what a letter ꞉ke this would do to people who loved him?

"Use your head, girl," Aaron Brennan snapped. "D you reckon the jailers would just hand them over to him Even if he got them, somebody else would likely take then away from him. Seth may be scrappy, but he's not real big."

"I know. I just don't know what else to suggest." Megan folded the letter and slowly handed it to Sarah Ann. Had anyone else noticed that Seth hadn't mentioned her at all She felt angry with herself for noticing, but shouldn't he have? He had remembered to send a message to his mother How much more trouble would it have been for him to in clude her own name as well?

Sarah Ann unfolded the letter and stared down at it. She couldn't read, but it was a link with her son.

Benjamin Grady, the preacher for the settlement, stepped forward. "We'll pray for him. That's the most we can do."

There was a shuffling noise as everyone went to thei knees. Megan could hear the people on the porch doing th same. The crowd was unnaturally quiet aside from the oc casional cough.

"Lord, our boy Seth Brennan is in the enemy's hands. W ask that you look out for him and protect him in Pharaoh' land. Seth is the apple of his ma and pa's eye and we all wan him back. His bride-to-be can't rest for wanting to see him."

Megan glanced up but the preacher wasn't looking at her She hastily closed her eyes again as the prayer droned on. I that how everyone saw her? Yearning to see Seth? It both ered her that she hadn't spent more time in miserable lone liness and aching for his return, now that she heard Brothe Grady put it like that. Was she unnatural for not missin him more? Although she would never have admitted it, sh spent more time worrying about Patrick than Seth.

It wasn't that she didn't love Seth. She had never love anyone but him. But they had known each other all thei lives and she had always taken him for granted, even whe he went off to war. It occurred to her that this could mea that she didn't really love him at all, but she put the though aside. This was no time for traitorous thoughts like that. Of course she loved Seth. Even if she didn't, she didn't want him mistreated.

Brother Grady was known for his long-winded prayers. When he prayed over a matter, he kept after it until he was certain he had God's attention. Megan's knees were numb by the time he said, "Amen." She heard sighs of relief as everyone got to their feet. Aaron had to help Sarah Ann haul her bulk back into the chair, where she sat rubbing her knees and staring at the letter.

Questions broke out all over the room about Seth and what was going to happen to him. Megan listened in silence. The questions were directed at the men, not her. Again she noticed she was on the outside, looking into Seth's life. Aside from mention in Brother Grady's prayer, no one seemed to connect her with Seth, even though they were promised to each other. She told herself it was only because almost every family in the settlement was related to the Brennans in some way and they were all naturally worried about their kin. All the same, she felt excluded.

In the cabin Caleb was struggling to get out of bed. He had no idea what emergency had called the settlement together, but there was a chance that Union troops were in the area. He managed to swing his legs over the side and stand. For a moment he waited, giving the pain time to subside. Then he reached for his neatly folded clothes, which Megan had left on a nearby chair. Once he was dressed he felt better. Caleb wasn't a prude, but there was something intimidating about being naked in a strange house.

His leg felt as if fire were coursing through it as he pulled on his underlinen, then his pants. He shrugged into his jacket and buttoned it as he limped to the door. He was right; Megan had left without remembering to lock it. He opened it and peered out.

The cabin was small, and a low fire burned in the fire-place. There was little furniture—only a rocker, a table and a couple of the straight-backed chairs that every house hereabouts contained. Bleached feed sacks hung as curtains at the windows and there was a braided rug on the floor, its colors still new and bright.

Caleb moved slowly over the floor, wincing every time he had to put his weight on his bad leg. He knew he couldn't hope to walk far on it, but if Union troops had passed the house once, they might do so regularly. If he could make it to the road and away from the house, someone might see him.

He reached the door and paused to catch his breath. Caleb hated feeling so weak. His muscles were trembling and he had only walked a few feet. He was beginning to realize how badly he was hurt and that his concern of never healing properly might be well-founded. He had been there almost two weeks and he couldn't see much improvement at all in his leg. Up until now he had thought Megan was exaggerating his condition.

Caleb opened the door and a blast of cold air hit his face and slicked through his heavy wool jacket. He had no coat and wouldn't steal one of Megan's quilts for warmth. Especially since that would make him easier to see.

The porch steps were particularly difficult and he half fell down them. For a moment he held to the porch and caught his breath as waves of pain ripped through him. Had he pulled the wound open again? He looked at his leg, but it wasn't bleeding. Limping painfully, he started across the yard.

Megan couldn't get away until everyone had exhausted their questions and suggestions and agreed that there was nothing they could do to get Seth back or to ease his suffering. More than once she had started to tell them about the prisoner in her cabin, but she was too afraid they would lynch him first and think later. No, this was the only way she could help Seth, and she was determined that nothing would undermine her plan.

She took a loaf of bread from her mother, who seemed to be the only one other than Bridget who was thinking about Megan's feelings. Bridget hugged her and patted her shoulder, her blue eyes glistening with unshed tears. Megan nodded. The women in her family were silent when they were most emotional.

Holding the bread under her arm, Megan started the climb to her cabin. Her thoughts were on Seth and his miserable conditions. Were the Confederate prisons as bad? Megan didn't know and she knew not to pose the question to anyone in the Hollow. It would seem traitorous to suggest their own men were as inhumane to their prisoners as were the Yankees. All the same, Megan wondered.

As soon as she topped the ridge, she saw Caleb struggling up the road ahead. She let one of Owen's expletives escape her lips and she ran to him. "What are you doing out of bed?" she demanded once she was beside him.

He ignored her and tried to drag himself farther up the road.

"What are you trying to do? Kill yourself?" She darted in front of him. "Look at you! You're as pale as a sheet!" Without giving him opportunity to argue, she slipped his arm around her shoulders and turned him back in the direction of the cabin. "You must be as crazy as a bedbug to try to walk to Raintree in your condition. What if you fell on that leg?"

He didn't answer, and when she looked up at him, she saw a white line of pain around his lips. "You must be purely crazy!" she muttered.

After several long minutes, she had him back inside the cabin. "Don't you know someone could have seen you?" she demanded as she helped him back to his bedroom.

"That was the general idea," he finally answered. "I was hoping to see Union troops."

"You would have a long way to go before that happened. It's a wonder no one from the settlement decided to walk me home. The only people around here are Confederate and they would rather shoot you than not."

"Then the emergency wasn't Union soldiers in the area?" He braced himself on the doorframe to the bedroom.

"No, it wasn't. It was a letter from Seth. Can you stand here while I put a fresh sheet on the bed? Of course you can. You were bent on walking to Raintree, weren't you?" She left him at the door and stripped the sheets from his bed. "Of all the fool things for you to do!"

She moved quickly, but he was trembling visibly by the time she had his bed ready. She helped him limp to it and sit on the raised pallet. "Your skin looks like a wax candle!" She was deeply concerned. "Why are you being so quiet? You're never quiet."

"I'm hurting like hell," he said through clenched teeth, "and I'm right back where I started."

"And you're staying here, too." She helped him take off his jacket and the trousers that were binding his leg, but left him his underlinen. A fine sheen of sweat lay on his pale skin. He wasn't lying about the pain. Did it usually take gunshot wounds so long to start healing? Megan couldn't ask anyone and Caleb apparently didn't know either.

When he was lying in bed and able to relax through the pain, he said, "You say you got another letter from Seth?"

Megan hesitated. "His parents did. They let me read it."

He looked at her. "He wrote them, not you?"

"It doesn't mean anything." Megan bent to pick up the sheets she had taken from the bed. "Most likely he didn't have two pieces of paper or he was in a hurry to send it out. Besides, he knows his mother worries more than most would."

"Surely he enclosed a message for you."

She glanced at him. He seemed genuinely curious. "Now you're talking too much again. I guess that means you're feeling better." She left the room and took the sheets out to the service porch in back.

She sat on the back steps, despite the cold, and hugged her knees to her chest. Why hadn't Seth at least sent her a greeting? How long would that have taken? For that matter, why had he sent the letter at all? Didn't he know it would upset his family and only make his mother worry more? How like Seth to think only of himself.

Megan hated these thoughts but she knew they were true. Seth had always put himself first. Even that night in the clearing when they had made love the first and only time. He must have known then that he was considering joining the army and he had taken her anyway, even if a baby might have been the consequence. What on earth would she have told her parents and everyone else in the settlement? Sex before marriage was strictly forbidden, even to couples who were engaged. But Seth had wanted her and he hadn't thought beyond that.

For the first time, Megan let herself think of her future if she backed out of marrying Seth. For one thing, she would probably have to give up her cabin and move back in with her parents. It made more sense for Bridget and Patrick to have the cabin than for her to stay there alone. Megan liked being away from the others, even if it was lonely or even frightening at times. Cabins were too difficult to build and the men's time was too precious for her father to be willing to build Bridget and Patrick another one.

Megan rested her chin on her knees. On the other hand, if she married Seth, would she be happy? She was rather surprised to realize she had never thought about that before. Like everyone else in Black Hollow, she had always assumed she would marry him. Her future had been more or less ordained since she was twelve or so. The only real surprise had been that she and Seth had waited so long to announce their intentions of marrying. Did that mean he had reservations as well? Megan had certainly never thought of that. Maybe he didn't love her at all, but was simply taking the easy route.

The chilling wind crept into her and Megan got up shivering. She knew her thoughts were more the cause of her trembling than was the temperature. These were thoughts she should never have had. Not when she was living in the cabin, using the things from her hope chest and waiting for Seth's return. She would be shunned if she backed out now. Assuming, of course, that Seth returned at all. He had said in his letter that men were dying around him every day.

She went into the house and finished peeling the potatoes to boil. Doing routine work helped. It was harder to think when she had to keep her mind on the sharp knife and her fingers.

"Megan?" Caleb called.

"What is it?" She dropped the potatoes into boiling water and went into the room.

"Who drew these pictures?"

She looked at the sketches she had hung from tacks on the wall. "I did. Why?"

"You drew them? They're good." He was studying them as if he hadn't noticed them before.

"There's no need for you to make fun of me. I'm busy." She turned to leave but he called her back.

"I'm not teasing you. Why do you always get so defensive?"

"Why would I believe you mean these things? I'm not a fool. Didn't you just try to escape? Don't you remember we're enemies?"

"If you were in my place, wouldn't you try to get away? As for us being enemies, that's not the way I think of you."

She frowned at him. "You must think I don't have any sense at all. You're North and I'm South. If that's not enemies, I don't know what to call it."

"You might think of me as a person."

"I'm busy." Again she turned to leave but this time she paused of her own choice. "You really think my drawings are good?"

"Of course I do. They look as if they could walk off the paper."

Megan went farther into the room. "I like to draw. Papa says it's a waste of time and that it's sinful to waste anything. But sometimes I just can't help doing it." She glanced at him to see if he was laughing at her. "I only draw when I've finished with the chores for the day."

"You don't have to make excuses for me." His eyes met hers and she had to look away. "I've seen Felicity's drawings and they aren't nearly as good as yours, but she's considered to be quite talented."

Megan went to a drawing of two puppies tumbling in play. "These are two dogs Papa raised. They're coonhounds but there's not much for them to hunt these days. They spend most of their time sleeping under the porch." She smiled. "That's about all coonhounds do, sleep and hunt. And howl. You can hear these two from miles away when they pick up a scent. A good hunter can tell one dog's voice from another and know just what they're tracking."

"I've done some hunting, but living in a city, I don't own hounds."

She studied him. "I can't imagine living like that."

"It's not a bad life," he said with a wry smile.

"I didn't mean that. What do you do all day? I don't see how you get the things you need. Surely you can't afford to buy everything. Where do you get food?"

"From stores. We buy whatever we need."

She shook her head. "Brother Grady would have a field day with that! He says it's sinful not to work for everything you have and that you're supposed to grow your own things. We try to be as self-reliant as we can be in the Hollow. There isn't much we have to buy." She smiled. "I guess that's a good thing since the only thing we can't seem to grow is money."

Caleb didn't comment.

"Are you hurting very bad now?"

"I'm better."

"I could go get you some willow to chew. I've heard that helps with pain."

He shook his head. "I'm all right." He hesitated. "Megan, I wasn't escaping from *you*. I have to try to get back to my unit. Otherwise, I'm a deserter."

"I understand. I guess I would do the same thing." She added, "Dinner will be ready soon. You'll feel better once you've eaten."

"You know your plan to trade me won't work, don't you?"

"I don't know any such thing. It only stands to reason that they would want their own officer more than a private like Seth."

"How do you intend to make this trade?"

"I don't know yet," she admitted.

"Crossing Union territory, even with a few Confederate sympathizers around, will be dangerous. Traveling with me as a prisoner and returning home safely will be nearly impossible. Even if we reach the right prison, there's no guarantee that they'll give you Seth. They might just keep me and send you away."

Megan felt the tears rising and she fought them back. "I have to do something!"

"Because you love Seth that much?"

She didn't answer for a long time. "No," she said finally. "Because I don't love him enough." She left the room before he could ask any more questions.

Caleb lay there listening to her make supper and thought about what she had said. Certainly she was honest. She hadn't been forced to tell him that. "If you don't love him that much, why are you set on marrying him?" he called out.

"It's not something you'd understand," she called back.

"Explain it to me."

She came slowly back into the room and sat on the edge of the bed. "I was intended for Seth most of my life. I can't explain it to someone who didn't grow up in the Hollow. I guess it's different elsewhere. You see, most of us are related in one way or another so we don't have many to choose from. Seth and I are one of the few that aren't kin and that are the right age to marry. His cousin, Patrick, married Bridget. Seth was to marry me."

"So it's an arranged marriage."

"In a way. I care for Seth. Our lives fit together. Our families are friends and the family lands are side by side. After we marry, the land will all be one, for all intents and purposes, though our fathers will control it as long as they're alive. Do you understand?"

"I'm beginning to."

"If I don't marry Seth, there's no one else eligible. Not unless I want to settle for a widower and have to raise his children from a previous wife. There are two men I could marry who already have families, but both of them are Papa's age and I don't care for either of them. Since I don't have a brother to look after me as I get older, I have to marry. It wouldn't be right to expect Patrick to take me in since he has younger sisters of his own that may need to live with them."

"You have a brother. Maybe your family will forgive him after the war is over."

"Not Papa. He never changes his mind. Mama would take Owen back right now. He was her favorite. Owen and Papa never saw eye to eye on anything. He probably would have left the Hollow for another reason if it hadn't been the war. Owen is too rebellious." She smiled faintly. "He and I are alike. Bridget is more like Mama. Papa has always said that Bridget will be happy in life because she doesn't ask for all that much.''

"And you?"

"He says I never will be. Maybe he's right in the long run, but I'm happy now. I like my cabin and I even like not being with the others.'' She looked at him. "Can you understand that?"

"I can understand it easily. From what you've told me, I wouldn't want to be with them, either.''

She shook her head. "No, you don't see. I love them. Or at least I care for most of the people in the settlement. But I like my independence.''

"And after you're married?''

For a long time Megan was silent. "I guess we all have to give up something. Sacrifice is supposed to be good for us.''

"I've never believed that. And I don't think independence is a bad thing. It hasn't hurt me any.''

"Of course not. You're not a woman.''

"Why couldn't a couple be independent together?''

"Now you're talking nonsense.'' She touched her drawing of the puppies. "If I tell you something, will you promise not to laugh?''

"Yes.''

"I used to pretend that when I became an adult I would write a book and draw pictures to illustrate it.'' She threw him a quick look. "Are you laughing at me?''

"No. I was smiling because I plan to write a book someday myself.''

Megan stared at him. "You want to write a book? Now I know you're teasing me.''

"Why do you think I'm ridiculing you at every turn? I've had stories in my head ever since I was a boy. I used to tell stories to Felicity and her friends all the time.''

"Men don't write. They build fences and repair barns and hunt for game.''

"Megan, the world is larger than Black Hollow. My father doesn't do any of those things. Neither do any of my uncles. Who do you think writes books if they're not written by men and women? Somebody does it and I don't see any reason why it shouldn't be me. Or you, for that matter."

"I can just see me now, writing stories between milking the cow and churning the butter and gathering the eggs. Maybe I could do the illustrations while I scrub the floor."

"Suit yourself. Far be it from me to convince you to be free."

She frowned at him. "The world isn't so accommodating. I'm surprised you've grown this old and have not noticed that."

"The world also isn't full of nothing but work and responsibilities. If some of us don't dream and work to fulfill our dreams, we aren't any better than cattle."

"Why is it that we end up arguing if we talk more than a few minutes? I'm going to see how supper is coming along."

"Supper can wait."

"You talk twice as much as any man I ever saw. I'll bet Papa hasn't talked to Mama this much in the past year!"

"Then I feel sorry for your mother."

"Caleb, not everyone talks all day long. And what's more, I don't think your people are as idle as you say they are."

"They aren't idle at all. They just have different pursuits."

She nodded knowingly. "Yes, well, I'm going to pursue supper now." She left but she couldn't stop thinking about all he had said.

Could she really write and illustrate a book? She had harbored this dream for so long it was a part of her. Yet when she thought of how to go about it, she reached a dead end. Nobody in Raintree was a book publisher—they didn't even have a newspaper. How would she ever go about getting a book published, assuming it was good enough for others to want to read it? No, she told herself. Being a writer would just have to be a dream.

But would Caleb write? He seemed certain that he could do it. Did he know how to go about it? Whatever her own experience, Megan knew men and women wrote books because she had read their names on the covers. How did they have time? Perhaps once she had several children to help out with chores, there would be time, but she didn't want to wait and she hadn't seen her own mother's work lessening over the years. Work seemed to expand to fill all the hours of the day no matter how many hands were whittling it down.

The idea of writing never left her all the time she prepared the meal. No matter how hard she tried to tell herself it was a foolish idea, it stuck in her mind.

When she took Caleb's supper to him, he was lying very still. She knew him well enough by now to know this meant he was in pain. He didn't mention it but sat up, and she handed him the plate. She admired him for that.

"Will you bring your plate in here and eat with me?"

"I suppose I could do that," she conceded. She had never had a meal in her life that wasn't consumed in the kitchen, but who was to know?

She joined him and noticed he had waited for her. "Mama baked the bread," she said.

"She's a good cook. So are you."

Megan smiled. "Mama insisted that Bridget and I learn that even if we never learned anything else. She also taught us to sew."

"And to read."

"No, that was one of my aunts. Papa wasn't too pleased that Bridget and I learned that. Owen was the one who was supposed to be learning to read."

"Megan, why didn't Seth write to you instead of to his parents? What's the real reason?"

She pushed the food around on her plate. "I don't know. I've asked myself that all afternoon. He had to realize that I would know the letter came. I can understand him writing his parents instead of me the first time—maybe. But I can't see a reason at all for him not even mentioning my name in the second letter."

"Not even a greeting?"

She shook her head. She felt too close to tears to answer aloud.

"I know it doesn't mean much to you, but I would have written to you." His voice was softer than she had ever heard it.

Megan's eyes met his and she found she couldn't look away.

"I know it's hard for you to believe, but all Northern men aren't barbarians, just as all Southern ones aren't knights in shining armor. I would be more thoughtful of my fiancée than that. Even if it was more or less an arranged marriage."

She managed to avert her eyes. "Maybe I made a mistake in not letting those soldiers find you that day. Maybe I'm wrong in keeping you here."

"I'm your pawn in this game of war," he said with an attempt at lightness. "Remember?"

"I remember. All the same, it may have been a mistake. Maybe I should have let you go on down that road. A Yankee patrol might have found you."

"Or I might have died of shock or exposure. I left the house thinking there was a regiment in the area. Like you said, I couldn't hope to walk all the way to Raintree. But I had to try."

"Did you hurt yourself too badly?" she asked.

He thought for a minute before he answered. "That's possible. I know I'm hurting more than I was before I tried."

"You're a hard man to doctor," she said.

"I know," he replied.

"I want you to promise me you won't try anything like that again."

"I think I'd be a fool not to promise. I've had time to think lately. This is the most comfortable, even considering the pain in my leg, that I've been in months, maybe years. I think that's why I thought I had to try to escape."

"I don't understand." She didn't dare look at him.

"Let's just say I'm starting to enjoy the company. Perhaps a bit too much."

She nodded. She knew exactly what he meant. "I guess I should have let you escape after all." Suddenly she didn't dare stay in the room with him and she left quickly. He didn't call after her.

Sitting by the fire to finish her supper, Megan did quite a bit of soul-searching. She couldn't start to care for Caleb, not even if he were a Confederate. She was promised to Seth, and in the Hollow, that was as binding as marriage vows. Certainly she could never love him or expect him to love her. But could she stop the emotion that was coming to life inside her? Certainly Seth had never made her feel this way, not even that night in the clearing.

Megan was glad no one could read her thoughts.

Chapter Five

From Caleb's bed in the back room, he could see the fireplace in the main room. In the days he had been in the cabin, he had read most of *The Mysteries of Udolpho*, counted all the timbers in the walls, the wide planking flooring, and was starting to count the bricks in the fireplace. Megan fascinated him but she was busy most of the day, keeping the small farm and cabin in shape. Even though it was now winter, there were things to be mended and cloth to be sewn.

As he was counting the bricks for the second time, Megan came into his line of vision. She put down the armload of firewood and straightened as if her back were tired. Then she knelt and put a log on the fire and unhooked an iron spoon to stir the beans she was cooking over the fire.

He didn't call out to her, nor did she look in his direction. Caleb rarely had the opportunity to observe her without her knowledge. Megan untied her heavy outdoor shawl and hung it on a peg by the chimney and touched her smooth auburn hair to be sure none of it had strayed from its pins. In spite of the work she had been doing, her white blouse was still clean and her skirt not muddy. Megan was one of the neatest women he had ever seen. She was nothing like the stereotypical mountain women some of his fellow soldiers had laughed about around campfires.

Since coming to the cabin, Caleb had discovered other discrepancies in what he had been told. It wasn't difficult to figure out that the Union soldiers, in order to justify the hardships and dangers they were placing these women in, had to lessen their humanness. He assumed the Confederate soldiers were doing the same thing. For most people, war was only possible if one could convince himself that the enemy was barbaric.

Megan left his range of view but soon returned with a piece of paper. Still not looking in his direction, she sat on the low stool by the fire and began to draw. As her bit of charcoal moved over the paper, she started to sing.

Caleb had never heard her sing before. Her voice was clear and true and the song was an old one he had heard his sister sing on many occasions. Homesick, his eyes burned with tears he refused to shed while he listened to the strains of the familiar song. Felicity had never sung it so well.

Abruptly Megan broke off the song. She straightened and studied the paper in her lap. Then with a sigh, she started to crumple it and toss it into the fire.

"Wait!" Caleb called out.

She jumped as if she had forgotten he was in the house. As she turned to him, her eyes were wide and startled, her lips slightly parted.

"Wait," he said more gently. "May I see what you're drawing?"

"It's nothing." She hesitated, then came back into the back room and held it out to him.

The drawing was of a bird in a bare winter tree. Its feathers were fluffed against the cold and its beak was a tiny point sticking out of the feathers. Caleb smiled. "I've seen so many birds look just like this."

"It's cold out. It was trying to keep warm."

"You'd think it would head south for the winter."

"Perhaps it did. We don't know where it came from originally. Maybe it's a Canadian bird."

"Why were you going to burn this?"

"I burn most of my drawings. I only do them to amuse myself."

"Is it all right if I keep this one?"

She hesitated. "I suppose so."

He put it on the small table by the bed, where he kept the book he was reading. "I haven't seen much of you today."

"I've been busy. A shutter is broken on the front window and I've been trying to fix it. I didn't have much luck. I don't dare ask Papa to come do it. He might see you and shoot you."

"I'd just as soon not have that happen," he said with a smile. "You have a beautiful voice."

She glanced at him as if she hadn't expected him to say that. "I'm sorry. I forgot you were here. Did I wake you?"

"No one could sleep as much as you seem to think I do. No, I was awake. And don't apologize. I enjoyed hearing you."

She came nearer and started untying the bandage on his arm. "How are you feeling?"

"My arm is almost well."

"And your leg?"

"That could be better," he admitted. He didn't tell her that it felt as if it were on fire every time he tried to move it. He was beginning to think he had further injured it the day he had tried to escape.

Megan made no comment but pulled the covers aside. They had reached a compromise in his clothing. He wore a pair of her brother's pants with one leg cut away. Owen's shirts had been too small, however, so he was still bare from the waist up. His wool uniform had been too scratchy to wear in bed and he couldn't allow her to cut the leg out of his only pair of pants.

When she uncovered the wound, he saw her frown. "What's wrong?" he asked, pushing himself up on the bed so he could see the injury.

"Probably nothing," she said in a voice that didn't fool him for a minute. "I suppose all gunshot wounds heal this way. Right?" She looked at him anxiously.

He made a noncommittal sound. A streak of angry red was starting up his leg from the wound. The wound itself was puffy and scarlet. "I believe what we have here is the beginning of gangrene."

"Gangrene?" she whispered.

Caleb tried to calm his thoughts. Panic wouldn't help. "I've seen it before. In the hospital tents."

"What do the doctors do for it?"

For a long moment he couldn't answer. "They amputate."

"No. I won't do that to you."

"Good," he said wryly. "I was hoping you'd say that. Unfortunately, you may have to. Or you may have to get me to a doctor, no matter which side he's on." His eyes met hers.

"No. You're my prisoner and I'm going to take care of you."

"How do you intend to do that? Do you know what happens if gangrene is left unchecked? The person dies."

Megan covered the wound and avoided his eyes. "I'm not going to let that happen. I need you."

He watched her go back into the main room and bring in the clothes she had taken from the line. They were still stiff from being frozen. She put the basket down by the bed and started folding them. In a brisk way that told Caleb she was very concerned, she said, "I'll walk down to Mama's and get some medicine."

"And how will you explain needing it?"

"I don't know yet. That's why I'm folding clothes while I think. I could tell her I need it in case I cut myself."

"That might work. Sulfur is what we need, I think. Sulfur cures most anything."

"When Papa's horses get cut, he uses a carbolic acid wash. if that doesn't work, he has a stick of lunar caustic."

"I'm willing to try anything. Even veterinary medicine."

She dropped the sheet she was folding and said, "I'll be back soon."

She took her heavy shawl off the peg and, after a glance at the fire to be sure it was safely contained and likely to keep burning, she left the cabin.

The wind was so sharp it almost hurt her lungs. There would be a heavy frost before morning, if not a light snow. The clouds were heavy, but to Megan's practiced eye it looked as if a storm would pass them by this time. The top of the mountain had been dusted several times but so far snow hadn't reached into the Hollow.

When she reached her parents' cabin, she smelled the familiar scent of wash being ironed. Bridget had the irons set up on end to gather the heat while she shoved one over the shirt on the board. As on so many wash days before, Megan heard their mother grumbling about the ironing.

"When I was a girl in the old country," Jane was saying, "we had a different way of doing it. We'd spread the clothing on the clean floor and smooth it with our bare feet. Nobody got burned and there were never any scorch marks on our clothes. You'll never convince me that this way is better. This is the English way!"

Bridget winked at Megan. They had heard this many times. "My feet would likely freeze today, Mama," she said.

"Nonsense. Our feet never froze." Jane glanced up. "Hello, Megan. I didn't hear you come in. I thought you'd be ironing today."

"I'll do that later." Now that she was here, she wasn't at all sure she could get the medicine she needed. "Do we have any sulphur?"

"Not likely. The Yankees have cut off all our supplies. I think I used the last when your papa cut his hand on the fencing." She looked at her older daughter closely. "You've not cut yourself, have you?'' Even after spending most of her life in Black Hollow, she still retained the brogue of her youth.

"No, Mama. I just thought I should have some on hand.''

"And well you should. Sometimes I think this infernal war will go on forever.'' Jane turned back to the bread she was kneading. "In the meantime, you'd do well to be careful with your knife.'' Jane was never in the best of moods on ironing day. She honestly believed the Irish way of ironing was better and it was only by Samuel's edict that she used the heated irons.

"Are you sure you haven't cut yourself and just don't want us to worry?'' Bridget asked as she exchanged the cooling iron for a hotter one.

"No, I really haven't. I was just asking.'' If there was no sulphur, she would have to use the veterinary medicine. "Mama, it wouldn't hurt a person to use medicine meant for a horse, would it?''

"Depends, I suppose. We're all animals.'' Jane jabbed her fists into the mound of dough. "You must have started your chores early if you're free to talk at this time of day,'' she observed tartly.

"I have to get back up the hill. I haven't started my ironing yet.''

Jane made an admonishing sound. "I raised you better than to go gallivanting off in the middle of the day. What would your papa say if he was to come in?''

"I'm leaving. I'll see you on Sunday.''

"Aye, that you will. You recollect when the service starts?'' This was a reminder that Megan had almost been late for the service on the preceding Sunday.

"Yes, Mama.'' She waved at Bridget, who smiled and nodded. They were used to their mother's moods when her Irish upbringing didn't match the ways of the Hollow, and they knew she wasn't angry with them.

Megan circled the house and went toward the barn. This would be trickier since she had no reason to be out here if she were seen. Samuel was nowhere in sight and she was able to slip into the cold darkness behind the door. She paused for her eyes to grow accustomed to the dimness. There were no animals in the barn—not since the soldiers had started stealing them. The family horse and mule were hidden in a meadow that only the people of the settlement knew existed. Otherwise they would have disappeared long ago.

The liniments and tack were kept in a room near the double doors. She was as familiar with the barn as she was with the house. Samuel was a man of habit and he never rearranged anything. That enabled Megan to find the correct bottle that contained the carbolic acid. She felt along the shelf, shuddering when her fingers encountered cobwebs and something that felt a bit too much like a mouse. Finally she touched the stick of lunar caustic.

This was all the acid and caustic that Samuel still had, but she thought he might not miss it. Since he was able to work less often with the horse and mule, they were less likely to need doctoring. She would probably be able to get it back on the shelf before it was missed.

She put it in her pocket and wrapped her shawl about her more warmly. The barn kept out the wind, but the coldness seemed trapped inside without animals to heat it. She was glad to leave its darkness and go back into the light.

Walking as quickly as she dared, she headed back up the mountain. She knew the wound on Caleb's leg was worse than he had admitted. Cuts were a part of farm life and she had doctored other wounds. A gunshot couldn't be all that different. She also knew what gangrene was. One of her cousins had lost part of a foot several years back and he had considered himself lucky.

When she reached the cabin, she hurried into Caleb's room. He wasn't reading as she had expected. That meant he was as nervous as she was. She gave him a reassuring smile. "If this is good for horses, it will be good for you as well. You'll see."

He sat up and gingerly untied the bandage. Megan poured the carbolic acid on a clean cloth and hesitated before pressing it on Caleb's leg. He winced and she knew he was hurting, but there was no way to prevent that. When she thought the acid had done all it could, she removed the cloth and took the stick of medicine from her pocket.

"What's that?" he asked suspiciously.

"Lunar caustic. Don't you use it where you come from?" She bent over the wound and touched it with the stick.

Caleb caught his breath sharply. "Give me that. You're enjoying this too much."

Megan was glad to hand it over. "Rub it in good. Then we have to let it dry before we bandage you again." She took a fresh bandage from the clean ones she had stacked on a shelf. "Papa always lets it dry before he does anything else to it." She could tell by the pallor of Caleb's skin that he was in a great deal of pain.

Finally he handed the stick to her in silence. He lay back on the pillow and closed his eyes.

"I know that hurt," she said softly. "And I wasn't enjoying it."

"I know." He didn't open his eyes.

"Are you all right?"

He nodded. "I will be."

"I could bring you some chicory coffee," she suggested hopefully. "Would you like some?"

"There is almost nothing I'd like less than chicory coffee," he said with a small smile. "How you drink that stuff is beyond me."

"I don't. I was making it because I thought you liked it. I hate the taste. Papa drinks it and so do most of the other men," she added. "Mama started making it when Raintree ran out of real coffee."

"As far as I'm concerned, you never need make another cup."

Megan sat on the edge of the bed and studied him in concern. There was nothing she could do to ease his pain and she knew his strained silences were due in large part to well-founded worry. "I'm not going to let anything happen to you," she promised again.

He opened his eyes. "I'm going to hold you to that."

"Do you have any idea where your brother may be?" Caleb asked as he watched her knit the shawl she was making for her sister for Christmas.

"No," she said, then paused. "That's not really true. I think he will settle somewhere around Cat Springs, Ohio."

"Oh? He went to Ohio? That's where I'm from." Caleb thought for a minute. "I think we went near a place called Cat Springs on the way to Tennessee. Do you have other family there?"

She laughed. "Of course not. We all live right here in Black Hollow. Papa used to have some cousins in Oak Ridge, but they moved and we have no contact with them anymore. No, I think Owen will stay in Cat Springs because he wrote us from there and said he likes it better than anywhere else he's been." She frowned at the dark brown yarn in her hands. "Papa burned the letter as soon as he heard it had come. I had time to read it, though."

"You miss Owen a great deal, don't you?"

"Yes, I do for a fact. We were always close. He was older and he always looked after me. He taught me a lot of things a girl probably doesn't have any business knowing."

"Such as?"

"How to whistle. Mama says it's a wonder anyone wants to marry me at all since I can whistle like a man. It's supposed to be bad luck or something. And I can swim." She smiled at him as if she knew he would be scandalized.

"You can swim?" He grinned. "I've never known a girl who wanted to learn."

"Maybe it's different when you live in the country. We aren't as formal, I mean. Anyway, I used to follow Owen to the swimming hole, and when he found out, he taught me. He tried to teach Bridget, too, but she was afraid and told on us. After that Papa and Mama said I wasn't to swim, either." She frowned. "I still don't know what harm it would do."

"Neither do I." He had a sudden vision of how she would look in a wet chemise. He tried unsuccessfully to put the picture from his mind.

"And I can skip rocks."

"You have to have a good pitching arm to do that."

"I know. That's what makes it improper. Girls are supposed to be taught more useful things. But I can make rocks skip better than Owen ever could."

"You'll have to show me sometime." He watched her fingers flying in the yarn. "Will you finish that in time for Christmas?"

"I think so. It doesn't matter if it's a few days late. We don't give presents in the Hollow."

He furrowed his brows. "No Christmas presents?"

"Sometimes the smallest children get something special, like an orange or a top their papas whittled, but we don't make it a day for giving gifts. It's for going to church, according to Brother Grady. Since he took over the church, he's tried to stop us from giving presents on Christmas at all."

"That's terrible!"

"Does your family exchange gifts?" She looked up at him, never losing a stitch on her softly clicking needles.

"Of course we do. We go to church as well, but that's only part of the tradition. I can just imagine Felicity if she thought she wasn't going to get or give gifts on Christmas! She would be beside herself!"

"She actually *tells* you she wants a gift? I can't imagine that."

"She knows we'll give her things. She just drops hints as to what would please her the most. You don't do that?"

"Papa says that's worse than anything, asking for something as a gift." She blushed slightly. "I didn't mean to speak against your sister."

"I didn't take it that way. No, it's part of the fun. For instance, if you could have anything at all, what would it be?"

Megan thought for a minute. "A music box." She laughed and lowered her eyes as if the admission were embarrassing. "I shouldn't have said that."

"Felicity loves music boxes. All women do, as near as I can tell. What would be wrong with asking for one?"

"It's so frivolous! It wouldn't serve any purpose at all." Her voice softened. "I saw one once in Raintree. I couldn't stop looking at it. It was round and had painted horses that circled it and it sounded like fairy music when it played. I've often wondered who bought it and where it is now."

Caleb was surprised at how much he wanted to find such a music box and give it to her. "Didn't you ever tell Seth about the music box? Maybe he would have bought it for you."

"No, not Seth. He's much too practical for that."

"Buying something a woman wants is perfectly practical if a man wants to please her. Gifts are best when they aren't practical at all."

Megan shook her head. "It's a good thing Brother Grady can't hear you say that. He says money is too hard to come by in the Hollow and that it's a sin to squander it."

"From all you've told me, he thinks everything is a sin. Are you happy living such a Spartan life?"

She pretended to be busy counting stitches in the pattern. When she looked up again, she said, "Tell me about Felicity. You said she's about my age. Is she engaged to be married?"

"She wasn't when I last heard from her. I haven't had a letter from my family in months. She could be married twice over for all I know."

"Maybe you'll be with them soon." Her eyes strayed to his leg, then moved away quickly.

Caleb didn't need any reminders. It was hurting him constantly now. "Megan, I don't know how any of this is going to work out. Even if your crazy plan works and you're able to trade me for Seth, I don't know if my leg will heal. For that matter, I could be shot before I reach Ohio, even if it does mend. So I'm going to tell you what I feel."

She looked up, her eyes apprehensive.

"You shouldn't marry Seth."

"What?" She tried to laugh at the idea but failed. "Not marry Seth? The idea never crossed my mind." Then she said, "Why do you say that?"

"Because you don't love him."

"There's no way for you to know that. You don't even know him!"

"No, but I know people like him. If he loved you, he would have bought you that music box instead of spending his money on drink and loose women. Don't look at me like that. You told me he's wild, and that takes money. If he loved you, there wouldn't have been reason for you to tell him you wanted that music box. He would know it all by himself."

"That's not fair." She avoided his eyes, as if that had occurred to her, too.

"And if you loved him, you would talk about him in a different way. You talk about him as if he were a brother or a cousin, not a lover!"

"We aren't lovers!" She turned bright red and wadded the knitting in her lap.

Caleb suddenly realized the women in Raintree weren't the only ones Seth had seduced. "I meant two people who are in love, not two who had made love together."

"Well, of course that's what you meant." She was still flushed and ill at ease. "I didn't think for a minute that you meant ..."

"Megan?" He watched her closely. "I get the feeling that I stumbled onto something no one else knows."

She sighed. "It happened just before he left for the war." She stood and went to the window. It was at her eye level and she put her hand up on the ledge as she gazed out sightlessly. "I never told anyone, not even Bridget. I thought we were going to be married in a few days. He said that we were."

Caleb wished he had Seth within reach. He could hear the pain in her voice.

"It happened in the very clearing where I found you. Of course this cabin wasn't built then. There was no place we could go to be alone. Besides, I would never have come up here with him. The entire settlement would know before I returned!" She drew in a deep breath and held it for a moment. "It happened before I knew what was going on."

"I'm sorry."

She lowered her head. "It's all right, I guess. When he comes back, we'll be married and that will set it right. No one else will ever know. Except for you."

"I meant that I'm sorry that he was so inept at making love."

Megan looked over her shoulder at him. "How do you know that he was?"

"If he wasn't, you'd have known what he had in mind."

She turned away again. "I shouldn't be having this conversation with you." After a moment she said, "Are you saying it's not supposed to be so... fast?"

He smiled at her, memorizing the curve of her slender shape, the way her hair was woven into a bun on the back of her graceful neck, the way the sunlight made her skin creamy and peach-hued. "Making love should take much longer. Hours are not unreasonable."

"Are you teasing me again?" She frowned and her brows furrowed over her straight nose. "I should have known not to confide in you."

"I'm not teasing you."

She started to leave the room but he caught her wrist and pulled her down to sit on his bed. "Why did you confide in me?"

She shook her head but he didn't release her. "I suppose it was because I know you won't be here long and that you can't possibly tell anyone in the Hollow. And I've needed to tell someone."

"Megan, don't marry him. He's not worth it."

"You can't know that!" she protested again and tried to free her wrist.

"Yes, I can. You should marry someone who is capable of giving as much love as you are. There are two kinds of people. Those who take and those who give. Takers don't make good husbands." He paused and rubbed his thumb over her inner arm. Beneath her sleeve her skin felt soft and warm. "Since you've told me this much, did you enjoy the lovemaking?"

"You shouldn't ask me a thing like that!"

"I know. Did you?"

She stopped struggling. For a while he thought she would refuse to answer and that he had gone too far. "No," she finally said in a low voice. "I didn't. Maybe there's something wrong with me?" She turned the statement into a question and looked at him for verification.

Their eyes met and Caleb felt his soul spinning to meet hers. He hadn't intended for this to happen. Her brown eyes held him and promised all he had ever yearned for in a woman. As if by instinct, her lips parted and he could see the line of her white teeth. "No," he said gently. "There's nothing wrong with you. Nothing at all."

He put his hand on her neck and felt her frantic pulse throbbing beneath his fingers. Her skin was smooth and tender and he wanted her more than he had ever wanted any woman in his life. He slipped his hand behind her neck and drew her toward him.

Their lips paused a breath away, then touched. She tasted sweet in his mouth. Caleb ached for her. He kissed her and she responded eagerly. She was small in his arms and incredibly inviting.

Suddenly she pushed him away and rushed from the bed. She stood, her back to him, her hands pressed against her lips. Her shoulders trembled and for an awful moment he thought she was crying.

"I'm sorry," he said. "I should never have done that."

Megan didn't answer.

Painfully Caleb swung his legs over the side of the bed and he tried to go to her. "Megan?"

She went to him and tried to push him back into bed. "Lie down! Do you want to hurt your leg even more?"

He pulled her to him. She was so much shorter than he had remembered, and she was willow slender. "I didn't mean to frighten you. Or to hurt you."

"I'm not hurt. Or frightened," she added after a pause.

"Then why did you pull away?"

"I had to. We can't..."

"I wasn't going to. I was only kissing you." He put his fingers under her chin and tilted her face back so he could see her troubled eyes. "I would never do anything to hurt you."

"If I hadn't pulled away, something might have happened that would be all wrong. I can't want you!" Her anguished voice told him that she did want him, right or wrong. "You can't care for me!"

"I already do."

"No! We're enemies!"

"You know we aren't. The war doesn't have anything to do with us. With how we feel." Tears glazed her eyes and he wanted to hold her and kiss them away.

"I can't love you," she whispered. Then she pulled away and hurried from the room.

For a moment Caleb stood there. He slowly lowered himself back onto the bed, his leg hurting as if demons were playing in it. Love? Until she had said the word it hadn't occurred to him. Now it refused to leave his mind. Love. He was falling in love with her—the one woman in the world he couldn't have. And now that he admitted it to himself, he realized he had known he loved her all along.

Chapter Six

Megan pulled her white cotton nightgown over her head and hung it on a peg. She shivered in the cold of the bedroom as she poured water into the basin on her washstand. There was a thin film of ice on the water that broke and caused the water to splash in the bowl. Dipping a cloth into it, Megan started her morning sponge bath.

All her life she had hated cold baths. Only the alternative of going dirty made her take one. Most of the people in the settlement waited until spring to bathe, her father included. He was of the opinion that too many baths were bad for the health and he had discouraged his daughters from taking them. Megan had often heard him say that immersing in a tub was a sure way to bring on sickness and that baths were only to be used as a medicinal treatment. When she had pointed out that both views couldn't be true since they contradicted each other, Samuel had threatened to take her behind the barn and whip her.

Now that she had her own place, she bathed every day, even if it was only a sponge bath. It was hard to bathe in the washtub when Caleb was in the house, though she had done so when she was positive he was asleep.

She paused and listened. She couldn't hear any sounds coming from the back room. Now that his arm was almost healed, he bathed himself in the mornings and, as early as she got up, he was usually awake ahead of her.

Megan hurriedly finished her bath and dressed in her brown wool dress, her heaviest stockings and her warmest shoes. She unbraided her long hair and brushed it until it lay in smooth waves on her shoulders. Was it possible, she wondered, that Caleb had already bathed and was reading?

Coiling her hair into a heavy bun, Megan pushed in the pins that held it and picked up the washbasin. She crossed the main room and tossed the water out the back door. It splashed on the dirt and beaded into brown pearls in the dust. As cold as it was in the cabin, it was much colder outside.

Megan put a log on the fire to warm the house and went in to see about Caleb.

He lay sprawled on his bed, his eyes closed, his muscular arm thrown out of the covers. A two-day beard darkened his square jaw—he hadn't felt well enough to shave lately. Since he never neglected keeping himself clean, Megan had wondered about this. Now she realized he must have been in much more pain than she had thought.

When she touched him, she drew her hand back reflexively. His skin was burning to the touch, but he shivered as if her hands were freezing to him. He didn't open his eyes. "Caleb?" she said tentatively. He didn't respond.

With growing dread, Megan pulled back the covers. His leg was still bandaged but now the dangerous red streak extended beyond the bandage and up his thigh. Her hands trembled as she covered him again. The gangrene was taking hold. Caleb might die.

Megan ran to the hook where she kept her heaviest shawl and wrapped it around her. Then she went to the shelf by the dry sink and took down the sugar bowl where she kept her money. She had been saving for a new book, so her stash was larger than it ordinarily would have been. She shoved the money in the pocket of her dress and ran from the house.

While there was no doctor nearby, there was an old Indian called Elk Woman who occasionally sold medicinal concoctions to the settlement. The only problem with Elk Woman was that she was half-crazy and hated whites.

Megan had never been to the hut where the old woman lived, but she knew the way. She had been warned by her parents never to go there for fear Elk Woman would shoot her. Only the men of the settlement went there, and they seldom went alone.

She ran through the familiar woods behind her cabin. Each step increased her fear for Caleb's life. Should she have stayed with him and tried to break his fever first? A high fever could be as dangerous as gangrene. Megan had seen a little girl have fever so high that it left her mind damaged. The girl was older than Megan, but had the mind of a small child and would never be able to have a normal life and a family of her own. Megan found she was crying silently as she ran in search of the Indian woman.

Soon she left the woods she had known all her life and was in unfamiliar territory. She searched until she found the branch of Medicine Hat Creek that parted from the main stream and eventually wound around to Elk Woman's hut. It wasn't hard to follow the creek but the minutes seemed as long as hours. What if Elk Woman had moved away or died? Everyone knew Indians came and went without notice or even apparent reason.

Suddenly Megan found herself in a small clearing. Across the meadow she saw a squalid hut with a pale stream of smoke curling from the mud chimney.

Elk Woman was the widow of a trapper who had come to the area before the settlement was established. He had been many years older than Elk Woman and had long since died. No one knew for certain what she had done with his body, but it was supposed she had cremated him in the way the local Indians did their dead. He had been even more anti-social than his wife and no one had asked too many questions. Since that time Elk Woman had lived alone.

Megan had reached the center of the clearing when the hide covering the hut's doorway was shoved aside. An ancient woman appeared, a scowl on her face and a rifle in her gnarled hands. Megan stopped abruptly.

The old woman silently leveled the rifle at her.

"I've come to buy medicine," Megan called to her. Her heart was pounding with fear and was making a knot in her throat. "I don't mean to harm you."

Elk Woman stood still for a moment as if she were letting the words sink into her brain. Then her eyes darted past Megan in search of others. When she was satisfied Megan was alone, she lowered the rifle and motioned for Megan to come closer.

On legs that seemed to be made of jelly, Megan closed the distance between them. "I need medicine," she repeated.

Elk Woman was tall and more wrinkled than anyone Megan had ever seen. Her eyes were like black beads in her face and had no more expression than if they were made of obsidian. Her hair hung in lank strings that reminded Megan of dirty hanks of wool. A bedraggled feather was stuck in the greasy leather headband she wore, along with a tuft of fur from some long-dead rabbit. Her dress was of deerskin but was so greasy it was shiny and mottled with stains. Megan tried not to identify the odor that emanated from the woman.

"Medicine. For what?" Elk Woman finally said.

"A gunshot wound. It's gone bad. It has gangrene in it."

"Not know gangrene. Has red streak? Long, like so?" She drew an invisible mark on her puckering flesh. Elk Woman was a person of few words, none of them gentle.

Megan nodded.

"He die." Elk Woman turned to go back into her hut.

"No!" Megan caught the woman's arm but released her at once.

Elk Woman glared at her as if she might shoot her after all. "He die!" she repeated.

"I have to have medicine!" Megan insisted. Somehow she knew the woman was more knowledgeable than she was willing to admit. "I've brought money."

"What good is money to me?"

"It can buy you things in Raintree. Pretty things," she said desperately.

Elk Woman was silent for a moment. "I give you medicine. You give me shoes."

"My shoes?" Megan looked at her feet.

"No shoes, no give medicine."

"All right." Megan sat on the winter grass and began unlacing her shoes. She wasn't sure she could walk home barefoot with her feet in one piece and not frozen, but she was willing to pay any price.

Elk Woman kicked off her filthy moccasins and chortled like a child as she grabbed the shoes. "You take mine," she said magnanimously.

Megan managed not to wrinkle her nose as she put her cold feet into the moccasins. She was thankful she was wearing thick stockings.

Elk Woman turned and went into the hut. Megan didn't want to follow, but she wasn't going to let the old woman take her shoes and refuse the medicine after all.

The interior of the hut was worse than Megan could have imagined. A low cot stood against one wall and was heaped with smelly skins. Everything else the woman owned lay in the corners. In the center of the hut, beneath the smoke hole in the roof, was a circle of stones on the dirt floor and in it burned a low fire. Every gust of wind filled the hut with acrid smoke. Megan's eyes burned and her nose rebelled at the stench. Could anything from this squalid hut cure anyone?

Elk Woman went to several leather bags, each marked with a crude design drawn with Indian paints. She studied them carefully, then took one and opened it. Her grimy finger dipped in and she pulled out a quantity of something that looked like shredded bark. Silently she handed it to Megan.

Megan took it and closed her hand over it. Could she believe the woman? What if this made Caleb worse? "What do I do with this?"

"Make tea. He drink it." Elk Woman held up her hand, her fingers spread. "Five times, you do it. Use it all. Boil it over and over until water no have color."

Megan nodded.

Elk Woman dug through the bags until she found one with a blue bolt of lightning on it. She dumped its contents into Megan's other hand. Megan looked down at the sickly white root. Bits of dirt still clung to the hairy tendrils that grew off it. In shape it was similar to a man.

"Boil this. Make soft." Elk Woman made a grinding motion in the palm of her hand. "Mash in hand. Put on wound."

"Will this make him well?"

Elk Woman nodded. "Medicine from my tribe. It make him well." She held up her hand again. "Five days."

Megan put the root and bark in the pockets of her skirt. She wondered if Elk Woman knew how to count or if she merely said "five" to indicate any amount and passage of time.

"Go away now." The old woman turned her back and shuffled to the fire.

"Thank you," Megan said, and backed out of the hut.

She was glad to step outside and gulp in fresh air. Her head was spinning from the odors and closeness inside the hut. She ran across the clearing and into the woods.

When she reached the cabin, she kicked off the filthy moccasins and ran in her stocking feet into the house. She didn't even want to touch the moccasins long enough to burn them.

A glance in the back room told her Caleb's condition hadn't changed. She went to the fire and poured the pot of ready water into two smaller pots to boil. Carefully, she put the root in one and the bark in the other. Again she wondered what the objects were and whether they would cure Caleb or make him worse. But she knew others in the settlement had used the Indian's medicine, and as far as she knew, none had died from it.

Taking a pan of cold water, Megan went in and started bathing Caleb's face and chest. He groaned and tossed his head, but she persisted. If the fever didn't break, he might die. Her feet were like ice on the floor, but she didn't want to take the time away from caring for him to get her other pair of shoes. Nor did she know how she would explain the loss of her shoes to her family. Among people who had so little, every change was noticed.

The fever was persistent. As fast as Megan cooled one part of his body, another heated. Megan had little experience with fever since she and her family were usually healthy but she drew on everything her mother had ever told her. Jane had been thorough in her instructions to her daughters. Someday they would have families of their own and it was up to the woman to know enough medicine to take of the others.

"You're not going to die," she said to him. "I won't let you." She felt tears spring to her eyes and she brushed them away impatiently.

When the water had boiled, Megan poured off enough to give Caleb. It was a dark, muddy color and had an odd smell but she had to chance it. Most of the people she knew believed that for medicine to be strong, it had to be unpleasant. If that were true, she thought this must be potent indeed.

She let it cool a bit, then carried it to Caleb. Slipping her arm under his head, she lifted him against her. Carefully she put the cup to his lips and poured some in his mouth. Caleb frowned but reflexively swallowed it. Megan kept giving it to him until the cup was empty. Had Elk Woman meant he was to drink five cups or to drink it for five days? Megan decided she would make tea of the bark until there was no color to the water and hope she was following the instructions properly.

Caleb sighed when she laid his head back on the pillow. A fine sheen of sweat slicked his brow. It was a change but she didn't know if it was one for the better.

She went back to the fire and fished the root out of the water and onto a clean cup towel. When it was cool enough to pick up, Megan held it in one hand and mashed it to a pulp with the other. It felt slick and gelatinous.

Going back to Caleb, she removed the bandage on his leg. It looked much worse than the day before and her worry increased. She had never seen a wound that looked so bad. Trying not to hurt him, she spread the root on the infected flesh and covered it with a fresh bandage.

Then she started sponging away his fever once again.

Her arms and shoulders ached from wiping the cold cloth over him and she sat on the bed to reach him more easily. Her hip made contact with his and when she leaned forward, her breasts brushed his bare chest. The contact with his skin was affecting her in ways she hadn't expected. "You're going to live," she said over and over as she worked on him. "I'm not going to lose you! Not now."

Methodically she worked with him. His skin was still burning with fever that didn't seem to break no matter what she did. She put a cloth across his forehead to keep it cool while she bathed his chest. If fever affected the brain, it only made sense to keep his head as cool as possible. Against his skin and black hair the cloth was startlingly white.

"I care too much for you to let you die," she said, knowing he couldn't hear her. "You aren't like anyone I've ever known and I don't want you to leave me." She wiped at her tears with the back of her hand as she dipped the cloth into the bowl. "It scares me when I think how much I care for you. I find myself thinking about you all the time. I don't know what I'll do when I have to go back to living without you." She paused and studied his still face. "Please don't leave me, Caleb. Please don't die."

By midafternoon he was cooler and seemed to be more asleep than unconscious. Bending over him, knowing she shouldn't, Megan kissed his forehead, his cheeks, then his lips. There was no way he would ever know. He stirred when her lips left his, but he continued to sleep.

Wearily, Megan went into her bedroom and put on her shoes. Her feet were so cold they tingled but she was too tired to care. How long would it be before she knew if Caleb would live? And what would she do if he grew worse? She knew the answer. She would have to go to the settlement and find someone who knew more about medicine than she did. That would probably mean that Caleb would lose his leg, despite her promise to him. Even then he might not live.

She lay down on her bed and drew her knees up to her middle as she had when she was a girl and overcome with worry or sadness. She was no longer concerned that she would lose a lever to regain Seth's freedom; she might lose Caleb.

She wasn't sure when he had become so important to her, but she could no longer deny it. When she closed her eyes she could hear his voice, deep and melodious. He liked talking more than any man she had ever known. Did men in the settlement talk so much when they were away from their women? She didn't know if he was simply bored or if he really enjoyed her company. Whatever the reason, he talked to her and she liked it.

Memories of Seth came to her and this time she examined them critically. Seth almost never talked to her about anything he was feeling. He might tell her about a new calf or a horse he wanted to buy, but not about sunsets or her drawings. Megan's interests were second to his and up until she met Caleb, Megan had never questioned this. She had never heard her father talk to her mother about emotions or abstract ideas so she had never missed it. Seth wasn't a bad person, he was simply behaving the way all the other men in the settlement did.

Megan knew she would have to give Caleb up eventually. There was no way on earth for her to be with him once Seth came home. Caleb would go back to his people and she would stay in Black Hollow with hers. Thinking about it made Megan feel an emptiness inside. Caleb was becoming an important part of her life.

When she heard a sound from the back room, she felt a stab of fear. Was he worse?

She ran to him and put her hand on his forehead. To her amazement, it was cool. Caleb opened his eyes and looked up at her, squinting as if he were having trouble focusing. "Megan?" he asked in a cracked voice.

"I'll get you some tea!" She hurried to pour up more of the bark tea and brought it to him.

He sipped it as he frowned. "That tastes terrible!"

"How do you feel?"

"Worse than that concoction tastes." He tried to shift in the bed and flinched as pain shot through him.

"Why didn't you tell me you were worse?" she demanded as she made him drink the rest of the tea. "You've had me worried half to death!"

"I didn't want to upset you." He opened his eyes again and tried to smile. "I hate to be a bother."

She found herself smiling as tears gathered in her eyes. "No one in the entire world is more of a bother than you are. Why would you start to worry about it now?'' But she touched his face gently. She felt a tear roll down her cheek.

''You're crying,'' he whispered.

''You nearly died! I thought I had lost you.''

''Is that why you decided to poison me with that tea? You were putting me out of my misery?''

''If you were feeling better, I'd hit you.'' Her voice softened. ''*Are* you feeling better?''

He nodded. ''I guess this is better. I really did think I was going to die for a while there. I guess I should have mentioned it.''

''Tonight I'm going to make myself a bed in here. I can't hear you well enough from my room.''

Caleb smiled, though his eyes were closed again. ''Why, Miss Llewellyn, you shock me.''

''You must be better. You're being a pain in the neck again.'' She carried the cup to the sink to wash it. Relief swept over her and she let her tears fall into the water. He might have a chance now.

Late that afternoon, Bridget came running into the cabin. Megan was startled and hurried to her, pulling the door to the back room shut. Had she seen Caleb?

''Mama says you have to come to the settlement! Union soldiers were seen up the creek and they're heading this way. She's afraid for you to be up here alone.''

''Union soldiers!'' Megan glanced at the closed door that hid Caleb.

''Hurry! They could be here any minute. Mama says some awful things were done to a family over toward Spring Mountain and she thinks these may be the same men!''

Megan tried not to panic. ''They might not even know my cabin is here.''

''Megan, use your head! There's smoke coming out of your chimney, and anybody traveling on the road has to pass right by here! Come on!''

"I'm coming. Tell Mama I'll be right there. I have to tamp my fire down."

"No, you haven't got time to do that!"

"I have to!" Megan snapped. "My house could burn down! Go home and tell Mama I'll be there soon."

Bridget hurried out but she gave Megan a peculiar look. Megan knew she would have to answer questions about this later. They both knew the fire was perfectly safe just as it was.

As soon as Bridget was gone, Megan started locking up her house. She couldn't leave Caleb. Not in his condition and certainly not with nearby Yankees he could signal. She looked in on him and was relieved to find him asleep.

She pulled the shutters firmly into place and ran the iron strap into the braces to lock them. The broken shutter posed a problem, but she thought if she could wrestle it into place and get the latch set it would look sound to a casual observer. If she could get the iron bar lined up inside it might even hold in case of an attack. She went out on the porch and was still struggling with it when she heard a sound behind her. Wheeling, she saw two men coming into her yard. She backed toward the door.

"Wait a minute, ma'am," the one in charge said. Although he wore what appeared to be a cavalry arm patch, he was on foot and he was unkempt. The other man was downright dirty. "Do you have any food?"

"No." She almost had her hand on the door latch behind her.

"You'd better stay where you are," the dirty one said in a threatening voice. To his comrade he said, "They always say that. You'd think these Rebs are living on air, to hear them talk."

"I believe I smell something cooking," the other said. He came up onto the porch, and Megan hastily moved away.

They seemed too large and rough in her cabin, as if they were entirely alien. Megan wondered if she could reach the rifle she had standing behind the door. She moved closer to it.

"Just stay where you are," the first one repeated. He fixed her with a glare. "Jobe, see what that is cooking on the hearth."

Megan watched the soldier go to the pot of stew she was cooking for supper.

"What's this?" the dirty man asked. "This looks like food to me! I believe she was lying to us, Frank."

The one he called Frank gave her a mean smile. "I believe you're right, Jobe."

"It's rat!" she blurted out as the other man lifted the dipper to taste it. A man would have to be desperate to eat something like that, she reasoned.

"Rat!" He dropped the ladle back into the pot.

"I ran out of food. All I have left to eat is whatever I can trap out in the barn." She held her breath. They didn't look as if they were hungry enough to eat rat meat.

"You Rebs will eat anything!"

Megan edged toward the door.

"Watch her, Frank. She's trying to get away."

Megan lunged behind the door and grabbed the rifle. In one quick movement she had it pointed at them. "Get out of here!" she commanded, her voice shaking.

"You wouldn't shoot a man, would you?" Jobe said as he stepped nearer.

"I'd shoot a Yankee!" She aimed the barrel at his face. "Do you want to gamble that I'd miss at this range?"

Frank patted at the air in a calming motion. "Now don't get so riled up. We're going. Aren't we, Jobe?"

"Sure we are. We just thought you might have something to eat."

"Well, I don't have anything I'm willing to share with the likes of you, so get out of here." She didn't let the rifle barrel waver.

The two men circled her and went out onto the porch. She watched them cautiously from the comparative safety of the cabin. Even if they were outside it didn't mean much if they decided to rush at her. She couldn't shoot them both and they knew it.

Suddenly Jobe gave a shout and charged at her. Automatically Megan squeezed the trigger. There was a loud report. Because she was inside the house it sounded even louder. Jobe shouted and fell back off the porch and to the ground, a red patch spreading across his chest. Frank paused only long enough to scoop him up, then he ran with him into the woods.

Megan was trembling as she leaned against the doorframe. She heard a noise and she turned to see the door to the back room open. Caleb stood in it, his pistol gripped in his hand.

"Are you all right?" he demanded. "What happened?"

"Nothing! I was shooting at a squirrel." She hurried to him. "Get back in bed." She helped him lie down again and covered him up. "Stay there!"

"That wasn't a squirrel I heard shout." He grabbed her skirt so she couldn't run from the room. "Did you just shoot someone?"

"Turn me loose! Papa and the other men will have heard the shot and they'll all be here in no time. You have to stay in here and be quiet or they may lynch you!"

"I'll be damned. You shot a Union soldier, didn't you?" He stared at her.

"A deserter, more likely." She hurried out and latched the door behind her. She didn't trust Caleb to stay put.

Frantically she moved about the room, hiding anything that might suggest she wasn't alone in the cabin. For a man that had been confined to the bedroom, Caleb had left his mark all about the room. His bandages were soaking in the wash bucket, two bowls and two spoons were drying on the drainboard. His uniform pants were folded with her aprons and dish towels where she had been ironing.

She tossed the pants under her bed and put away everything else in the cabinet before she heard feet running into her yard. She went to meet her father, Aaron Brennan and Benjamin Grady. They were armed with hunting rifles and looked as if they had expected to find her dead.

"Megan! Are you all right?" Samuel said as soon as she stepped out onto the porch.

"I'm fine, Papa. Two soldiers were here!"

"Bridget came to fetch you. Why didn't you come back with her the way you were supposed to?"

"I didn't have time. She came when I had just built up the fire and I was afraid the logs might roll out onto the floor while I was gone." She wrapped her arms about her against the cold.

"There's blood here, Samuel," Aaron shouted. "Look!"

"I shot one of them. With my squirrel gun. I don't think I killed him. The other one carried him away."

"Are you sure you aren't hurt?"

"I'm positive, Papa. They asked for food and I told them I didn't have any but they didn't believe me." Now that she was relatively safe, Megan was starting to tremble. "They tried to come in and I grabbed the rifle and shot one."

Samuel stared at her. He opened his mouth as if he didn't know quite what to say to a woman who was able to shoot a man in broad daylight, then he closed it again.

"If we head after them, we might be able to find them," Aaron said.

"That's right. We're wasting time," Brother Grady said. "They're getting away."

Megan pointed in the direction the men had gone. "They went that way, toward the south bend in the creek."

Samuel backed away to join his friends. "I'll have to talk to you about this later, Megan. Maybe I was wrong to say you ought to live up here. You should move back home."

"We'll talk later, Papa. They're getting away!"

She breathed a sigh of relief when the men left in pursuit of the soldiers. Closing and barring the door, she went back to Caleb.

"You didn't have to lock me in. I'm not fool enough to get myself lynched."

"No, but I didn't want them to come in and wander in here." She sank down in the chair by the bed and buried her face in her hands. "I shot a man!"

He reached out and pulled her to him. "I'm glad you did. I'm moving too slow. I might not have been able to get in there in time."

"You heard them? You weren't asleep?"

"I don't sleep that soundly, even after drinking that vile tea of yours. I think you were right about them being deserters. Regular army men wouldn't have been saying the things they were and there would be more of them."

"Do you think they'll come back?"

"I don't know. If they do, we'll be more prepared next time."

"I have to fix that broken shutter. I've tried everything I know how to do but it's just too heavy for me to lift and nail at the same time. I may have to get Papa up here to mend it. But if I do that, he might see you." She sighed. "No, I can't take the chance."

"We'll worry about it later. They won't be back tonight. I gather you killed one of them?"

"I don't know. It all happened so fast!" Her eyes were wide. "Do you think I may have? I hit him in the chest."

"It all depends. If you did, it wouldn't be a loss. Not if they're deserters."

She shook her head. "I'm not used to having to shoot people. I have enough trouble shooting food!"

"I hope it will all be over soon." He put his arm across her shoulders. She leaned nearer. She was so close she could see the darker flecks in his silvery eyes. His eyes were mesmerizing and she was losing herself in their depths.

Suddenly she drew back. She had been about to kiss him! "I have to go. Papa will expect me at the house. I have to convince him that I'm safe living here alone." She knew he was watching her but she didn't dare look back. Somehow she sensed the threat he represented was almost as dangerous in its way as the deserters were.

Chapter Seven

"You're up!" Megan said as she came into the main room.

Caleb was standing by the hearth, a log in his hands. "I'm feeling better. I had hoped to get the cabin warmer before you woke up."

Megan watched him bend to place the log on the fire. Except for the stiffness in his right leg he looked perfectly healthy. And dangerously sexy. "You shouldn't be on that leg." She tried to make her thoughts behave.

"It's much better. Whatever you did to it a few days ago worked."

"Let me see." She pulled the rocker closer to him and untied the bandage. When Caleb was on his feet, his muscles were taut and rippling when he moved. He made her think of things she had no business dwelling on. Like how his skin felt when she bathed him or brought down his fever and how his weight felt draped over her when she had helped him walk to the back room. She had preferred it when he was lying on the pallet in the back room. Then she had been able to convince herself he was a patient, not a virile and exciting man.

Trying not to touch his skin any more than necessary, she pulled the cloth away from the wound. Her mouth dropped open. "It's healing! The red streak is almost gone!"

"I know. What exactly did you do to it?" he asked as he bent to examine it.

"There's an old Indian woman who lives back in the woods. I went to her for medicine. I didn't expect it to work so fast! I was afraid it wouldn't work at all!"

"I don't remember much about that day." He was watching her closely.

"There's no reason you should. You barely opened your eyes until late afternoon when those deserters came here."

"Have you heard any more about them?"

"Yesterday when I went down to the settlement, Papa told me there's news about some men camping down toward the valley. The oldest Grady boy saw their campfire and got close enough to see several men. One of them seemed to be wounded or asleep. I guess I didn't kill him."

"Too bad."

"They're supposed to be on your side," she said. "I should think you'd be glad they're still alive."

"Deserters aren't on anyone's side but their own. They're a disgrace to the uniform they were wearing."

"Speaking of clothes, I need to get you something else to wear." She tried not to look at his broad chest. "It was all right as long as you were in bed, but you can't go around like this." She avoided his eyes. "It's not proper."

She went into the back room and rummaged through the few articles of Owen's clothing that she had saved. Most had been given away after he left that terrible night. Samuel had refused to let Owen take anything with him, and as soon as he was gone, her papa had ordered them to get rid of every reminder of him. Megan had slipped out some clothes and had hidden them in the root cellar in case Owen came back and needed them. When her cabin was finished, she had brought them here. She no longer thought Owen would come back for anything, but the clothes were a link with him. Besides, she couldn't admit to her father that she had gone against his orders and saved anything of her brother's. Now she was glad that she had.

"I can find only one shirt. Will it fit?" She took it to the main room and handed it to him.

Caleb pulled it over his head and the muscles in his lean frame rippled and knotted. Megan found she couldn't look away. Suddenly she realized he was watching her, and she turned from him to pump water into a glass.

"It's a good enough fit."

She glanced back at him. The shirt was open in a deep V on his chest, which disturbed her almost more than his naked skin had. "You'll find a lace in my room on a peg by the washstand." She was amazed how steady her voice sounded. Her heart was fluttering painfully and her pulse was racing.

He went into the bedroom and came back with a leather thong. As he laced it into the shirt's neck, he said, "Tell me what happened the day the deserters came."

"You got out of bed and tried to shoot them."

"No, I mean before that."

"Nothing much. I brought down your fever and gave you the medicine Elk Woman sold me." She smiled wryly. "She took my most comfortable shoes as the bargain."

"I'll find a way to send you another pair."

"That's not necessary. Not at all. Besides, how would I ever explain that to my family? And to Seth?"

"I seem to remember something else. I don't think it was a dream. I remember you saying you weren't going to give me up."

Megan's hands stopped in the act of washing the glass. He had heard her? "I meant I wasn't going to let you die. I was only reassuring you."

"I seem to recall it being a bit more emotional than that."

"You must have been dreaming."

"It's an odd thing for me to dream. I even recall that you were about to cry."

"I don't cry easily. Bridget can get teary over burned bread. Not me. It was a dream."

"I also felt you kiss me. And I'm positive that was no dream."

She put the glass down but didn't dare turn around. "I would never do such a thing."

He touched her and she jumped. She hadn't heard him cross the room. His fingers seemed to burn through the fabric of her dress. "Don't lie to me, Megan." Gently he turned her to face him.

She looked up at him. His black hair was falling over his forehead and his gray eyes were touched with silver. He was so handsome she felt her heart skip a beat. He touched her cheek and let his finger trail along the curve of her jaw. Fire seemed to be left in its wake. Her breath grew ragged and she had to restrain herself from leaning in to him. "I never lie." It didn't sound believable, even to her.

"Perhaps 'lie' is too strong a word. Did you kiss me?"

"I felt of your face to see if you were still feverish." She tried to step aside but he put his other arm around her waist to keep her there. "It may have felt like a kiss."

"Nothing but a kiss feels like a kiss."

She felt the blush rising and put her hands on his chest to push him away. Instead, she left them there. He felt so good.

He put his fingers under her chin and lifted it. For a moment he only gazed down at her, his thumb tracing the line of her lips. Then he bent and kissed her.

Megan had been kissed many times by Seth, but no kiss had ever affected her like this. His lips were warm and soft, yet firm. Her lips parted beneath his and the taste of him filled her mouth, exciting her with a hot rush. Dizziness spun through her. If he hadn't encircled her waist with his other arm, she would have stumbled. His other hand was laced through her hair, guiding her in the kiss.

When at last she could pull back, she leaned weakly against his chest. "We can't do this!" she said breathlessly.

"I know we shouldn't." His voice sounded tight and strained, as if the kiss had affected him as much as it had her.

"You can't ever do this again."

"I don't know that I can promise that."

His fingers continued to caress her and to weave in her hair. Megan realized her bun must have come loose when he first touched it. Until now she hadn't noticed. Instead of being embarrassed that her hair was flowing unrestrained down her back, she found it added to the sensuousness she was feeling. Certainly Caleb seemed to be enjoying it as he gathered masses of it in his hands and rubbed it on her cheek.

"You have beautiful hair," he said as his cheek rubbed the top of her head. "So thick and so soft."

"It's red." She felt she had to deflect his compliments or she would be lost. "Not as bright a red as Bridget's but enough to count. Enough to keep it from being beautiful."

"I've always been partial to red hair."

"In the Hollow, we feel—"

"Hush. I don't want to hear about the narrow-minded attitudes of the Hollow. Most women would kill for hair like yours." He wrapped it around the palm of his hand and watched it fall like silk against his fingers. "You're beautiful."

"My hair..."

"I'm not referring to just your hair. You're beautiful all over, inside and out."

She drew in a shaken breath. "No one has ever said that to me before."

"Are all your people fools or just Seth?"

"I can't let you talk to me like this." She tried to push against him but her heart wasn't in it. "It's sinful to hear compliments like this and you should know not to say them."

"You're wrong."

Megan laid her cheek on his chest and heard the steady beating of his heart. Did it always beat so strongly or was he as excited by her closeness as she was by his?

"Compliments are a part of loving. Are you telling me Seth never tells you that you're beautiful?"

She silently shook her head.

"Damn!" he whispered. He sounded frustrated, almost angry. "Don't marry him, Megan. It will be a huge mistake."

"Is spinsterhood a better choice?" she asked, finally managing to find the will to put distance between them. "What sort of life would that be?"

"You could come north with me."

Megan stared up at him. "Leave Black Hollow? Leave everyone I know? I could never do that." Her mind was whirling. It had never occurred to her that she might live somewhere else. "My place is here."

"It doesn't have to be."

"What are you saying exactly?" She had to be very sure about this. His reply might shape the rest of her life.

"My family would give you a place to stay. You could make a different life for yourself."

"Until you came here, my life was just fine the way it was." She walked to the hearth and gazed into the fire. She couldn't tell if he was asking her to marry him or if he was only offering her a place to live until she could make another life for herself. "I know what to expect from people in the Hollow. My father would disown me just the way he did Owen. There would be no coming back."

"Perhaps you could find Owen."

Megan closed her eyes and leaned her forehead on her hand upon the mantel. "I can't leave Black Hollow," she repeated to convince herself.

"It's not something you have to decide today."

"And what about us? What are you asking me?" she insisted.

He hesitated, then came to her. Gently he rubbed her shoulders and neck. "I care a great deal for you." He seemed to be choosing his words with care. "I don't know what will come of it. I only know I don't want to leave you."

She closed her eyes. "That offers me nothing. If I were to choose to be a spinster, I would rather be one with my own family than among strangers. No, Caleb. I won't consider going north with you." Taking a deep breath, she pulled away. "I have work to do."

Caleb watched her as she went into the bedroom and closed the door. Then he struck the mantel with all the pent-up frustration inside him. Why had he said that? He knew all too well that he was falling in love with her. Why hadn't he told her? True, he had only known her a short while, but it felt as if it would last forever. But Caleb had always prided himself on his logic; he never made rash decisions. Up until now he had considered that a virtue. Muttering a curse at himself under his breath, he limped into the back room and closed the door.

"I think all girls should be sent to school along with their brothers," Caleb said as they sat watching the fire dance in the hearth.

Megan looked up from her knitting. Since their kiss the day before, she had avoided him. It hadn't been an easy task when the cabin was so small. "No school would teach girls."

"They do where I come from."

"We don't have a real school in the Hollow. Whoever has the most education teaches the children in their family. That's how I learned to read. I listened in while my aunt was teaching Owen. Later I made him teach me to write, too. He knew he could get into trouble for doing it, but he taught me." She smiled in remembrance. "I could always talk Owen into doing just about everything. We stayed in trouble half the time."

Caleb shook his head. "I can't understand people wanting to continue their ignorance. Why don't any of you rebel? Insist that someone start a real school. Teach not only reading but arithmetic and geography and everything else that schools are supposed to teach."

"Who would be the teacher? I don't want to brag, but I have more education than anyone else in the Hollow and I certainly couldn't be a schoolteacher."

"Why not?"

She laughed. "I thought you had noticed. I'm not a man."

He grinned. "I noticed. But you don't have to be a man to be a teacher."

She stopped knitting and looked at him. "Is that true?"

"I always tell you the truth."

"Did you have a woman as a teacher?"

"No, Felicity and I had a male tutor the first few years. When I went to the higher grades, all my teachers were men."

"There. You see?" As if she had won a point, she continued knitting.

"But that doesn't mean they don't exist. Felicity even considered being a teacher at one time."

Megan humored him with a smile. She didn't believe a word of what he was saying. "Of course she did. What a utopian place you live in. I'm amazed you don't all have angel wings and live in the clouds."

"The world is a bigger place than Black Hollow. You have to know that from your reading."

"I know that novels are fiction, too. Besides, that's one reason Papa and the others settled in the Hollow. They were trying to get away from the world. They wanted to set up a place of their own where they could believe as they chose and have more control over what their children would see and do."

"That's narrow-mindedness at its worst."

"Not at all," she objected. "Papa told me his own ancestors came to America in order to worship as they pleased and to live however they thought best. Black Hollow is a place for people who think alike and who want the same sorts of things."

"But you're not one of them. You want to read and write stories and draw pictures. I think you should move away and become a writer."

"Don't make fun of me."

"I'm serious. I've seen your drawings and I've read one of your stories."

"You have?" She frowned at him. "When did you do that?"

"I told you it was lonely in there. I was trying to find something to do other than wade through the mysteries of *Udolpho*. I found some papers with your handwriting on them and I read them. The story is very good."

"You had no business doing that. Why are you admitting to it? You ought to be ashamed, reading people's private thoughts." She frowned at him. "You really liked it?"

"Yes, I did. It never occurred to me that you would mind or I wouldn't have read it."

"I should have burned it. Bridget has always fussed at me for being so careless. I just couldn't seem to get rid of that one. I'll have to before Seth comes home."

"Damn it, Megan! Why would you be so set on marrying such a closed-minded man?"

"You don't know Seth! You're hardly one to judge him!" She was angry because she had been asking herself that same question lately. "I don't want to die a lonely old woman. And I don't want to move back in with Mama and Papa. I love them, but I also love my freedom. Nobody watches what I do here." She glared at him. "Nobody but you, that is."

"You wouldn't have to die a lonely old woman," he argued.

"No? Who would marry me? Some old widower who wants me to raise a cabin full of children or who is only looking for someone to be his housekeeper?"

"You could marry someone your own age. Just not Seth."

"That's not possible. Not in Black Hollow." She lowered her eyes. "You're forgetting what happened between Seth and me in the clearing."

"No, I haven't. Not for a single minute lately." His voice sounded strained.

"Word of what happened would get around if I didn't marry Seth. No other young man would have me."

"Seth would tell?"

She could feel his eyes on her. She refused to look up. "You don't understand how it is here. We're our own guardians, so to speak. If there's something the congregation needs to know, a person tells. Seth would be honor bound to tell so everyone could pray for the redemption of my soul."

Caleb mumbled a word Megan thought she must have misunderstood. "You're not going to marry him. You're coming north with me."

"No, I'm not. I'm going to trade you for Seth and come straight back to Black Hollow."

"Are you telling me you really want to live like this? Where your fiancé would embarrass you by telling your entire congregation that you're no longer a virgin? Where you have to hide the fact that you read and draw and write stories? Is that how you really choose to live?"

"No!" The word came out more forcefully than she had intended. "It's not what I want. But the alternative is to leave everyone I know and love! I want to be here to see Bridget's children and to have babies of my own who can know their grandparents and aunts and uncles and cousins. Mama is getting older and her joints pain her. Someday she will need me to care for her. And Papa wants grandsons to teach to hunt and fish. My world doesn't contain only me!''

"Neither does mine. And you can have babies anywhere. If you raise your children in Black Hollow, they will grow to be just like the rest. Like Seth!''

"I'm marrying Seth of my own free will! He would have married me in a few days if he hadn't enlisted! We thought it wouldn't matter if we jumped the gun a bit.'' She realized her voice was rising in anger. She jerked up the knitting and began stabbing at the stitches, her needles clicking in fury.

"I didn't mean to anger you.''

"Yes, you did.''

"All right. So I did. But only in order to make you think. Otherwise you're determined to do something that will make you miserable all your life.''

"You don't know that!''

"I know from the way you kissed me that you need more from lovemaking than a quick roll in a clearing!''

Megan stood up abruptly. "I'm going to bed.''

He glared at her and didn't answer.

Megan stalked across the room and took pleasure in slamming her bedroom door. It was early. The sun had barely gone down and she wasn't at all sleepy. She couldn't read because Caleb still had her book in his room and she wasn't going to ask him for it.

Angrily she peeled off her dress and tossed it onto the chair. She stripped to the skin and pulled her white gown over her head. With quick jerks she pulled the pins from her hair. Even though the door to the bedroom had been open all day, it was cold enough in the room for the sheets to feel icy as she slid into bed. She glared at the closed door. She had to open it at some point or she would half freeze before morning, but she had no intention of doing so until Caleb was in his room.

She reached under the bed and brought out the paper she hid there. Taking her treasured pencil, she started to write a story such as she had never written before. Her anger sparked it to life and she captured it all on paper. She was positive she would have to burn this one. Ladies didn't write about murder and mayhem.

When the door to her room opened, she jerked her head up.

"I'm sorry."

"There's no need for you to apologize," she said stiffly. She wrote about a cannonball that blasted a tall, dark-haired man to bits.

"Yes, there is. I shouldn't goad you like that. I don't know what gets into me."

"It's rudeness, I expect." She had the cannonball bounce and flatten a man who resembled Seth.

"You're right. If you want to marry Seth and have a houseful of children, all like him, you're welcome to do it."

"Thank you. I will." Her pencil wheeled another cannon into place.

"It's admirable of you to want to take care of your mother as she gets older."

"I'm not doing it for praise."

"You're not going to forgive me?"

"I've accepted your apology. What more do you want?" She began writing a scene where several men, some looking like Caleb and the others like Seth, were exploded by gunfire and cannonballs.

"Nothing, I guess."

She put down her paper to glare at him. "You can be completely insufferable. Did you know that?"

"You seem to be the only one who affects me that way. Most people think I'm a perfect gentleman."

She made a disgusted sound and picked up the paper again.

Caleb came to sit on the bed beside her. Too late Megan remembered she was in her nightgown and that this was entirely too intimate. "What are you doing? Get out of here!"

"Not until you stop being angry with me."

"You can't possibly stay here that long. The war will end long before that."

"Megan," he said with a smile. "Are you really that angry?"

She shoved the pencil and paper away. "Yes, I am!"

He only looked at her, his eyes lit with amusement. "I think something else is bothering you."

"You make me think about things that I don't want to think about." She glared at him and folded her arms over her chest. "My world was all nice and orderly before you came and now it's turning upside down! I was content to wait for Seth to come home and to marry him and to live here forever. Now I can see that there will probably come a time when I want to have things my own way and not his. That I may want to teach my daughters to read and to draw and that Seth won't like it. I don't want to think these things!"

"It's better that you should think them now than after it's too late."

"Are you that dense? It's already too late!"

He reached up and took a tendril of her hair. She had been so angry she hadn't taken the time to braid it properly and it hung about her shoulders just as it had fallen from her bun. "You're talking about the clearing again?"

She nodded. She could feel tears welling in her eyes. "I knew better than to do that. I *knew* better. And I let him do it anyway. Ever since that night I've regretted it and there's nothing I can ever do to change what happened." She shoved at the tears as they filled her eyes to overflowing and ran down her cheeks. "That's one thing you don't ever have a second chance at. I was stupid and I've ruined myself for marrying anyone but Seth. Even an older man who needs a housekeeper and child raiser wouldn't want me if they knew I'm not a virgin!"

"They probably won't be able to tell."

"Of course they can. Everybody knows that!"

"Trust me. If you don't tell and Seth doesn't tell, no one will ever know."

She looked up at him. "Is that true?"

He nodded.

"But all the same, I'm damaged goods now. Even if no one else ever knew, I would know."

"I don't consider you damaged goods."

She stopped talking and stared at him. At last she said, "Don't do this to me, Caleb. Don't sweet-talk me knowing you're soon going to go away and never see me again. Leave me alone so I can put my life back the way it was before you came."

"I don't think you really want that."

She laid her head back on her pillow, then realized how intimate that seemed and abruptly tried to push him aside and sit up. "You shouldn't be in here. You certainly shouldn't be playing with my hair and leaning across me like this!"

"Why?"

"It's not proper!"

"Is that the only reason?"

Megan had always been honest. "No. It's not the only reason. But it's the only one I'm willing to give you."

Caleb sat back but he continued to look at her. "You're beautiful, Megan. Even when you're angry with me. Your skin gets paler and your eyes grow darker and they seem to have sparks in them. Being near you is like the feeling you get when you can feel lightning in the air and you know a really earthshaking storm is on the way."

"I know. I'm feeling the same thing." She said the words grudgingly because she didn't want to admit it.

"What are we going to do?" He seemed genuinely to be asking her opinion. "We seem to be spiraling up into something that has no end. Or at least not an end that contains the futures we had planned for ourselves."

"That's why my way is best. There are no highs that are too high or lows that are too deep. Flat ground is safer."

"And it's also boring." He grinned at her. "Nothing with us would ever be boring."

She found herself smiling. "No. It wouldn't be boring." For a forbidden moment she allowed herself to think of Caleb living here as her husband, sharing her cabin openly, plowing the garden, raising calves to sell in Raintree. Sharing the bed she lay in.

As if he were thinking the same thing, he said, "You'd be happy with me. I'd do anything to make you happy."

"I can't—"

"Hush. I know what you're going to say and it's not true. You're not a prisoner here. You could leave if you wanted to. You could leave with me."

She shook her head. There was no way she could make him understand that she had never been farther than Raintree and that the rest of the world seemed foreign to her. That she needed her family roots the way she needed food and air.

"Just think about it." He bent forward and kissed her on the temple.

Megan closed her eyes as warmth washed through her. It took a great act of will not to put her arms around him.

Caleb walked out the door, leaving it open so the fire's warmth could heat the room. She could hear him by the hearth putting logs against the back of the chimney so they would smoulder all night. It sounded so domestic. So right.

But with all his suggestions that she leave, he had never mentioned love and he had never spoken of marriage. Megan was already falling in love with him, but she had more respect for herself than to leave her home and have to live on crumbs all her life.

In all honesty, she found herself thinking, had Seth mentioned loving her? He had said he did when he asked her to marry him and he had said it again in the clearing that night she had given herself to him. But weren't those the only times? And both times hadn't the words given him his way? Words could be so treacherous.

Megan wadded up the paper she had been writing on and squeezed it into a tight ball. As tight as her insides felt when she thought of Caleb leaving without her.

Chapter Eight

Caleb had progressed to the point in mending where Megan allowed him to sit with her in the main room by the fire in the evenings. She gave him the rocker since that was the easiest chair for him to lever himself into and out of, and she sat across the hearth on one of the straight-backed, armless chairs.

She was drawing a picture of a rabbit on the back of the brown paper that had wrapped the last parcel she had bought in town. "I saw this rabbit earlier when I brought some of the meat up from the woods and hid it in the hayloft. It was crouched by a stump with its fur ruffled against the cold. I was able to get quite close to it before it ran away."

"You should write a story about it."

She laughed shyly. "Write a story about a rabbit? That would be a waste of time. Who would ever see it?" But the idea drew her. "Do you think I could do it? When Bridget was little, she liked the stories I made up about animals."

"Of course you could write it. You know more about the woods and animals than anyone I've ever known. All children love stories about rabbits and the sort."

"You're encouraging me to fritter my time away. You're a terrible influence on me. I have more than enough to do as it is." She looked up from her drawing. "I could make up a story about a bunny who became lost when winter was coming on." For a minute she thought, the story already taking shape in her mind. "No, no one would want to read it."

"I disagree. If you sold it to some publisher, it could make you enough money to buy some of the things in town that would make your life more pleasant. A music box, for instance."

She ducked her head. "I never should have told you about that. It was frivolous and foolish for me to want a music box. What could I possibly do with it?"

"You could listen to it and enjoy it."

"It's a good thing you aren't going to be around much longer. You have a real talent for tempting me to do the things I know I shouldn't."

"Does that mean you're getting ready to make the trade?" His voice became much more serious.

"Not yet." She avoided his eyes. "You're leg isn't healed enough yet."

He flexed it experimentally. "It's better than I ever thought it would be. I'll always have a limp, though."

"Not a bad one. You're lucky to have your leg at all."

"I know. And I know I have you to thank for it."

She hadn't wanted the conversation to become so personal. It was dangerous for her to think of Caleb in those terms.

He lifted his head and looked out the window. "Someone is coming."

Megan leaped to her feet. "It's Bridget! Quick! Get into the back room. And for goodness' sake, be quiet! If she hears you, she may tell Papa. I haven't nursed you along this far to lose you now!" She pulled him to his feet and watched him limp across the floor. "Keep the door shut tight!" she added in a loud whisper. She could hear Bridget's footsteps on the porch.

Bridget came into the room on a gust of cold air just as Caleb closed the door to the back room. "My goodness, but it's cold!" she said as she hurried to the fire. "I thought I would freeze before I got here."

"I didn't expect you. Is something wrong?"

"Of course not," Bridget said with a laugh. "Can't I visit you without bringing bad tidings?" She picked up the drawing of the rabbit. "How wonderful! He looks as if he could hop around the room." She looked at Megan in commiseration. "I guess you get awfully lonely up here. Why don't you move back home just until winter is over?"

"No," Megan said with what she hoped was a calm smile. "I don't draw because I'm lonely. I enjoy the privacy."

"I just don't understand you. I don't at all. If I were up here all by myself, I'd be half-crazy by now." She looked back at the drawing. "It's a shame there's nothing you can do with this. The children in the settlement would love to see it, but Papa wouldn't be pleased. You know you promised him you wouldn't squander your time up here."

"I have to rest sometime," Megan said more sharply than was necessary. "I'm sorry, Bridget. Sometimes I wonder if Papa is right in everything he taught us."

Bridget looked shocked. "How can you question that? If Mama heard you, she would have to bring up your name in church next Sunday and Brother Grady would have to pray publicly for you."

"I know." This had happened to her before and Megan had been thoroughly embarrassed. In a lower tone, she said, "Bridget, do you believe all we've been taught?"

Bridget pulled her shawl from her shoulders and hung it on the back of the chair. Her bright red hair was escaping its pins and she automatically tucked it back into place. "Of course I do." Her voice wasn't convincing.

"Other people don't live like this, working from dawn to well past dark every day, with no time to do the things we simply want to do."

"How do you know how other people live?"

Megan caught her mistake. "I read books. If you took the time to read, you'd know this, too."

"Reading has always been easier for you. Besides, Papa doesn't want me to read, unless it's the Bible, of course—and even then he prefers to read it himself. I've never enjoyed it like you do."

"You just don't practice it enough."

Bridget looked back at the sketch. "It really is a shame the children can't see this."

"I've thought of a story to go with it." Megan leaned forward eagerly.

"Speaking of writing, that reminds me why I came up here in the cold." Bridget laughed. "I'm already getting as absentminded as Aunt Pauline. I have a letter from Patrick!"

"A letter?"

Bridget scooted her chair closer so Megan could look over her shoulder as she read. "He's in Virginia. Did you ever think any of us would go so far from home? He's homesick and says that he will never leave the Hollow again once he gets back."

"I wish the war were over now," Megan said with a sigh. She thought of Caleb in the other room. She didn't long for the end as fervently as she once did because that would mean he would be out of her life forever. Immediately she felt guilty. "What else does Patrick say?"

"A battle is coming up. It hasn't happened yet—I got the letter that quick! Can you imagine? A calvary unit passed through the valley and they had brought the letter directly from Patrick."

"He's going to be in a battle?" As always when she heard one of her people would be in danger, Megan felt fear curl in her middle.

"Let me read you that part." Bridget held the letter close to her eyes. She had always been nearsighted. " 'We're camped on a rise above the James River outside of Richmond. A Yankee troop is expected by the end of the week, carrying supplies to Richmond, then south to Petersburg. From the way we're dug in, we can intercept them and get the supplies for ourselves. Captain Hightower says the Yankees will come from Fredericksburg. Our plans are—'"

"I don't think you should be reading me this!" Megan interrupted. She was all too aware of Caleb listening just beyond the door. He might be her prisoner, but he was also a Union officer. If he got free, he might be able to wire a warning to his side and Patrick's company wouldn't get the supplies they so desperately needed.

"It's all right. I'm not reading you the personal part." Bridget bent over the paper again. "'—to go to Lynchburg, where we'll meet with troops from—'"

"Bridget, can I get you some tea? I made some from the dried rosemary and it's not bad if you add honey. That will warm you right up." She got hastily to her feet.

"I'm already warm, thank you. Don't you want to hear Patrick's letter?"

"Of course I do. You know how I worry about him. I just don't think he should have written you in such detail about his company's intentions."

"Why not? It can't hurt for us to know. We aren't the enemy."

"What if the letter had fallen into Union hands? He could be placing the others in danger."

"But it didn't." Bridget frowned slightly. "Are you all right? You aren't acting like yourself."

"I may be coming down with a cold," Megan said, glad of the excuse. "The past few days I've felt a bit low."

"You should come back with me. There's nothing you have to do up here that can't wait for a few days. Mama will ply you with that awful treacle tonic and have you feeling better in no time."

Megan smiled at her sister. "I hate that tonic. That's reason enough for me to stay where I am."

"Papa says snow is on the way. He heard it from Uncle Mose and he's always accurate. Ever since he broke the large bone in his leg he's been as good a weather barometer as anyone could wish for. He can predict rain or snow almost to the very hour."

"I noticed all the signs were pointing toward snow. I brought up some of the smoked meat and hid it in the hayloft this morning. I didn't want to wade through drifts if the snowfall is a heavy one."

"We're due a storm. It's held off longer than I expected. The top of the mountain has already been white several times, you know."

"I know." Megan thought for a minute. "If it snows hard, I may not be able to get to church on Sunday. It's a long, cold walk from here. In a heavy snow it will be really difficult."

"Neither Mama nor Papa would agree to you endangering your soul just because of snow. I'm surprised you would even think such a thing. It's not like you're too old to wade through drifts or in the family way."

Megan put her hand on Bridget's shoulder. "Don't you ever question what Brother Grady tells us? I just don't believe I would go to hell simply because I don't want to wade through knee-deep snowdrifts for an hour to reach the church. And coming back up the mountain will be even more difficult. How much can it matter if I miss one Sunday?"

"Brother Grady says it matters, and he ought to know. He's the one with the calling. If it's too hard for you get to the settlement, that's all the more reason for you to move back in with us until spring thaw. Should I tell Papa to come up and get your trunk before the storm sets in?"

"No. I'll be able to get up and down the mountain just fine. I was only talking."

Bridget shook her head. "You shouldn't even talk about such things. What if you said them to someone other than me? You'd be in a lot of trouble!"

"I know. That's why I only talk to you about my feelings and the questions I have."

"You shouldn't talk to me about them either. I'm your younger sister and you're supposed to be a good influence on me." Bridget was perfectly serious, even though she was grown and had married. That was the way the Hollow worked. Everyone older was responsible for everyone younger.

"I'm sorry. Sometimes I think I'd be a better influence if I taught you to be more independent."

Bridget smiled as if she thought Megan must be joking. "There you go, teasing me again. It's a good thing I can see through your silly words." She reached for her shawl and flicked it around her shoulders. "I have to be going. I just wanted to share the letter with you."

"Thank you for reading it to me." Megan hoped Caleb had heard less than she knew he must have. There was a loud bumping sound from the back room, and she froze.

Bridget turned and looked in that direction. "What was that?"

"Squirrels. I have a family trying to move into the eaves."

"Papa should come up here and get rid of them for you."

"No, no. I can chase them away myself. Or have less far to go for squirrel stew," she added. "They aren't bothering me."

"They would me. That sounded almost like a person dropping something." Bridget looked again at the closed door. "Are you sure you don't want me to take a look? I'm never sure there aren't deserters creeping up on us ever since you shot that one."

"I doubt a deserter could slip into my back room and me not notice him. I've been in here most of the day." Megan put her arm around Bridget and walked her to the door before her sister could decide to look anyway. "Don't tell Mama that I'm coming down with a cold. She would only worry."

Bridget laughed. "That and send me back with that treacle tonic. I can see past your wiles."

"You always have," Megan said, thankful that it wasn't true. "Give Mama and Papa my love."

"I will." Bridget hesitated at the door. "Will you at least think about moving back for a while? I miss you. Mama is good company, of course, but she's not you. We always used to have such long talks, and it made the work pass easier."

"I know. I miss you, too. I'll consider it." She stepped out onto the porch with Bridget. The wind seemed to cut into her with its icy blasts. "Hurry home and stay warm."

"I will. Get back inside before you get a chill." Bridget hurried down the steps and was running as she left the yard.

Megan waited until she was sure Bridget wouldn't double back, then went inside. As she closed the door she sighed with relief.

The back door opened. "Is she gone?"

"Yes. What was that noise?"

"I dropped your book. I saw it falling but I couldn't grab it quickly enough."

"At least she thinks it was squirrels."

"I know. I heard."

"How much did you hear exactly?"

"All of it."

Megan frowned up at him. "Now I have to keep you here until after Patrick's company leaves Lynchburg or you'll tell your army where they are."

He smiled at her. "I guess you're right. You wouldn't want me passing information to my superiors."

She had the feeling that he was seeing through her excuses to keep him. "Besides, a storm is coming. It's a good thing I decided to keep you until your leg is stronger. I wouldn't want to lose you to the cold before I get Seth back.''

"No, we certainly wouldn't want that." He went back to the rocker and sat down. "It's much better that I be imprisoned here for the time being. I'll just have to make the best of it." He smiled at her before leaning forward with the poker to stoke the fire.

"You needn't be so smug about it. I'll send you on your way as soon as I can. Make no mistake about it."

"I know." He sounded as unconvinced as if he had looked into her mind and had seen the confusion he created there.

Megan watched him relax into the chair. In the cabin's dim light he was partially silhouetted against the firelight and looked disturbingly virile. She tried to think about something, anything, else.

"I also heard what you said about not believing what this Brother Grady preaches."

"I didn't say I don't believe in any of it, just some of the details," she said defensively.

"I doubt that I would, either. Most reasonable men, including preachers, would take deep snowdrifts into account. God certainly would."

"I have no intention of discussing this with you. Brother Grady has our best interests at heart. The settlement is founded on a religious principle and it must be adhered to. Everyone seems to agree with it but me, so I must be the one who's wrong."

"Not necessarily. Everyone doesn't march to the same beat."

"What does that mean?"

"It means that I understand." He looked at her and smiled.

"Well, don't. I don't want you to understand," she said as she turned away.

"How do you want me to be, exactly?"

"I want you to be the enemy! I don't want you to be so agreeable and understanding and..."

"And?" he prompted.

"I'm going out to the barn. I have chores to do." She grabbed her shawl and flung it around her shoulders angrily.

The cold wind felt sharp against her face but Megan welcomed it. Caleb shook her world and made everything she tried to believe in and depend upon seem to be built on quicksand. She had already gone too far with Seth for her to consider loving someone other than him. She had to hold to that thought and not let her emotions run away with her. If she was rid of Caleb soon it was possible that neither he nor anyone else would know how traitorous her feelings had become and she could somehow put her life back together. She could fall back in love with Seth.

She went in the small door of the barn, rather than wrestle the large double doors against the wind. Taking up a pitchfork, she started jabbing at the hay. There was no reason for moving the hay into the far corner since there were no animals to feed, but it would have to be done eventually and the exercise would keep her warm. She had only come out here to avoid Caleb.

She was so intent on expending her frustration on the hay, she didn't notice three dark shadows in the back of the barn. The shadows came together, then separated to circle around her.

As she shoved the pitchfork in the hay she heard a shuffling sound. Instantly she was alert. Any sort of wild animal could have come into the barn looking for shelter from the coming snow. She had once accidentally cornered a bobcat in her father's barn on just such a day.

Suddenly two men rushed at her. Megan cried out and brought her pitchfork up in defense. They were wearing Confederate uniforms but their clothing was so dirty and ragged it took her a moment to realize which side they were on. "Get out of here," she said in a warning voice. "I'm on your side and I've nothing to steal."

"We think maybe you do," one said. "You look real pretty to me. It's been a long time since we had us a woman."

"Yeah," the other one said with a leering grin. "We thought we would just find a warm spot to sleep, but looks like we hit pay dirt."

"Get out of here," she warned again. "Just go away and leave me alone." She wondered if she could get past them and across the yard to the cabin. Once inside she would have Caleb and her rifle, as well as doors she could lock. She thought fast. "I'll go back to the house and get you some food, since you're Confederate soldiers, but you have to get out of my way."

"See, Matthew?" the first one said. "I told you she has something to steal. Something other than herself, that is."

"I reckon we ought to take both. I'm more hungry for a woman than I am for food." He edged around her side, opening the space between him and his comrade.

Megan glanced at the opening they made and started to run. Immediately two arms grabbed her from behind. A third man lifted her from the ground and tossed her into the hay. Megan screamed in fear and tried to scramble away but he caught her ankle and pulled her back.

"Hold her down, Matthew," one man said as he imprisoned her hands over her head. "Catch her legs."

Megan felt their hands on her and revulsion rose in her stomach. Her throat hurt from screaming but she wasn't aware of making a sound. She fought them as hard as she could but she was no match for three men. They soon had her pinned in the hay.

One of them stood between her legs and started opening his trousers. He was grinning down at her as if he were taking great pleasure in her terror. Megan called them every name she could think of but they only laughed. He reached down and ripped her blouse open and began pawing at her breasts. Megan was almost in shock, telling herself it couldn't be happening, but unable to escape into unconsciousness. With one jerk he tossed her skirts up and started to kneel.

Suddenly the double doors to the barn were thrown open. Caleb stood there, his army pistol in his hand. "Get away from her," he said in a tone that said he would rather shoot them than breathe. "Now!"

The men scrambled away and slunk like animals toward the shadows. Caleb went to the nearest one and put the pistol to the man's forehead. "Listen to me very carefully," he said. "You're not to come back here for any reason. You're not to even stay on this mountain. If I ever see you again, I'll kill you. Do you understand?"

The man nodded, sweat rolling down his face in spite of the cold.

"I have a good mind to shoot you anyway, just to prove my point to your friends here." The muscles in Caleb's hand flexed as he cocked the pistol. The barrel never wavered from the man's forehead.

"Don't shoot me!" the man started crying. "I didn't mean no harm! We was just having some fun!"

Caleb's finger tightened on the trigger. "You call rape fun? You're worse than yard dogs!"

"Shut up, Matthew!" one of the others hissed. "Just shut up! Mister, don't shoot us. We'll get out of here and never come back!"

Caleb drew back half a step and motioned with the pistol. The three men raced for the door and shoved one another in their effort to put distance between Caleb and them.

Caleb knelt beside Megan, who was sobbing in the hay. She tried to pull the torn blouse over her breasts but she was trembling so hard she couldn't do it. He reached for her shawl and covered her. "Are you hurt?" he asked. His voice was deep with concern.

She shook her head. She wasn't able to speak.

"Come on. Let's get back into the house."

"Are they gone?" she whispered, clinging to his arm. "Are you sure they're gone?"

"They must be halfway down the mountain by now." He stood and pulled her to her feet. Half-supporting her, he led her toward the yard. "They won't be hanging around here."

Megan found it difficult to breathe and she couldn't stand alone. She had never been so frightened in all her life. "Why didn't you shoot them?" she demanded, her voice quivering.

"I found the pistol but I couldn't find the bullets."

Her knees almost buckled under her. There were no bullets in his gun? For a dreadful moment she thought she was going to be sick.

Caleb helped her into the cabin and firmly locked the door behind them. "Are you sure you're all right? They didn't have time to hurt you?"

"I'm all right." She watched the room dip and spin. "Maybe I should lie down for a minute."

He helped her into the bedroom and she sat on the edge of the bed. He pulled the shawl around her more securely and she remembered her blouse was torn. Everything seemed to be happening to someone else, far away.

"Where is another blouse?"

"There. In the trunk."

He found a blouse and gently took the shawl from her. His jaw knotted as he saw faint bruises already appearing on her pale breasts. They might not have raped her, but she was hurt. He was worried because she was moving so slowly and speaking so vaguely. He had seen soldiers in shock and she had all the symptoms.

Removing her blouse affected him more than he wished. He was her protector and shouldn't be thinking how warm and smooth her skin was and how beautifully she was made.

He helped her put on the blouse and buttoned it up for her. "Lie down."

She did as he said and he covered her up to the chin with her blankets. As he did, she started to shiver. He went into his room and gathered up an armload of quilts. He had to get her warm.

He piled the quilts on her and tucked them around her, then reached under to remove her shoes. Her toes curled in his palms and she pulled away from him. Caleb wished he had found the bullets. Seeing how frightened she still was, he wished he'd shot all three men.

He sat on the edge of the bed and gazed down at her. "You're safe now."

"Why am I so cold?" Her teeth were chattering.

"You were badly frightened and you're in shock. It will pass soon."

"You saved me." She said it as if it were almost a question.

"Of course I did."

"But they could have killed you. There were three of them."

"Fortunately they were too scared to notice the pistol's chambers were empty." He smiled at her. "I've always been a good gambler."

She shivered again. "Did you lock the door?"

"Of course. You're safe. By the way, where are my bullets?"

"In the sugar bowl above the dry sink. With my money."

"I think it would be a good idea for me to have them. Just in case."

She nodded. "Every time I think—"

"Hush. Don't think about it." He drew her up into his arms and held her against his chest. "I'll keep you safe, Megan."

"It shouldn't be this way!" she whispered against his shirt. "People have begun acting like animals! Worse than animals!"

"I know. War is like being in hell. But it can't last forever."

She put her arms around him and held him close. He knew she was crying silently and thought it was because he was there and not Seth, who should be her protector. "You'll have him back safe soon. Don't cry."

"That's not why I'm crying." She shoved at him but he continued to hold her gently. "You don't understand!"

That was true. Caleb didn't understand anything that was happening between them. Megan awakened his protective spirit to an astonishing degree—if he knew which way the men had run, he would be tempted to go after them even now. At the same time, she excited him beyond all reason. Every time he closed his eyes he saw her on the hay, her skirts tumbled up to expose her legs, her breasts bare in the faded light in the barn. The memory made him more protective, even as it aroused his desire for her. "You're safe with me," he repeated. "I won't hurt you and I won't let anyone else hurt you, either."

"I'm glad you're here," she murmured against his chest.

Caleb thought she was referring to his having saved her from the bushwhackers. "Glad to be of service, ma'am," he said with a tender smile. She sighed as if he still didn't know what she meant, but she didn't explain. Caleb wondered if it was possible that she was starting to feel for him what he was feeling for her. He was afraid to hope.

He left her in bed and went back into the main room. In her shaken state he didn't want to say or do anything that might further alarm her. He rested his forearm on the mantel and looked into the dancing fire. How could he ever bear to leave her? Especially since he had no respect for Seth from all she had told him.

She needed him. Caleb knew that wasn't strictly true, but it was true enough. Megan would be safe with Seth and her own people. But there was more to caring for a person than merely keeping them safe. The part of Megan that he saw yearning to fly free would never take wings if she had to stay in such strict mental confinement.

But what could he do about it? Damned little, he had to admit. He struck the mantel and glared out the window. There was too damned little he could do to set her free.

Chapter Nine

Megan soon recovered from her fear but she still felt dirty. Even though Caleb had arrived in time to keep the bushwhackers from raping her, they had touched her and looked at her and she felt soiled. She decided to take a bath that night when Caleb was asleep.

After he went into the back room and closed the door, Megan went to her own room and waited for the sounds to die down. She heard the makeshift bed creak under his weight, and slowly the cabin took on its usual night sounds.

On tiptoe, she went to the water she had left in the large kettle over the fire. It was almost boiling. Careful not to make any sounds, Megan went out onto the porch and got the large tub she used for rinse water when she washed clothes. She carried it into her room. Then she began the laborious task of bringing the water to fill it. Once it was deep enough, she got her bar of soap and poured in the boiling water to warm it and firmly closed her door.

She quickly shucked off her clothes and stepped into the tub. The warmth seemed to seep into her bones as she sat down and slid as low as possible. For a minute she closed her eyes and enjoyed the luxury of a complete bath.

Caleb had never been a sound sleeper. He heard the soft sounds and lifted his head in the darkness, trying to identify them. Was someone moving about the house? If it were Megan she would have no reason to move so furtively.

He swung his long legs off the bed and pulled on his pants before stepping into his boots. He reached under the mattress and took out his pistol, now loaded and ready. If the bushwhackers had returned he had every intention of shooting them.

When he opened the door, he saw that the cabin was dark. Megan's door was shut and that was unusual, but he thought she might have forgotten to open it. The glowing embers on the hearth told him the main room was empty.

He crossed to the back door and looked out. Pale moonlight made the yard silver and blackened the woods beyond. He slipped out, making no more noise than the shadows.

Although he listened carefully, he could hear no sounds outside. He circled the house and noticed the light in Megan's room. To see if she was all right, he looked in the window. He wasn't prepared for the sight of her in the washtub.

She was slowly washing her body, soaping her slender arms and the rounded fullness of her breasts. Her hair was piled high on her head unlike the way she wore it during the day. He had never seen a woman so beautiful.

Although she was small, she was perfectly proportioned. Her clothing hid many of her charms. As he watched, she rinsed the soap from her breasts and droplets of water glided over her skin, hung momentarily from her nipples, then fell away. Caleb was achingly aware of how long it had been since he had made love to a woman. But even as he thought this, he noticed that Megan was stirring more than mere lust in him. He wanted to really make love with her, not just satisfy their bodies.

Megan lifted her arms and removed the pins from her hair. It cascaded down, waving over her shoulders and mo-

mentarily hiding her breasts. She tipped her head back and
wet her hair, then started soaping it.

Caleb knew he shouldn't stand there in the dark and
watch her, but he couldn't tear himself away. Even the cold
on his bare chest didn't matter as much as the sight of Megan naked in her tub.

Suddenly she paused and lifted her head as if she had become aware of him. Caleb knew she couldn't see him. Her
room was filled with lamplight and he was in deep shadow.
But she looked toward the window and somehow directly at
him. Caleb froze, wondering if she could see him after all.
Then she looked away and he relaxed. The glance had
brought him to his senses, however. He had no business
staring at her this way. Only a cad would stay.

He circled back the way he had come and let himself into
the house. Taking even more care to move silently, he
crossed to the back room. For a long time he sat there, on
the side of his bed, his forearms resting on his thighs as he
thought. There were decisions he had to make regarding
Megan and he was a bit surprised to find some part of his
mind had already made most of them.

He was in love with her. That was beyond question. He
also wanted, in the same degree, to protect her. There was
no question there, either. But what was he to do about it?

Staying with her was unfeasible. From what he knew
about the settlement, he would be as unwelcome as a rat-
tler. Especially once he voiced his opinions on the education of women and on Brother Grady's repressive religion.
No, it wouldn't do to stay here.

He smiled as he looked around the room at the rough log
walls and wide plank floor. He couldn't imagine his family
visiting here. Not that they were snobbish, far from it. But
they had never been in a log cabin in their lives and would
feel too foreign to it. Besides, he didn't want Megan to work
hard all her life. Not when he could give her so much more.

On the other hand, he didn't want to wonder in the years to come if she had married him for his money. A life of luxuries might be too tempting for any woman who had lived a life of drudgery. There was an easy way around that. He simply wouldn't tell her he was rich.

Did she love him? At times he thought she was at least beginning to, but then she would lose her temper at him and he would no longer be sure at all. She was still adamant that she was going to trade him to get Seth back. This didn't sound like the decision of a woman in love. But then, Caleb had never pretended to understand the workings of a woman's mind.

He took off his pants and looked down at his leg. It was almost healed. There would be a scar, of course, and he would probably always walk with a slight limp, but it was almost well. Once Megan had used the mysterious Indian herbs, his recovery had been remarkable. Caleb hadn't told her. As far as she knew, he was still too wounded to leave and his limp verified the fact. He viewed it as a small and necessary deception.

Caleb had managed to justify staying with her. He knew he shouldn't be away from his regiment any longer than necessary. He had sworn an oath to protect his country and to fight against Confederates until he died or the war ended, whichever came first. But he was no longer so eager to do so.

The issues had seemed so clear back home in Pollard's Crossing, Ohio. Slavery was wrong and all the Northern views had been right. While slavery was still an evil, he no longer saw all Confederates as agents of the devil. Now that he was accustomed to the soft cadence of Megan's speech, it didn't sound so foreign to him. While he might not agree with the ways of the settlement, they were people to him now and not just "the enemy."

Caleb lay down and stared up at the now-familiar roof. Even if it meant staying in Black Hollow, he didn't want to leave Megan. But how did she feel? If she didn't love him now, would she learn to? He had asked her to go north with him before, but he had offered it as a refuge and a new beginning, not as a proposal of marriage. Now he was ashamed that he had thought she needed refuge from her own people and her way of life. That, he knew, had been his own brand of snobbishness speaking. A type that was difficult to recognize because it was wrapped in the trappings of care.

He heard a splash and knew she was pouring clean water over her to rinse away the soap. The ache increased in his groin. He couldn't put the mental image of her out of his mind. Not that he was trying that hard. His major effort was centered in staying where he was and in not going to her.

After a while, he heard more of the furtive noises and knew she was dipping water from the tub and carrying it out to toss out the back door. Soon he heard a metallic clang that meant the tub was empty and back on its peg on the porch. Her light footsteps were on the floor and he was surprised to see his door open.

For a minute she stood framed in the doorway, her voluminous nightgown hiding all the lovely secrets he now knew she possessed. The lamplight behind her made the gown just transparent enough to tantalize him, but to show him nothing. She opened the door wide enough for heat to reach the room, then hurried back to her warm bed, leaving her own door open.

Caleb forced himself to stay where he was. Naturally they slept with the doors open. The mornings were cold enough without shutting the heat out all night. But he hadn't realized she opened his door when he forgot. Having always lived in a house with a fireplace in each bedroom had spoiled him.

He heard her bed creak on its rope slats and the sound of her snuggling into the layers of sheet and quilts. Caleb found his fists were knotted in his effort to remain alone in his room.

Wide-awake, he measured most of the hours of that night.

Megan sang softly as she cleaned the cabin. Caleb was unusually neat for a man. Or at least the men she knew were more messy than he was. Her father never picked up his own clothing or carried his plate to the basin. Caleb did both and more. He seemed to think he had as much responsibility in keeping the cabin clean as she did. Megan thought she could be terribly spoiled if this kept up.

"I remembered a hickory tree down past the bend in the creek," she said as she finished her ironing and folded the last of the clothes. "I didn't gather the nuts last fall and I doubt anyone else did either. I may walk down there and see if any are still on the ground."

"Alone?"

"It's too far for you to go on that leg. Besides, if you leave the cabin, there's a chance you'll be seen. We can't see the settlement from here and people don't often walk this way, but there are plenty of people who could happen upon us by the creek."

"Take my pistol."

"I can take the rifle. That way, if I see a squirrel I can shoot it. I'd like a change from horse meat."

"So would I," he said with a smile. "Almost anything would be a nice change."

"I know. I try not to think what we're eating, but it's not easy."

"Maybe the war will be over soon."

"Maybe." She looked over at him. If the war ended, he would leave. "Will you be all right while I'm gone? You won't try to escape?"

Caleb laughed. "Megan, if I were going to escape, all I would have to do is leave in the middle of the night. You wouldn't miss me until morning."

She shook her head. "I have very good hearing. No one could leave the house without me hearing." She put her head to one side. "Why do you find that funny?"

"No reason. Is there anything you want me to do around here while you're gone?"

"No. Just stay out of sight."

She put the clothes away and left the cabin. Although wild animals had probably picked over the nuts by now, it was worth going to see if any were left. With sugar so dear, nuts were almost like sweets to her these days.

Like the day before, the sky hung low and heavy. Leaden clouds encased the top of the mountain and lay in foggy fingers in the meadows. Megan knew the nuts would soon be buried if she didn't gather them today.

When she reached Medicine Hat Creek she followed it around the bend. The water was running slowly as if it were of a mind to freeze at any moment, though the creek was large enough that it never froze completely. In the clearing ahead, she saw the walnut tree.

It stood alone as if someone had deliberately planted it in this spot. Its large limbs branched out and up. Even with the limbs bare, it was magnificent. Megan tied the tow sack at her waist to leave both her hands free and started wandering over the ground, searching for walnuts.

As she had expected, most of the nuts were gone and many of the ones left had gone bad, but even a few would help break the monotony of their diet. Christmas was only a few days away and Megan wanted to have some special dish for Caleb since he had told her that his family always made Christmas a lavish tradition.

She circled the tree and knelt to pick up a walnut when she heard a low growl. Megan froze. Raising her eyes, she saw several wolves at the edge of the woods. They were all watching her, their yellow eyes intent. She had her rifle, but she knew there was no hope of shooting them all and wolves used almost human intelligence when they were hunting.

With game so scarce they would be hungry and determined.

Her eyes darted to the tree. There was a fork fairly low to the ground and she had been good at climbing as a girl. The wolves made another of the soft growls as if they were discussing how to bring her down. Megan reached between her legs and caught the hem at the back of her skirt. Moving as slowly as she could, she brought it up between her legs and tucked it securely in the waistband to free her legs for climbing. Then she darted for the tree.

The wolves leaped into action as soon as she moved. Megan threw herself at the fork in the tree, her hands scratching at the bark. As she hauled herself into the air, she heard a distinct click of teeth inches from her ankle. Fear improved her climbing skills.

She didn't stop until she was well above the wolves' ability to jump or climb. They circled the tree, looking up at her and making a mumbling howl that told of their frustration at missing her. Megan held on to the limb above her perch and wondered when it would be safe to climb down.

The leader of the pack, an animal with a paler coat than the others, seemed to be considering the situation. It reared on the tree and even jumped onto the lowest fork, but it wasn't able to climb to where she was. One of the others saw her abandoned rifle and crept nearer to sniff at it cautiously. He shied away with a menacing growl.

Megan had been in the tree perhaps half an hour when the snow started to fall. Most of the wolves were sitting on their haunches, watching every move she made. Ice pellets mixed with the snow stung Megan's face. The tree's bark quickly began gathering a light crust of ice. Soon she would have difficulty staying on the limb and climbing down would be even harder. She had no hope at all of anyone coming along to rescue her. Not in this weather.

An hour later the ground was white and the tree limbs rattled like old bones in the wind. Megan hugged the trunk desperately to keep from falling. Cold had settled into her and she couldn't stop shaking.

Just when she was about to give up all hope, the lead wolf lifted its head and stared intently at the woods. One of the others did the same. She looked in that direction but couldn't see anything. The silent snow was making the woods black and impenetrable. Moving to a signal only they knew, the wolves loped across the clearing and disappeared like ghosts into the trees.

Megan stared after them. Were wolves smart enough to do this to trick her into coming out of the tree? Her father had told her many stories about their cunning. He thought they were only slightly less intelligent than humans.

After what seemed to be an eternity, Megan decided she had to risk it. She hadn't seen anything moving in the woods for a long time and if she continued to stay where she was, she would freeze.

Her hands felt stiff and her muscles almost refused to respond as she tried to leave her place of refuge. She went down to the next limb and paused, looking at the woods all around the clearing. It was snowing so hard she could barely see the trees now. After some difficulty she dropped to the ground and crouched there, ready to spring back into the tree at the least sign of movement. There was none.

Feeling the ground, she located the rifle under the snow and shook it off. The powder would be wet and it probably wouldn't fire now, but she couldn't leave it behind.

Megan hurried to the woods that hid the creek and started the return trip. The hill that had seemed to be such a gradual slope now seemed twice as steep. The thought of Caleb and a fire kept her going.

Several times she thought she had lost her way, but she knew if she followed the creek long enough, it had to lead her to the settlement. The snow was making the landscape alien but she continued to keep the creek on her left and not to be lured from it by the thorny brush and increasing snow drifts in the open areas.

Soon she was plodding along, barely certain that she was moving ahead at all. It was taking much longer to reach the cabin than she would have thought possible.

All at once she recognized where she was. There was the clearing where she had found Caleb! Her cabin was just past the rise beyond it. Eagerness gave her the strength to push on. She fought her way through the clearing where snow was accumulating fast. On the wooded slope the snow was less troublesome but patches of ice glazed over exposed rock and stump. Megan kept her thoughts firmly on Caleb and the warm cabin.

Just when she thought she must be lost again, she saw her cabin through the trees and smelled the wood smoke coming from the chimney. With a strangled cry, she stumbled into the yard and to the steps.

Caleb came to meet her. "What took you so long? I've been worried about you."

"Wolves." Her breath was coming in pants and her teeth were chattering. "They chased me up a tree."

"That settles it," he said as he gathered her in his arms and carried her up the steps and into the house. "You aren't going anywhere without me after this. Every time you get out of my sight, you end up in trouble."

The cabin seemed hot in comparison to the woods. Megan let him put her in the rocker but she held to her shawl until the fire's heat could penetrate her skin. "I'm so cold!" she said between chills.

"You should have at least worn my wool jacket over your dress." He got a cup and poured her some hot water. "Drink this."

"It's just water."

"It's hot."

Megan tried and found the warmth made up for a lack of flavor. She held the cup in both hands and leaned her forehead against it as well.

Caleb knelt at her feet and started unlacing her shoes. Megan didn't object. He pulled them off and started chafing her feet between his palms. "Can you feel this?"

"It feels good. Sort of." Her numb toes were starting to burn and tingle.

"Be still. I have to get the circulation going again. At least you were near a tree you could climb."

"I have walnuts, too. In my tow sack. Not many."

"I won't send you back for more," he said with a short laugh. He started rubbing her ankles and the calves of her legs. "You feel like ice!"

"I didn't think I would be gone this long. It's not that far to the walnut tree. But with the wolves not letting me climb down, and it starting to snow so hard, it took longer than I ever would have dreamed to get back." She tried to pull away from his hands. She knew she shouldn't let him touch her like this even if it did feel so good.

Caleb resisted her efforts and continued to rub her feet and legs until all the feeling had returned. Then he went to the bedroom and brought an armload of quilts to tuck around her.

"I'm all right. Really I am."

"I don't want you to get a chill." He pressed the covers tightly around her, then stared into her face as if he were trying to discover another course of action to take. "How do you feel?"

"I'm warm. Hot, almost."

"Good. You wait until all the cold is gone before you unwrap."

She smiled at him. "This is delicious hot water. You'll have to give me the recipe." She gave him a teasing glance.

"It may not have tasted good, but it warmed you." He took the cup and went to get the rosemary leaves she used for tea.

Megan untied the tow sack at her waist and looked in. "There are precious few walnuts, considering all the trouble I went to."

"It wasn't worth it. Not for nuts."

"I wanted to make you something special for Christmas."

He came back to her and put the cup of honeyed tea in her hand. "That's why you went to gather nuts? For me?"

"You've told me that your family makes a big to-do of Christmas and I didn't want you to be homesick. I can't make much of a meal with what we have on hand, but I planned to put together a walnut cake."

Caleb reached up and touched her cheek gently. Megan felt the caress all the way through her being. His hand was firm and strong but not rough with calluses the way men's hands were in the settlement. She wondered if he had worked outside at all before joining the army. Perhaps, she thought, he had been some sort of a clerk.

"You risked yourself for me?" he asked.

"I didn't think there was any risk involved," she said in all honesty. "I was only going to the walnut tree."

"If anything had happened to you, I would never be able to forgive myself." His voice was deep and gentle, his gray eyes dark with suppressed emotion.

She knew she should move away or lighten the growing tension with humor, but she couldn't think of anything except Caleb and how much she wanted to kiss him.

She wasn't sure who moved first. His face came nearer and she pushed the quilts aside to free her hands. She put her palms on either side of his face and stroked the hard line of his jaw. He felt so strong and vibrant beneath her hands. Slowly she touched his ears, his nose, his lips, trailing her fingers over his features as if she were blind and were memorizing him.

He took one of her hands in his and brought it to his lips, then turned it and put another kiss in her palm. He folded her fingers over it as if the kiss were a thing she could keep for later.

Gently he touched her face as well, rubbing his hand along her cheek to the back of her head. His eyes never left hers as he found the pins and released her hair. It fell over her shoulders and felt cool on her neck. Slowly he wound her hair in a skein around his palm and rubbed it against her cheek.

Words failed her. She knew she should tell him to stop but she couldn't possibly have done that. With all her soul she wanted him to continue.

Caleb came closer. Still holding her hair, he guided her lips to his. His kiss was gentle at first, then warmed into passion. Megan's lips parted beneath his and she heard a soft moan that she scarcely recognized as coming from herself. She put her arms around him and held him close.

Their bodies matched and molded together to a perfect fit. Caleb had drawn her to her feet and still continued to kiss her. Megan felt as if her heart would burst from her body. Fire seemed to race through her veins.

He bent and lifted her in his arms. Their eyes met and no words were necessary. Megan drew his face back to hers.

Caleb sat in the rocker with her in his lap. Slowly, as if he could never get enough of her, he kissed her. Megan felt her head spin from the wine of his lips. Between kisses he murmured to her, love words that meant little to her ears and everything to her heart. "You taste so good," he said, his voice low and mesmerizing. "You drive me to distraction."

"Am I dreaming this?" she whispered in return. "Maybe I froze to death out there and this is heaven."

"Any place we could be together would be heaven. What did I do before I met you? How did I live through the days?"

"Caleb," she murmured, using his name like a caress.

They kissed again and she felt his hand circle her to touch her breast. A quick breath caught in her throat as unexpected flames seared her soul. His fingers were gentle and compelling. She didn't want him ever to stop touching her, loving her.

Her nipples grew taut beneath his touch and throbbed deliciously. Megan pressed herself to his chest and let her tongue seek out his. This time the groan came from him.

Just as she was becoming eager for the next step, Caleb pulled her head down beneath his chin and his hand left her breast. Megan could hear the hammering of his heart and knew he was struggling for control. She kept her arms about him.

"I can't take you like this," he said in a husky voice. "Not knowing if you would regret it in the morning."

"Morning?" she said in a low voice. Words were difficult for her when she only wanted his loving. "It's barely midafternoon."

"If I take you into the bedroom, it will be morning before we stop making love."

She was marveling silently over this possibility when he added, "I don't want to rush you into anything, Megan. When you come to me—if you come to me—I want it to be with full knowledge of what you're doing."

"I know what I'm doing now."

He shook his head. She could feel the motion in her hair. "No, Megan, you're still thinking of Seth returning and of staying in the settlement. I can't live here, no matter what happens, and you don't want to come north with me."

"It's not that I don't want to. I can't." She pressed her cheek against his chest and breathed in the aroma that was all his.

"That's why I had to stop." He was silent for a long time. "What if our making love resulted in a baby? There would be no way to explain it except by telling them the truth. Your people might never accept you again."

She was silent. He was right and they both knew it. "You confuse me. You make me consider things I never want to think about."

"I know. That's what you're doing to me, too."

He held her in his arms and set the chair to rocking slowly. The familiar creak of the rockers on the wood floor brought tears to her eyes. She loved him so much and he had never spoken of love to her. It was admirable that he didn't want to chance leaving her with a love child, but she was willing to risk it for a night of making love with him. All night, he had said. Had that been an exaggeration? She had always assumed making love took very little time. But he had said it would last all night.

"Tell me what it's like where you come from—Pollard's Crossing, I mean," she said, as if she were a child coaxing him to tell her a story.

For a while he only held her. At last he said, "It's quite different from Black Hollow. Pollard's Crossing is a large town, almost a city. There are streets of houses, all decorated as pretty as dollhouses. Most of them are painted in colors with different color shutters at the windows."

"The houses are painted on the outside?"

"They look like Easter eggs, there are so many different colors."

Megan considered this. She couldn't imagine a house painted pink or blue. The buildings in Raintree that weren't brick were whitewashed, but none was colored.

"The yards have picket fences around them, all white. Ponies pull lawn mowers so the grasses stay trimmed, and there are flower beds with every color flower you can imagine."

"I love flowers. I hope someday to plant flowers here."

"Right in the middle of town is a park with a gazebo in the center of it. On warm evenings there's music there and everyone gathers around to listen or to sing along. The courthouse is just beyond and it's bigger than any building you've ever seen in Raintree. The churches have steeples on top."

"Our church has a steeple. It's not a tall one, but there's a cross on it."

"On summer evenings we sit on our porches and watch children chase lightning bugs."

"So do we." She smiled at the memory of summer evenings when she was a child, playing in the twilight with Bridget, Owen and the other children of the settlement.

"When fruits are ripe, Mama puts up jellies and relishes and the whole house smells sweet."

"I love that smell." Beneath her ear, his heart was relaxing into a steadier rhythm. So was her own.

"I had a dog when I was a boy. His name was Fetch and he knew all sorts of tricks."

"Do you still have him?"

He nodded. "He's old now. I wonder if he will still be there when I finally get home."

"I hope so. I had a dog that I loved once. His name was Toby."

"What happened to him?"

"We think he chased a raccoon into the creek and the coon drowned him. They'll do that, you know."

"I'm sorry."

"Someday I'll have a dog here. Cats, too. I love animals."

"I can't imagine my house without animals all about." His voice was soft, too, as if he were remembering his own childhood.

She nodded. "Cats are wonderful for keeping mice away."

"So practical. I have them around just for the pleasure of their company."

"I didn't want to admit that."

He tipped his head in order to see her face. Megan looked up at him. "I don't know what's happening between us, Megan, but you can believe me when I say that I'm being very careful not to hurt you."

"I trust you, Caleb." She wanted to say a great deal more, but she couldn't when he hadn't broached the subject. Certainly she couldn't say she loved him when he might not feel that way at all toward her. If he had to admit that he didn't, her heart would break. It was better not to say anything at all.

But she didn't make any move to leave his lap and he didn't seem eager that she should. At least, Megan thought, this was one memory she would treasure and keep close all her life. As the fire sang to them, they rocked, speaking softly and holding each other close. For once Megan never thought of doing chores.

Chapter Ten

Megan's thoughts were on Caleb even though she seemed, to all outward appearances, to be listening raptly to Brother Grady's sermon. He had ranted on for almost two hours and Megan had long since stopped paying attention. It was Christmas and she didn't want to hear how she was a miserable sinner and destined for hell if she didn't straighten out.

She had decisions to make. Important ones. Caleb had once offered to take her north with him and she was considering it. Her eyes flicked over the congregation. Her parents were on one side of her, Bridget on the other. Directly in front of her were Patrick's parents. Across the aisle were the Brennans, Sarah Ann looking uncomfortable as she took up the equivalent of two seats in the pew. Megan wondered how she had managed to get to church over the high snowdrifts. Megan had found it difficult herself.

The Grady children and their mother took up the entire front pew. Elvira did her best to keep her large brood quiet and attentive, but they were a handful at all times. Others from the settlement dotted the other pews, occasionally coughing or shifting on the hard wood seats. These were people Megan had known all her life. Except for Caleb she knew virtually no one that didn't live in the settlement.

If she left, she would almost certainly never see any of them again. Including Bridget and her parents.

Megan looked at Bridget out of the corner of her eye. By all rights she should be sitting with the Cassidys since she and Patrick were married. Usually she alternated services, sitting first with one family, then the other. They had been married such a short time before he left, it was hard to remember they were officially a couple.

Megan looked down at her own ringless hands. Her duty was plain. She had given herself to Seth and by all rights she had to marry him. That was practically the law in Black Hollow. Seth knew it as well as she did. Was that why he had made love to her in the clearing so soon before he enlisted and went away? He would have known that would prevent her from marrying one of the other young men before he returned. But if that was his intention, why hadn't he married her himself, the way Patrick had married Bridget?

She was beginning to face the possibility that Seth's reasons for making love to her that night were no more complex than simply that he had wanted a woman and she had been handy. The implication was deeply troubling to her.

For a long time she had known Seth was fond of going into Raintree and hiring women for his pleasure. She hadn't liked it and she had told herself all that would change once she and Seth were married. But with him gone, she was thinking more logically. Why would he stop something he had done for years, just because she was available? Love didn't change anything since he had still been making evening trips to Raintree after he had proposed to her. Megan didn't want a husband like that.

What would her family say if she didn't marry Seth? The answer was one of the reasons she was considering going north with Caleb.

Caleb. There was a man she could love. His kisses told her he cared for her, but he had stopped short of doing more than kissing her and touching her that one blissful afternoon when he held her in his lap in the rocking chair. Why had he stopped? Since she had made the mistake of telling him what she and Seth had done in the clearing, it didn't stand to reason that he had been trying to save her virginity. Megan hated that she had told Caleb because now he would never want to marry her.

Her thoughts drifted to his descriptions of Pollard's Crossing. It had sounded idyllic. She could picture white picket fences bordering manicured lawns with happy children playing games in them while indulgent mothers sat on deep porches sipping iced lemonade. Lemonade was a luxury in Black Hollow, but she was certain the ladies of Pollard's Crossing must drink it every day.

Then she tried to picture herself in that glowing picture. She had no family in Pollard's Crossing, no one to take her in. Caleb had said his family would welcome her, but as what? Hired help? Megan loved having her own home and didn't want to become a menial and work the rest of her days in a home where she couldn't even sit in the parlor.

But it would mean she could see Caleb from time to time.

Eventually, though, she would see him fall in love and marry one of the indolent young ladies and she would lose him forever. No, she shouldn't go north.

Brother Grady was finally running out of breath and winding down his sermon. Megan could recognize the signs from the tone of his voice. He even smiled a couple of times. After another ten minutes, he told the congregation to stand and sing a hymn they all knew. Christmas, other than as the day of Jesus's birth, had never been mentioned.

When the service was over, Megan filed out of the building with the others. The day was cold and the sky arched endlessly blue overhead. Against it the dark green of the pines and the bare branches of the other trees stood out in sharp contrast. At the side of the building, some of the boys were already engaged in a snowball fight. Their parents called to them sharply. It wasn't proper to throw snowballs at one another by the side of the church.

By the time the Llewellyns reached their cabin, Megan's spirits had climbed. With eager anticipation, she watched her mother go into the cabin, followed by Bridget and their father. She hurried to catch up. She almost had been late to church because she had waited until they left to put the gifts she had made in the cabin. Megan closed the door behind her and watched in anticipation as her mother went to lay her shawl on the bed.

"Why, what's this?" Jane asked in amazement as she held up the white collar embroidered with white thread that Megan had left there.

"And there's a shawl on my chair," Bridget exclaimed. "It's such a pretty shade of gold!"

"I made them for you," Megan confessed with a smile. "I've worked so hard to finish them in time." She nodded toward the place where her father always sat. "I made you a new tobacco pouch. I tanned the rabbit skin myself."

Samuel went silently to the table and picked up the pouch. "Is this a Christmas present?" he asked as he looked at her sternly.

"Not exactly," Megan said, her smile fading. "I just happened to finish them in time to give them to you today. I wouldn't call them Christmas presents, exactly."

"Weren't you listening to what Brother Grady said?" he asked in a no-nonsense voice.

"Of course, Papa," she lied. "But these aren't sinful. You've needed a new tobacco pouch and Bridget's old shawl is snagged in several places. She hasn't had time to make a new one for herself."

"And this collar?" he said, taking it from Jane's hands.

"I didn't think it would be too bright for her to wear. I didn't use any colors on it. I thought it would be pretty with Mama's Sunday dress."

Jane smiled at her. "I know you meant no harm, Megan. You've always been so thoughtful."

"I love my shawl," Bridget said as she wrapped it around her. "No one can knit as well as you."

"Give them back," Samuel said as he held out the pouch to Megan. "In this house we don't observe a secular Christmas. We aren't heathens."

"But Papa, I've worked so hard on them," Megan protested. "If it were any other day, you'd accept them."

"Not the collar. Your mother is a simple woman and not one to adorn herself. And it's not right for you to be tanning hides like some Indian squaw."

"Can I keep my shawl?" Bridget asked. "Please? It's so warm!"

He nodded grudgingly. "You may accept the shawl. But Megan, I'm warning you, this smacks too much of a worldly Christmas. Don't ever do this again."

She took the pouch and collar from him. "I won't, Papa." Inside she was foaming with anger. She had worked hard on them!

Jane patted her cheek in passing. "Help me get dinner on the table. I know your Papa must be hungry."

Megan did as she was told but her mind was rebelling. When Samuel went to the other side of the cabin, Megan asked her mother, "Why does it all have to revolve around Papa? Why does a meal have to be prepared because *he's* hungry?"

Jane stared at her as if Megan had started ranting. "It's mealtime. Everyone is ready to eat."

"I know. But you didn't mention everyone, only Papa!"

Bridget edged closer, her hands full of dishes. "Papa is the head of the house," she whispered. "You know that. Once Seth comes home, he will be the head of yours, and Patrick will be head of mine."

"It's not fair that he won't let you keep the collar I made for you, Mama." Megan ignored her sister. She didn't like the fact that Bridget was expressing another of the settlement's laws. The father was the head of the house and, therefore, its most important member. After him in importance would be sons, if any, then the mother, and finally the daughters.

Jane hesitated and glanced at her husband. "I know you must have put a thousand stitches in it, Megan. It's beautiful."

"I want you to have it."

"I could never wear it. He's forbidden it."

"You could still keep it." Megan thrust the collar in the pocket of Jane's dress. "Hide it somewhere."

For a minute Jane wavered between her husband's ruling and her own desires. "I'll keep it safe," she whispered with a quick smile. "For your sake," she added.

"Thank you, Mama," Megan said. She stirred the pot of beans and started ladling them into a bowl.

Samuel's blessing at the meal seemed as long as Brother Grady's sermon. Megan shifted her weight and willed her stomach to stop growling. No one ate before going to Sunday services and she felt half-starved. At last Samuel finished and they sat down to eat.

"Are you doing all right up there in your cabin?" Samuel asked, to show her he harbored no lasting ill will over her giving them all gifts.

"I'm fine, Papa. Some bushwhackers stole some of the meat I had hidden, but I think I have enough to see me until spring." She had decided on this small lie to explain her food being consumed at twice the rate it would be if she were alone in the cabin.

"If you run low, you come get some of ours," Jane said as she passed the corn bread to Samuel. "I don't want any daughter of mine going hungry."

"Yes, Mama." She was glad to see squirrel meat on the platter instead of horse. "You found some squirrels, Papa?"

"I did indeed. First ones I've seen in weeks. All the fighting nearby must have driven them away."

"Megan has a nest of squirrels in her eaves," Bridget said as she helped her plate. "I heard them making a racket last time I was up there."

"You shouldn't let them nest there," Samuel instructed. "They'll gnaw the wood."

"They've since run away." Megan hated to lie. Since Caleb came into her life, she seemed to be lying every time she opened her mouth around her parents.

The conversation drifted to safer subjects and Megan listened to the rise and fall of the familiar voices. How could she even consider leaving them and never seeing them again? It had been a foolish notion.

When the meal was over and the dishes washed and put away, Jane insisted Megan take some of the leftovers for her supper that night. Megan made only a token objection. Caleb would enjoy the change from her cooking. Jane was one of the best cooks in the settlement.

She climbed the hill, snow dragging at her long skirts and tripping her steps. Winter was Megan's least favorite season. She never seemed to be truly warm again until spring.

Her cabin soon came into view. At first she didn't know what was different about it, then she realized the front shutter was repaired. Her steps quickened. On the porch she paused to move it on its hinges. New nails held it in place as securely as it could be.

"You repaired the shutter," she said as she went into the house.

"Merry Christmas." He smiled at her. "It's not much of a present, but it's all I could think of."

"We aren't supposed to give presents." She showed him the tobacco pouch her father had rejected. "But I thank you anyway."

"He didn't want it?" Caleb had watched her work on the gifts and knew whom it had been for.

She shook her head. "I shouldn't have done it. I don't know what got into me."

"I'd be glad to have it." He took it from her.

"You don't smoke tobacco."

"No, but there are other uses for it." Caleb stroked the soft leather and smiled. "May I have it?"

"Of course." For a moment the silence grew long. Each had too much to say that couldn't be voiced. Megan put her basket on the table. "Mama sent our supper up. You're in for a treat. She's a wonderful cook."

"So are you."

Megan laughed. "Now I know you're teasing me. I can't hold a candle to Mama." She went to the pantry and took down a plate covered with an inverted bowl. Whipping it off, she said, "Here's your surprise. Walnut cake!"

He grinned. "And I know at what price you gathered the walnuts. You ought to call it wolf cake from now on."

"You're to remember that it's only a surprise, not a Christmas gift." She was still stinging from Samuel's upbraiding. "We don't observe a secular Christmas in the Hollow."

"Well, I do, and the shutter is my gift to you. If I had something to wrap, you'd have a real gift and maybe even a tree to put it under."

She stared at him. "Surely your family doesn't put up a Christmas tree!"

"Every year. We have connections in England, and as soon as the royal family started putting up a tree, so did we. You should see it with the candles lit and blazing away. It's a most marvelous sight."

Megan shook her head. "I can't picture a tree in the house. Especially not one with lighted candles on it!"

"And gifts wrapped under it. With pretty bows and colored paper. Mama and Felicity have made ornaments, too, out of cotton batting and the like to hang on the tree. It always makes Christmas seem magical."

"I can just imagine what Brother Grady and Papa would have to say about that!" Megan put the bowl back over the cake to cover it. "Magical indeed!" But the idea intrigued her. "What sort of ornaments?"

"Whatever popped into their heads. There are snowmen and snowflakes made of batting. Mama is good at embroidery so she stitched some angels with elaborate gowns and wings of gold threads. Felicity made some bells out of shiny paper. I wish you could see it."

"I would probably be run out of the settlement for merely looking at it." Still, her mind was working with vivid possibilities. "If only you could draw it for me. How did she know how to make the angels?" Angels were religious so she reasoned they couldn't be as sinful as the rest. "I'd love to see them!"

"I've never been much at drawing. I guess I'll just have to show them to you."

The words hung between them. All the decisions Megan had made in church about staying in the Hollow wavered. She turned away. "You shouldn't say things like that."

"How about this? I missed you like hell all day. When you came in the door, it was as if I were seeing a real angel. When you're not here the hours seem tedious in the extreme."

"I know you get lonely, but . . ."

"It's not loneliness. I used to enjoy being alone from time to time."

Megan was afraid to turn back to him. "The sermon seemed to last forever," she said in an effort to change the subject. "Brother Grady was in fine 'fiddle,' as my aunt says."

"I missed you."

"He was ringing hell and damnation from the rafters."

"Megan, look at me."

Reluctantly she turned. Their eyes met and she saw more than loneliness in his. "You're just homesick," she said softly, as if to convince herself as much as him. "You just miss your people."

He shook his head. "It's more than that. What do you feel for me, Megan?"

"I can't...I can't talk to you about this." She tried to pass him and go to her room. He caught her arm. She had no choice but to look up at him.

"This doesn't have anything to do with missing anyone or because it's Christmas or for any other reason you can fabricate. I find myself caring more for you every day. What are you feeling?"

"I..." Megan stopped and shook her head. "I can't tell anymore. You confuse me and you tempt me in ways that I never thought I could be tempted. I find myself thinking about you too much."

"Come with me when I leave."

"I can't." Megan knew she wouldn't be able to bear it if her only recourse were to work in his parents' house to earn her keep. She would come to hate living as a servant even if it did mean she could see Caleb from time to time. "Don't ask me to do that."

He put his arms around her and drew her close. "You confuse me, too. I've looked for you for years but I never expected to find you in the mountains of Tennessee." He didn't explain what he meant by that.

Megan laid her cheek on his chest. "You feel so strong, and when you hold me like this, I feel completely safe. It's been a long time since I felt so safe."

"The war has been hell for everyone."

She nodded. "At times it seems as if it will last forever. At others—" She stopped before she could voice her fears that he would leave soon.

"I know. I've had the same thoughts."

She didn't see how that was possible. Why would he dread leaving her? He said he cared for her, but that wasn't the same as love. It was what one friend said about another.

Caleb bent and kissed her hair, then her forehead. Megan lifted her face and joined her lips with his. The kiss swirled her into a world only she and Caleb occupied.

He bent and lifted her in his arms as easily as if she were made of thistledown.

"You'll hurt your leg," she objected.

"No, I won't." He carried her into her bedroom and laid her on the bed.

Megan's heart was pounding as he kissed her again. She knew she should object but this was beyond her capability. Instead, she kissed him in return.

Caleb sat up long enough to unlace her shoes and drop them to the floor. Then he removed her stockings and his own. Megan's mind told her to reprove him, to put an end to what was about to happen. She had no doubts that a single word would end it. The word was impossible for her to say or even think. She wanted him and she wanted him in the same way he wanted her.

He put his arm across her and gazed down into her face. "You're so beautiful. I can never look at you enough to satisfy me. And your voice. I hear your voice in my dreams and it's as if I'm hearing an angel. And your smiles and the way you laugh. I try to remember every move you make, every tiny thing that sets you so far apart from all the other women I've ever known."

"I dream about you, too," she confessed.

"What do I do in your dreams?" He touched her cheek, trailing his fingers to her mouth. "Tell me about them."

"I couldn't begin to do that."

"You don't remember the details?"

"I remember them too well."

He pulled the pins from her hair and, one by one, laid them on the small table by the bed. "I remember my dreams about you, too. Sometimes I lie awake for hours after, knowing you're in here and not knowing if I should come to you."

"Then why are you in here now?"

"It no longer seems like a risk as much as a necessity of life."

"Because I'm a woman, you mean." She didn't want to remember this later and convince herself he meant more by this than he really did.

"No. Because you're Megan." He drew out the last pin and unwound her hair so it lay like a fan over her pillow, dark red against the snowy white.

"Caleb, don't lie to me. Don't say things I want to hear in order to have your way with me."

"I've never lied to you and I certainly don't intend to start now. Men have more willpower than you seem to think, and I do in particular. I don't want you simply because you're a woman." His eyes ran over her. "But, God, what a woman you are!" Moving slowly, as if he wanted to relish every moment, he began to unbutton her bodice.

Megan couldn't take her eyes from him. This was so exactly like her dreams it seemed uncanny. Only the night before she had dreamed he was making love to her. She had woken trembling and hot for him. Now it was happening, and reality was so much better than her dream had painted it.

She felt the coolness of the air on her skin as he exposed it. There was a tug at her waist and he released her sash. Soon her dress lay open. He ran his finger from the base of her neck downward. Every inch felt as if he were lighting fires on her skin. Megan caught her breath at the sensation.

He drew her to him and kissed her as he pulled the dress from her arms. Through the thin fabric of her Sunday chemise she could feel the fabric of his shirt and the heat from his skin. Megan kissed him hungrily, letting her passion overwhelm her usual reticence.

He laid her back on the pillow and looked down at her. Gently he untied the pink ribbon that held her chemise together. The fabric fell away beneath his fingers.

"You're so beautiful!" He gazed down at her breasts as he exposed them. Almost reverently he touched them, curving his hands to cup their roundness. "So perfect!"

Instead of making her shy, his looking at her was heating her blood even more. The man she loved was making love with her and she could almost hear angels singing. There was nothing sordid about what was happening between them. Nothing could have felt more right. She lifted her hand and touched his face, loving the texture of his smoothly shaved jaw. She threaded her fingers in his black hair and enjoyed the way it fell silkily beneath her hand.

He caught her hand, kissed it and put it on the lacing of his shirt. Megan understood. She untied the thong and opened the neck of his shirt. His chest was lean and muscled, and she wanted to see more of him. She pulled his shirt free of his trousers and over his head. Her breath came quicker. "You're beautiful, too," she said. She drew her fingers down the muscles of his chest and lean belly. "You remind me of a puma I saw once. All lithe muscle and grace, but wild and dangerous." She was remembering how coolly he had put the pistol barrel to the bushwacker's forehead and threatened to shoot him.

"I'm no danger to you."

She smiled. "I think maybe you're at your most dangerous where I'm concerned."

He bent and kissed the swell of her breast then lower to take her nipple in his mouth. Megan caught her breath sharply. She had never known anything could feel so good! He pulled at it, drawing more into his mouth and making her arch her back to offer more of herself to him. His hand found her other breast and began to tease the nipple to throbbing eagerness.

Pulling his arm from beneath her, Caleb drew the wadded clothing away from her and tossed it to the floor. Megan lay naked before him. He looked at her, his hands following the pathway of his eyes. It was all she could do to simply lie there and let him gaze at her all he pleased. She wanted to kiss him and touch him and look at his body as he was gazing at hers.

Standing, he removed his pants and lay beside her, his naked body matching and molding to hers. Megan murmured in delight. He was so warm, so exciting! She ran her hands over him, wanting to sample all of him at once. Caleb kissed her and cupped her buttocks in his hands to roll her on top of him.

Megan put her hands on his chest and pushed up, her hair brushing his chest and trailing on the bed beside them. She straddled his middle, feeling his heat course through her. She wanted him so much she was trembling. He seemed to be in no hurry. Teasingly he touched her breasts, tempting each nipple to fullness as he watched. Then he slid one hand lower.

When he touched her Megan moaned and let her head roll back on her neck, closing her eyes in ecstasy. Never had anything felt so wonderful! He knew exactly how and where to touch her. A shiver of passion rippled through her and she whispered his name.

He drew her to him again and rolled so that his knee was between her legs. Megan opened herself to him, her eyes begging him for even more.

Slowly, enjoying every sensation, Caleb came into her. As they joined, Megan felt white-hot passion sear her. She could no longer wait. She began to move and he matched her, his body following the rhythm she set. The heat that had filled her body congregated in one area and Megan held to him tightly as she rushed nearer her completion.

Suddenly it was upon her. She cried out, partly in ecstasy, partly because it was over too soon. Waves of satisfaction pounded through her. She buried her face in his neck and held to him as if she could never let him go.

For a while she lay unmoving beneath him, not willing to release her passion. Then, to her surprise, he began moving again. Slowly at first, then more insistently. With a murmur Megan moved with him. Her desire leaped to life as quickly as before and she cried out as he gave her pleasure again.

This time when she reached her fulfillment, he rode the crest with her, holding her to him and pressing deep into her. He knotted his hands in her hair and said her name in a moan of pure pleasure.

Megan lay with him, her head cradled on his shoulder, her body curving perfectly to his. She couldn't speak for the wonder of what they had shared. Never in her wildest dreams had she thought it could be like this. When she opened her eyes, she found he was watching her, a small smile on his lips.

He touched her face, wonderment in his eyes. She knew he was feeling all the magic she was. This was too big for words. It was almost too magnificent for thoughts. She traced his smile and found hers matched.

"Megan," he said, making her name an endearment. "My Meg."

"My Caleb," she returned, her voice breaking with emotion. "I never expected anything to be so wonderful."

"Merry Christmas," he whispered, nuzzling her ear through her hair.

She knew Christmas would never be quite the same for her again.

By the next morning Megan was filled with guilt. She had made love with Caleb! Worse, she had fallen in love with him.

What could she ever tell Seth?

She slipped out of bed without waking Caleb and dressed hurriedly. At the doorway she looked back. He looked so large and virile in her bed. His tousled hair was black on the white pillowcase and his torso smooth and muscled. Even when he slept, he looked powerful, virile. Dangerous in the most delicious of ways. She wanted nothing more than to go back to bed and kiss him awake so they could make love again. With a suppressed groan, she left the cabin.

Although her kindling box was still full, Megan went to the woodpile and began making more long slivers of pine. Chopping at the wood helped somehow. Mentally she was doing the same to herself.

She couldn't marry Seth. That much was clear. Not because of what she and Caleb had done most of the night, but because now she knew for a fact she loved Caleb and not Seth. She wondered how upset her family would be, especially when she refused to move back to their house and stayed up the mountain in her cabin. During the night it had become hers and Caleb's, and she never wanted to leave it or to see another couple living in it. A young woman living alone was unheard of in the settlement and she knew there would be trouble over it. She was determined to do it anyway.

As she piled the new kindling in a stack by the stump she used as a chopping board, she heard a noise and turned to see Caleb watching her. She put down her hatchet and stared at him. He wore no shirt and the waist button of his pants was unbuttoned. He looked sexier than she had thought it was possible for any human to look.

"I woke up and missed you," he said.

"I had chores to do."

"You have enough kindling to set fire to the world."

Megan turned away. "It goes fast. Aren't you cold?"

He came to her. "I was afraid something had happened to you. I was in a hurry to find you." He touched her shoulder and she turned to him. "What's wrong?"

"We . . . I can't do this again." It wasn't what she wanted to say. Not at all. "We have our own lives. The war will be over someday, probably soon. You'll leave and I'll stay here. What . . ." She paused. She had been about to ask what if there were a baby born of their loving. But she would welcome that, settlement or no settlement. "What could I have been thinking of?" she finished lamely.

"I thought you were thinking of me." His voice was quiet and controlled. She couldn't tell what he was thinking or feeling.

She couldn't meet his eyes. "We have responsibilities, people to answer to."

"'No man is an Island entire of itself,'" Caleb quoted. "I know."

She couldn't help but smile since she had also read that in one of her books. "We have so much in common, yet there are so many more things that keep us apart."

"What are you saying exactly?" Was that pain in his voice?

"Only that we can't make love again." She risked looking at him and saw the hurt in his eyes. It almost broke her heart. "Please," she whispered.

For a long minute he only looked at her. "All right. I won't touch you again."

She felt tears sting her eyes. "Thank you." The words caused her great pain. Knowing she was doing the right thing didn't help at all.

He took the hatchet from her. "Go inside. I'll finish here."

"I have enough kindling."

"I know, but I need to do something with my hands." He turned his back to her and bent to get another chunk of pine heart. "Tearing up a dead tree seems like a good idea at the moment."

Megan watched the ripple of his muscles and remembered how they had felt beneath her hands. With every inch of her body she wanted to call back her words, to say she wanted him again, now, and that she would go north with him, even if it meant being a scullery maid in his mother's kitchen. Her pride prevented her.

Quickly she turned and hurried into the house.

Chapter Eleven

Megan's nerves had been on edge for days. Two weeks had passed since she and Caleb had made love. Every day she had to fight the demons that made her long to throw herself into his arms during the day and to slip into his room at night. At first she had attributed her uneasiness to this, but she knew it was more.

"What's the matter?" Caleb asked as she dropped the ladle into the pot of beans and examined her burned finger.

"I burned myself," she snapped. It wasn't bad, but it hurt.

"You wouldn't have if you hadn't been so angry. Have I done something to upset you?" He was whittling her a new ladle out of red oak and brushing the shavings into the fire. "I can do this on the porch."

"And have everyone in the settlement see you if they should happen to walk by? You know better than that."

"Why are you angry?" he persisted.

She spread a thin layer of butter on her finger and it felt a little better. "I'm not angry."

"You sound as if you are."

"Well, I'm not!" She glared at him.

He put his head to one side as if he found her state of mind interesting. "You've been upset for days."

Megan sat in her rocker and set it in motion as she stared at the fire. "This has happened to me before. I try to fight it, but it comes on me anyway. Mama is Irish and her grandmother had the second sight. I've inherited it. A bit of it, anyway. When I feel this way, something bad is about to happen."

"Maybe it's the end of the war," he suggested. "It could end any day now. For that matter it already may have happened and we just haven't heard."

She shook her head. "The settlement would know. Bridget would run up to tell me if there had been news. This is something else." She felt deeply troubled. "This is the way I feel when there's a death in the family."

Caleb leaned forward. "You can't possibly know that. Not without having talked to someone. Is anyone sick?"

"No!" In a more controlled voice, she said, "No, as far as I know, everyone is well."

"Maybe it's just that you're in a bad mood."

"I'm not in a bad mood!" she growled at him.

He grinned. "Whatever you say."

"I'm sorry, Caleb. I hate it when I get this way. Thank goodness it doesn't happen often."

"Does it always mean there's a death?"

"Don't make fun of me. Not today."

"I wasn't. I've heard of people being able to know this sort of information. One of my sergeants would always know when a battle was pending, long before we received orders or came upon a troop of Confederates. He was like a weather barometer."

"I feel sorry for him if it happened very often. I feel miserable." She bent and put her face in her hands. She wished he would come to her and comfort her, but since she told him they could no longer be lovers, he had kept his distance. It was what she had asked for, but not what she wanted. "It's odd," she added. "I never met my great-grandmother, of course, but we have this in common. I'm named after her. Maybe that has something to do with it."

"Would you feel better if you go to the settlement and see for yourself that everything is all right?"

"I have these beans to watch. I burned supper the past two nights and I don't want them to boil dry."

"I can stir beans. Go on down. You'll feel better once you see that everyone is well."

She smiled at him in relief. "Thank you for understanding. Not many men would."

"I wish you'd get it through your head that not all men act like the ones in the settlement." He picked up the spoon and stirred the beans to show her that he was capable of cooking in her absence. "Most of us treat women with dignity and respect. Especially when we love them."

Megan jerked her head up and stared at him. What was he saying? Caleb didn't elaborate. He had done this several times since that night of lovemaking, but he never came out and said what, if anything, he was feeling for her. Megan wondered in exasperation if he didn't realize that everything would be different if he loved her. All the decisions she had made hinged on that fact. Pride kept her from telling him. It would be tantamount to admitting that she loved him and she feared his rejection.

She took her shawl and wrapped it around her, then picked up an extra loaf of bread she had baked the day before. The bread would give her a reason for her visit. "I'll be back. If anyone comes . . ."

"I know. I'm not to be seen." He looked at her. "My leg is well enough to travel, you know. You could be rid of me."

Megan wrapped the bread in a clean cup towel. "I'll be the judge of that." She refused to admit that nothing was preventing her from trading him now. Nothing except her desire to be with him.

The day was warmer than usual for January and the brisk walk soon warmed her. The settlement lay hidden from view until she topped the ridge, then appeared, one cabin at a time, grouped near the Medicine Hat Creek. The path now circled past the cabins and on down the mountain, worn by passing troops into a road of sorts. Megan wondered what lay at the end of it. She had never been down into the valley itself. There must be other settlements, perhaps there was even a real town down there since the path had seen so much traffic.

She crossed the bridge and was surrounded by the cabins. Several dogs came to greet her and wagged their tails in recognition. A group of small boys were tumbling and running between the houses, using sticks like guns and making the noise that always seemed to accompany small boys. Megan watched them with amusement. She loved children and wanted to have a cabin full of them. The thought sobered her. If she didn't marry Seth, she would likely never have a husband or children. She decided not to think about that.

Her parents' cabin was near the water and was one of the first to have been built in the settlement. Its logs had silvered to a pale hue over the years and it looked permanent and solid and safe. The doors and windows were closed against the cold but a finger of smoke curled from the chimney and welcomed Megan.

She went to the door and opened it without knocking. Her family wouldn't know what to think if she knocked as if she were a stranger and not one of the family. That was why she had to watch for them constantly at her own cabin since Caleb had come there. They took the same liberty for themselves.

Jane looked up from the potatoes she was peeling at the table. "Welcome, Megan! I didn't expect you today."

"I brought you some bread."

Bridget took it from her and unwrapped it. "It smells so good. You make the best bread!" She held it out to their mother. "Doesn't it smell good, Mama?"

"It certainly does. What brings you down? I thought you'd be cooking your dinner by now."

"I am. I can't stay long. I left beans on the fire." She looked around. "How's Papa?"

"He's well. The weather settles in his joints in the winter, but that happens to all of us eventually." Jane dropped the potato into cold water and took another. "If you hadn't left beans cooking you could stay for dinner here. There's plenty."

"Thank you, but I'd better get back."

Jane looked up at her and her paring knife stopped in midslice. "I worry about you at times, all alone up there. Are you certain you aren't afraid?"

"I'm not afraid." She sat on the low stool by her mother. "Lately, I've had that feeling, Mama. You know, like the one your grandmother got from time to time."

Jane's fingers trembled slightly. "Oh?" She was trying to make her voice sound nonchalant. Jane firmly believed in the second sight since she had experienced it herself from time to time. "I don't suppose you know who the feeling is about, do you?"

"I never do."

"Maybe it's just the cold weather," Bridget suggested. Like Samuel, she was more prosaic. "When there's been no break in the cold, I feel out of sorts and sickly."

"This isn't the same." To Jane, Megan said, "Are you well?"

"Of course. I'm never sick."

Megan knew this was true. For a woman old enough to have grown children, Jane was remarkably healthy. She looked older than her forty years, but hard work and weather did that to a woman. All the women in the settlement aged more quickly than the women in Raintree.

"Has there been news about Patrick?"

"No. I haven't heard from him since the letter I showed you." Bridget's eyes widened and she stopped shelling corn. "You don't think it's Patrick, do you?"

"No, no. I don't have any feeling that he's in danger. I was only asking." She saw Bridget relax. When it came to Patrick, Bridget was less placid.

"Sarah Ann Brennan has been sick with a cold," Jane said, "but she's not bad off. Everyone gets a cold from time to time."

"The Brennans aren't family," Megan pointed out carefully. She wanted to start everyone thinking in terms of her not marrying Seth, but she wasn't willing to come right out and say it just yet. Not when she had a reason to keep them from dropping in at her cabin to talk sense into her. There would be time for that when Caleb was gone.

"They might as well be. You're going to marry Seth," Bridget said as she went back to pushing yellow kernels of corn from the cob into the pan. "That makes them sort of family."

"I've been having some doubts about that lately," Megan said.

"Doubts about marrying Seth?" Bridget exclaimed. "Tell me you're not serious!"

"Of course she's not," Jane said with a sharp glance at Megan. "She's promised to Seth and she will marry him as soon as he gets home."

"But what if I didn't?" Megan persisted. "What if I would rather stay in my cabin as a single woman?"

"Now you're talking foolishness." Jane let the last potato drop into the bowl of water. "It's a good thing your papa isn't in here to hear such talk. He and Aaron Brennan have struck a bargain, just as you and Seth have. Marriage doesn't involve just the couple, you know. There's the land to consider. Samuel and Aaron are already considering which of the pastures to combine and which to give over to you and Seth." She frowned at Megan and said very clearly. "Let there be no more such talk."

"Mama, I don't still love Seth."

Jane gave her a long look. "There's more to marriage than love, girl. You and Seth are a good match. Why, you've been keeping company since you were toddlers. There's not a passel of young men to choose from in Black Hollow. We consider it fortunate that you accepted Seth Brennan. He's a nice boy and you can grow old together."

"I suppose." Megan was no less firm in her decision not to marry him, but she had known it would be more difficult than to simply announce her changed intentions.

"Besides," Bridget said. "You couldn't live all the way up there if you were a single woman. What would people think?"

"I live there now and have for quite a while."

"Yes, but that's because you're tending the homestead until Seth returns. Brother Grady would never allow you to live there otherwise."

Megan frowned. "I don't think it's any of Brother Grady's business where I live or if I marry."

"Megan!" Jane glared at her daughter. "I'm going to forget you said that. What if it got around the settlement that you said such a thing?"

"Mama, he's just our preacher, not God himself!"

Jane looked as if she were on the verge of venting her temper but just at that moment Samuel walked in.

He looked from one to the other. "What's going on here?"

"Nothing," Jane snapped. "Nothing at all."

He wasn't convinced. "Megan, are you sassing your mama?"

"No, Papa." She frowned at her mother's rigid back.

Bridget looked from one to the other and Megan fixed her with a warning glare. Bridget had been known to blurt out information that was best kept secret. Miserably Bridget went back to shelling corn.

"Are you doing all right, Papa?" Megan asked. She had to put aside her anger. Exchanging sharp words with her mother would solve nothing.

"Just fine. And you?" Samuel was still watching them as if he were trying to figure out what had transpired just before he walked in.

"I'm well."

"Megan has been having the second sight," Bridget burst out. "She came down to see if anyone was ailing."

Samuel made a growling sound. "Superstition! Idle superstition. That's all it is. Godly folk don't have no second sight."

Megan frowned at her sister, who avoided her eyes. "I was just feeling edgy. That's all. I brought you some bread for dinner."

"Much obliged."

"I have to be going." She went to the door. "I wanted to pay a call on Mrs. Brennan while I'm down. Mama says she's been sick with a cold."

"If you see Aaron, tell him I said he can use the mule to haul out that stump as long as he gets him back in hiding before any Yankees confiscate him."

"I'll tell him."

She was glad to close the door behind her. As much as she loved her parents and sister, the cabin was frequently torn by strong emotions. After living alone, Megan had forgotten how easily arguments could rise among them. Samuel had always attributed it to the red hair the three shared. Megan was of the opinion that close quarters made tempers flare more easily.

The Brennan cabin was toward the back of the settlement and looked pretty much like all the others. Sarah Ann wasn't much on gardening because of her size so the yard was seldom scraped free of grass. She never bothered to rake the dirt into patterns the way most of the other wives did in their own yards. Instead straggly grasses, now browned by winter, stood in patches where the snow had melted. There were wagon ruts in the yard from the last time Aaron had used the mule and let the wagon bog down in the mud there. Megan stepped over the ruts gingerly so as not to trip.

She tapped on the door and heard Sarah Ann call out for her to come in. She opened the door and entered. The cabin was warm and smelled of onions, just as it always did. The Brennans were overly fond of onions and Sarah Ann was convinced they could cure most diseases. Sarah Ann was sitting by her cook fire and smiled when she recognized Megan.

"Come in this house!" she said in welcome. "Draw up a chair and warm yourself."

"Hello, Mrs. Brennan. Mama says you're not feeling well."

"I'm tolerable. I just ate a bowl of onion soup and that always fixes me right up." Her voice was stuffy as if her cold was very bad indeed.

"I like to make ginger tea when I have a cold. Should I bring you some?"

"No, no, child. I'll stick to my own recipes. I thank you though. You'll be a good daughter-in-law. Not like some I can name." Sarah Ann nodded her head and her chin tripled. "My neighbor, Mrs. Lukes, has had nothing but trouble out of that one her boy married. Esther always was a wild one. I never did see why Robert Lukes wanted to marry such a girl!"

Megan could figure that out but she kept her opinion to herself. It was well-known among her friends that Esther had found herself expecting a baby and had informed Robert that he would marry her or be denounced from the pulpit. "I don't suppose you've had another letter from Seth?"

"No, land's sake, I'd have sent word to you if I had." Sarah Ann sighed and her chair creaked in commiseration.

"It's terrible to have your only boy in the enemy's prison. It's real bad for sure."

Megan nodded. "I worry about him, too."

"I pray for him all the time, of course. And I have faith he will be restored to us," she added quickly. "I don't doubt that."

"Neither do I."

"But it's still hard to handle."

"How is Mr. Brennan?"

"He's fine. He had a bad cough for a spell, but it's done cleared up."

"I'm glad to hear that." Megan was at a loss to know what her premonition could mean. Everyone seemed to be as well as could be expected in the middle of winter. "Papa says Mr. Brennan can use our mule as long as he gets him back in the hiding place before he gets confiscated."

"I'll be sure and tell him. I don't know what he wants with the mule, but he don't confide in me." She laughed as if that were humorous. "It sure is good to see you. I didn't expect you to come down from way up on the mountain on such a cold day. I could put another log on the fire," Sarah Ann offered. "It's such a long walk!"

"I like to walk and it's not bad outside today. The sun is out and most of the snow is melted once you get out of the trees."

"I wouldn't know. I don't get out once the weather turns bad. Except for church, that is. I never miss a service."

"Have you seen the Cassidys lately?" It seemed a far stretch for her uneasiness to indicate them, but Bridget was a part of that family now so Megan thought it might be possible.

"I saw them last Sunday just like you did. They looked spry enough to me. I don't believe they've heard anything else from Patrick. These boys aren't much for writing, no matter how their families worry."

"Maybe it's just that letters aren't reaching us."

"That could be." Sarah Ann looked around as if she were at a loss as to a subject of conversation. She had never been one to visit and make small talk. "That could be," she repeated to fill the silence.

Suddenly the sight struck Megan harder than ever. Her hands were trembling as she drew the shawl closer. "I should be going. I only wanted to drop by and speak to you before I went back up the mountain."

"I'm much obliged. Can you let yourself out?"

"Of course. Keep your seat." Megan went to the door and lifted the iron latch. "If you hear anything else from Seth, you could send Bridget after me."

"I'll be sure and do that."

Megan was glad to step out into the cold air. The uneasiness subsided a bit but she was still shaken. What could it mean? Sarah Ann didn't look healthy, but she seemed to be in as good health as she ever was. She had said Aaron had been sick, but that he was getting better. Was it Seth?

A sick feeling settled in the pit of her stomach. Could her indiscretion with Caleb somehow have brought on trouble for Seth? She cast a quick look at the cabin with a steeple on top. Brother Grady was forever telling them that such things happened. If a wife argued with her husband and sent him out to the fields in anger, it was a miracle if he didn't die before she saw him again, and if he did drop dead, it was all her fault. Megan had been taught this principle since babyhood. So didn't it follow that she could harm Seth by making love with Caleb?

She went to the church and pushed open the door. It was empty and as cold as a tomb. Without people in it, there was an almost frightening atmosphere about the place. Megan wanted to slip into a pew and say a prayer, but she found she didn't know what to pray for. She couldn't in all honesty ask for Seth's speedy return to her since she no longer intended to marry him. Nor could she pray for Caleb with a clear conscience. She compromised by asking that Seth be returned to his parents and that he be in good health.

The door opened behind her and Megan gasped in fright. She felt foolish when she saw it was only Brother Grady.

"Megan, what are you doing in here?"

"I just wanted to say a prayer. I'm leaving now."

"You know you're not supposed to be in the church except for the appointed times. Excesses aren't holy." Brother Grady frowned down at her as if he didn't believe for a minute she meant no harm here. "You'd better be on your way. If you need to pray for something special, you have my permission to speak out in Sunday meeting and ask all of us to pray along with you."

"Thank you." She backed toward the door and hurried out. Once outside, she breathed a sigh of relief. She had always been afraid of the preacher and he had startled her. She certainly had no intention of asking for a public prayer over what was troubling her concerning Seth and Caleb. Life had gotten considerably more complicated since she took Caleb in.

That night Caleb was aware Megan was still upset. She had returned from the settlement more irritated than when she had left. "Are you going to tell me what happened?" he finally asked.

"I don't know what you're talking about." She put away the last of the supper dishes. "All right. Mama and I had words."

"Over what issue?"

She avoided his eyes. "It doesn't matter."

"You're awfully upset for it to be of no concern."

"I don't want to talk about it."

"I finished carving your ladle." He went to the mantel and brought it to her.

Megan's dark eyes lit. "It's beautiful! I'll always treasure it."

He watched her as she touched the wood gently. She had received so few gifts in her life. He wished he had more to give her than a hand-carved ladle. More than anything, he wanted to give her a music box. Was there any way to send her one once the war was over? But how could she explain it to Seth and her family?

She put the ladle on the shelf above the drainboard. "I'll put it here so I can see it when I'm doing dishes." She picked up the pan of dishwater to toss it out back.

He took it from her. After he tossed the dirty water out into the night, he hung the pan on a peg on the service porch to dry. She was watching him when he came back into the house. As if she wished to conceal her thoughts from him, she moved away and sat by the fire.

Caleb sat opposite her and picked up a bridle he had found in the barn while she was gone. The chin strap was broken and he was mending it for her.

"There's no need to do that. I don't have a horse anymore."

"You will someday."

"Not for a long time, I imagine."

"I like to keep busy." He measured a length of leather and cut it.

She took up her knitting and began to put stitches in the yarn. She always seemed to be working at something. He could count on one hand the times he had seen her sit idle, doing nothing.

"What are you making?" he asked.

"Stockings for Bridget. She has never liked to knit. I make her knitted things and she sews me a dress or a nightgown whenever she can." She blushed and he wondered if she were remembering the night they had spent together. He rarely forgot it.

"My sister knits. Mama doesn't care for it. She would rather do embroidery."

"Oh? Does she sell it?"

He laughed. "No."

"What does she do with it? Give it as gifts?" Megan looked at him as if she were really curious.

"She gives some as gifts and uses the rest in her house."

Megan's fingers slowed. "We don't use embroidery much in the settlement. Other than on christening gowns for babies or the collars of wedding dresses. It's too frivolous."

"My mother has embroidered every conceivable surface all over the house. My sister's hope chest is crammed full of pillowcases and runners and tablecloths and napkins, all filled with embroidery and lace."

"Really?" She frankly stared at him. "I've never known anyone at all like your family. Are you telling me true stories about them?"

"Of course." He looked up from the leather strap and met her eyes. "You could come with me and see for yourself."

"No." She lowered her eyes abruptly.

Caleb sighed. Since that morning when she told him there was no hope for them to be together, she had kept her distance. Until now he had forced himself to honor her wishes and had kept his as well, but it hadn't been easy. He tossed aside the strap and stood. "Damn it, Megan! Why do you make it so difficult?"

"What do you mean?"

"You know what I mean." He took the knitting from her and stuffed it back in her basket. "I'm asking you to leave with me!"

"I've already told you that I can't do that." She folded her hands in her lap and refused to meet his eyes.

"You don't love Seth! You can't love him and have made love to me the way you did. You're too honorable to have done that!"

"No. I don't love Seth," she admitted.

Hope sprang in him. "You don't?"

"Why do you sound so surprised? What you said was true. I would never have made love with you if I loved him."

"Then why in the hell won't you come north with me?"

For a long time she was silent. Caleb waited for an answer.

"Because of Owen."

"Owen? Your brother?"

"I saw him disowned. Papa says he's dead to us. I loved Owen and he was always Mama's favorite. Mama loves all her children but it's been hard on her to be without him. Family means so much to her since she can't be with her own kin. It nearly broke Owen's heart when he left. I could see it in his eyes. But Papa was adamant. Owen was a Yankee sympathizer and he couldn't stay in the settlement. If he had, some of the other men might have lynched him, so I guess it's just as well that Papa forced him to leave."

"Maybe we could find him."

"There's no telling where he settled. Just because he wrote about Cat Springs, Ohio, doesn't prove he plans to live there." Her eyes beseeched him to understand. "I can't break Mama's heart again. And there's Bridget, too. We've always been friends as well as sisters. I've shared all my secrets with her. Well, nearly all my secrets."

"Maybe your father will change his mind."

She shook her head. "Papa never changes his mind. Not about anything. If he disowns me, it will be for the rest of my life."

"Is that more important than I am?" He knew he was risking a great deal by asking this question, but he had to know.

Megan stared at him. "I don't understand."

"How can you not understand? I've asked you to leave with me many times!"

"Can't you see that I couldn't possibly be a servant in your mother's house? That I have more pride than that? Yes, I'd like to see the fine things you've told me about—the white fences and the Christmas trees and the clipped lawns—but I have my pride!''

"Whoa! Hold on! Who ever said you'd be going as a servant?''

She gave him an exasperated look. "How else could I earn my way? I can't do anything else!''

"You could be my wife!'' He stared at her, comprehension dawning on him. "Is that what you thought I was offering? A position as a servant? Megan!''

"Your wife?'' she whispered.

"Of course.'' His voice was softened with love. "Megan, why didn't you tell me this was what you thought?''

She shook her head slowly as if she were stunned. "Your wife. You want to marry me?''

"Of course I do.''

She doubled her fist and struck him on the arm. "You let me think I would be a servant? How could you do that?''

He caught her hand before she could hit him again. "How was I to know what you were thinking? I'm no mind reader!''

"I have to know exactly what's in your mind now. Is it because you're grateful to me for saving your life?''

"Of course I'm grateful! You saved not only my life but my leg as well. I'd be an idiot not to be grateful!'' He frowned at her in confusion.

"I can't marry you.'' To his amazement, he saw tears well up into her eyes.

"Why not?'' he demanded.

She pulled away from him and ran from the room. The slamming of her bedroom door jarred through the cabin.

Caleb hurried after her but stopped short of barging in. "Megan? Megan, come out here and tell me what's going on!''

"Go away!''

He knew she was crying but for the life of him he couldn't figure out why. Carefully he went over their conversation.

He had asked her to marry him. She had been under the impression that he was offering her a job before, but that was cleared up as soon as he proposed. He had told her he was grateful to her for all she had done for him and she had started crying and had run from the room.

Shaking his head, he went back to his chair and dropped into it. Women and the workings of their minds were a complete mystery to him. Certainly he had never expected his proposal of marriage to be met with this reaction. Again he went over what had happened but he was no closer to an answer than he had been before.

In her room, Megan cried into her pillow. What could have been so right, so perfect, had gone so wrong. He had offered to marry her out of gratitude. That was worse than offering her a job! He didn't love her. He had never said he did or even implied that he might come to love her in time. No, he had never mentioned love at all.

Megan refused to lock herself into a loveless marriage even if it did mean she would be with Caleb. In time he might fall in love with someone else and grow to hate her for the loss of his freedom. It wouldn't be the first time she had heard of something like this. Usually the man was trapped by an unfortunate pregnancy, but in that case, he would at least have a child to love in the marriage. In one of only gratitude, the marriage would be built on even shakier ground.

The words she had hoped with all her heart to hear had brought her no happiness at all. Caleb didn't love her.

Chapter Twelve

"It's time for you to leave." Megan tossed a change of clothing into a tow bag to carry with her. "You should wear Owen's clothes until we cross into Kentucky, then you'll put on your uniform." She placed the folded uniform in the bag. "I've already packed some food for the trip."

Caleb looked at her in silence, then said, "Do you really want me to go?"

"Yes." She didn't elaborate. His offer of a loveless marriage proved to her that she was only prolonging the pain of separation.

"Do you intend for us to walk all the way to Kentucky?"

"Of course not." She couldn't look at him. Her resolve was too weak. "I'll take Papa's mule and the horse that's hidden with him."

"You don't know the way to Corbin, Kentucky."

"No, but you do."

"You'll trust me to lead you there?"

"Once we're there, you'll be with your people. It's what you want." She didn't tell him that there was more to her plan. Megan was smart enough to know the Yankees wouldn't be likely to turn Seth over to her and let them simply ride away. She would need safe passage, such as a hostage. Caleb wouldn't be free to go until he brought them safely back to Black Hollow. Megan tried not to think of

Seth and Caleb together on the return journey. What if Caleb told him they had made love? Megan no longer intended to marry Seth, but she didn't want anyone in the settlement to know what had been going on in her cabin. But she had to take the chance.

She left him and went after the animals Samuel had hidden away from the settlement. She remembered Aaron had wanted to borrow the mule, thus she was relieved when she reached the place and saw he had either returned the animal or hadn't taken him yet. Her father would be angry over her taking them, but she knew she would be forgiven when she arrived with Seth. Or at least she would be forgiven until she told Samuel her intention of living alone in her cabin.

The horse was easy to catch and the mule not much more difficult. She had no saddle with her, but she knew how to ride bareback. She led the mule to the nearest stump and jumped onto his back. During the night she had decided Caleb should ride the horse because it would look strange for a Union officer to be on a mule and she on the better animal. Besides, she knew the mule well and had ridden him more often than she had the horse.

She rode the animals to the barn and tied them before she put the saddle on the horse. He snorted as if he weren't pleased at being ridden again. With the necessity of being kept hidden, he had done little work over the past few years.

Caleb came out with the tow bag of clothing and the other of food. Without speaking, he reached around her to draw the girth tight on the saddle. Then he tied the sacks on either side of the saddle horn.

Megan went back into the barn and measured out several days' worth of grain for the animals and put it into bags. Then she tied the bags together and hung them over the mule's back. She tied the quilts she had rolled into a tight bundle behind the saddle. Caleb watched all this in silence. Then he held out his hand to help her mount the horse.

"I'm riding the mule." She found herself perilously close to tears.

"We don't have to do this."

"Yes, we do. You've been well enough for several weeks and we both know it. I've been putting it off and last night proved to me that it's time."

He frowned at her. "Will you at least tell me what I said that upset you so?"

"No." She started to lead the mule to the mounting block. Caleb put his hands on her waist and tossed her onto the animal. Megan caught her breath in surprise and grabbed at the mule's sparse mane. She glared at him as he mounted the horse.

They started up the road toward Raintree. Megan looked over her shoulder at her cabin. There was no smoke spiraling from the chimney, which made it look vacant and unused. Since she cooked all her meals in the fireplace, there hadn't been a single day, winter or summer, that smoke hadn't risen from the chimney. When she faced forward, she found Caleb watching her. Megan tried to ignore him.

Before they reached Raintree, Caleb turned onto a path worn by army wagons and horses. In spite of herself, Megan felt a rush of adventure. She was about to see country that she had never seen before. But at too dear a price. For a minute she considered telling him to turn back, that she couldn't go through with it after all. Megan held firm. If they returned to the cabin, she might weaken and agree to marry him whether he loved her or not, and she couldn't allow herself to do that.

Although it hadn't snowed lately, winter hung in the air. Megan's breath puffed out like smoke and her skin felt wet and cold. Where would they find a place to spend the night? She had no money for a boardinghouse, even if she dared go to one with Caleb. A Confederate one wouldn't let him in and a Yankee one would be dangerous for her.

"I'd feel better if I were carrying my pistol," he said.

"You're my prisoner. Why on earth would I let you have the gun?" She had Caleb's pistol tucked in the waistband of her skirt, with her shawl knotted to hide it. Spare bullets were in the bag that held their clothing.

"It's not like I would use it against you," he said in a curt voice. "Can you shoot a man?"

"If need be. I've done it before, you'll remember."

He made no comment.

"How far do you think we'll get today?" she asked.

"We should be halfway if the weather holds and we ride steadily. I've ridden through this area before. It's an easy ride—no rivers to ford or difficult mountains. For the most part we'll have roads."

"Maybe we should stay off the roads so we aren't seen."

He shrugged. "We look like a farm couple on our way to market. No one will bother us. Unless someone decides to take our horse and mule. We don't have anything else worth stealing."

Megan leaned forward and patted the mule's chocolate brown neck. "I wouldn't want to lose Papa's mule or the horse. I've known this mule for a lot of years and he's a good animal."

"The horse isn't much, as horses go, but that's not important these days. Any horse is valuable." He sighed. "I have to admit, I miss the horse that was shot from under me. He was bad-tempered but he rode more smoothly than this one."

Megan smiled. She knew the horse had the roughest trot she had ever experienced. "Too bad you can't ride the mule. He's not bad."

At noon they stopped by a stream to eat. Megan was glad to get off the mule but she was determined not to let Caleb know. Her muscles weren't accustomed to riding for hours and she was already getting sore. She noticed his limp was worse and she knew he must be in pain. Immediately she felt bad about him being stuck with the rough-gaited horse.

They sat on a log and Caleb carved off a slice of the dried meat and handed it to her. Megan scooped up water in one of the tin cups she had packed and gave one to him. There were also dried apples and a loaf of bread. The meal wasn't tasty, but it would be good enough.

Caleb cut meat for himself. "Too bad we can't rest longer. You move as if you're tired already."

"I'm fine. We have to get to Corbin as soon as we can. This time of year snow is too likely."

"Have you given any thought as to where we'll sleep to-night?"

"Of course I have." She frowned at him. "I have two bedrolls tied behind the saddle."

"You plan to sleep outside?" He smiled as if he found that amusing. "Have you ever slept outside in winter?"

"I've never slept outside in my whole life, but how difficult can it be?" she retorted. "You spread out the quilt, lie down on it and sleep. I can do that."

"It's going to be cold."

"We'll build a fire."

"Let's turn back. We can be home by supper and no one will ever be the wiser."

"No. I have to get Seth. If we're cold, he is, too. I doubt there are fireplaces in that Yankee prison."

Caleb didn't answer.

"Are you all right?" she asked grudgingly. "If you're hurting too much, we can go back, I guess."

"I'm just fine," he said in a tight voice. "I can do it if you can."

"I'm used to privations. We thrive on them in the settlement. You've said so many times. This is like a picnic for me." She pretended to be enjoying herself.

"You must want Seth back very badly."

"Of course I do."

"Are you going to marry him?"

"I don't see that it's any of your business. Have some apples?" She held out the dried fruit.

He took a leathery circle and studied it as he said, "I think it's very much my business."

"Well, it's not. You'll be gone to your picket fences and Christmas trees and I'll be here. You'll never see me again so it doesn't matter what I choose to do with my life." The admission cost her a great deal because it was true. She would never see Caleb again. Or hear him laugh or taste his lips, or watch and memorize the thousand small things he did each day.

"It's your decision. Not mine."

"Seth may be wounded or sick. I can't bear to leave him in that place longer than necessary. I've waited too long as it is."

"I could go get him for you." Caleb didn't look at her.

Megan studied his profile. "You'd do that?"

"I'd do it for you."

"No. I'd rather do it myself." Megan thought the settlement might be more favorable toward her independence if she could deliver Seth herself. If she was going to step out of the rut Black Hollow women lived in, she had to prove something to the others.

"Suit yourself. It's not going to be that easy."

"It might be. We don't know that yet."

He shook his head. "They aren't going to simply hand over a prisoner just because you ask for him. Not even with me to trade. The guards are under orders. You'll have to go through military channels."

"That's where you come in. I'll tell them I'll shoot you if they don't give me Seth."

"You wouldn't shoot me," he said confidently.

"They don't know that."

"If you are able to get Seth, which I doubt will happen, what's to prevent him from shooting me?"

"I will. I won't give him the gun." She frowned. She hadn't thought of that possibility. There would be the trip home to consider and it would take longer to return. Three of them on two horses, even assuming Seth was in good health, would take an extra day. Seth would see Caleb as the enemy and might very well shoot him as soon as they were safely home. "I'll worry about Seth," she said with more confidence than she felt.

"You know what I think? I don't think you'll marry Seth."

"Why not? I loved him once. I can fall in love with him again."

"That's not the reason. You won't marry him because you are too fond of reading and drawing."

Megan tried to laugh. "Now you're just being silly. I loved books and drawing before I ever agreed to marry him. That's no reason at all."

"Yes, it is. You've had months of freedom in your cabin. You can read and draw whenever you like and not have to hide it from anyone. Why, you could even write that book of yours if you were alone."

"I told you I'm not going to write a book. That's a foolish idea for a woman."

"Maybe for a woman in Black Hollow. Lots of women write books."

Megan drank her water and didn't answer.

"I think you should come with me. We could just keep riding north until we come to Pollard's Crossing. I would have to go back to the army until the war is ended, but that won't be much longer. Then I would be back."

"No. Don't keep asking me."

"Why not? Are you starting to weaken?"

"Never." She stood and tried to ignore the ache in her back and legs. "Besides, I can't steal Papa's mule and horse. I'm only borrowing them. I couldn't send them back to him from Ohio."

"You could send him money to buy several mules and horses."

She laughed. "Now I know you're teasing me. I don't have any money to send him. None at all."

"I could send it. If you married me."

"I'm not going to talk about this any more." She started putting the leftover food back into the sack. Why did he always say these things at the times when she was weakest? Caleb had a talent for reading her feelings and at times it made her uneasy.

When Caleb led the animals to the stream for a last drink, she noticed he was limping much more than he usually did. Also, when he didn't know she was watching him, his face was drawn as if he were overcoming pain. She hated the thought of him hurting, but there was nothing to be done about it. Privately, she thought his wound would keep him out of the army, but she had no experience to go on.

She led the mule to the log and threw her leg over his back. It made her muscles cry out but she told herself it was worth it. When Caleb mounted his face paled, and she almost offered to return home. Maybe he hadn't healed as much as she had thought.

They resumed the ride north. Megan was surprised to find Caleb seemed to know the area so well. From time to time she found herself wondering suspiciously if he was taking her to Ohio in spite of herself or if they really were heading for Corbin, Kentucky. She had no choice but to trust him since she didn't know the way herself and had no one to ask.

They avoided towns and settlements. The danger of losing their animals was too great to risk being around people. Caleb could never walk all the way to Kentucky, or even back to her cabin, so without the animals they would be stranded.

By late afternoon the country looked different to Megan. The familiar slopes of mountains were rolling smoothly into foothills, though it was still heavily wooded. More farms were in this area and the fields were larger than the ones around Black Hollow. The fields lay fallow now and not only because it was winter. All the able-bodied young men were gone from here, just as they were gone from the Hollow.

From time to time they came upon a burned hull of a house, some of them larger than any building Megan had ever seen before. "The waste of it!" she exclaimed as she stared at what remained of a house large enough to hold two barns. "How could anyone burn a place like this?"

"It's war. I can remember my great-grandfather talking about the Revolution. As bad as it was then, it was different. This war has brothers fighting brothers. The property we destroy belongs to our own country. It's a far more personal war than the Revolution."

Megan looked in the fire-streaked windows. She could see a chandelier lying in the rubble, its candle holders burned and dirty. A table with delicate woodwork stood nearby, half its design burned away. One wall still retained some of the wallpaper, and the pink roses seemed incongruous in that setting. "It's awful," she whispered. "I had no idea it was like this."

"The Hollow has been spared most of the hardship. Most of the men are even still there. I've seen entire settlements where every man from ten years old to eighty has gone to fight." A muscle clenched in his jaw. "The South is running out of men. Some of the schools have sent their student body into uniform. They may be only boys but they're shooting and killing like men."

"Have you had to fight any of the school units?"

"No, thank God. I'm not sure I could do that."

They rode on. The countryside was also curiously empty of animals. Food was a serious shortage everywhere. There were some farmhouses that had been untouched but that were abandoned nevertheless. Their owners had been starved out or had died of the sickness that seemed to accompany armies. Fields were trampled into seas of dirt where skirmishes had taken place.

"Cannon were set up over there," Caleb said, pointing to ruts in the ground in hollowed-out places. "The enemy came from those trees, more than likely."

"Which side was the enemy here?"

"It doesn't matter."

"You sound as if you hate this war as much as I do."

"Everyone with a grain of sense hates war. People die. Not just men, but boys and civilians as well. A cannonball doesn't know a woman from a man or a house from a stronghold. And something happens to men when they see too much combat. They lose some of their civilization and it's terrible when that happens. I wonder sometimes if we will ever really recover from this war. I know none of us who fought in it will ever be quite the same."

"You seem civilized to me."

"Maybe it's because I'm smart enough to see through the lies that are spread in order to make us able to shoot our fellow men."

Megan heard the pain in his voice. Caleb hated being a soldier as much as he hated the devastation. "I hope it ends soon," she said sincerely.

"So do I. The Confederacy can't win. We have them outnumbered and we still have supplies. I hope it ends while there are still men left to return home."

By dark they were completely out of the mountains and in the mounding terrain of the lower lands. Megan saw her first sunset that wasn't half-masked by the mountains that surrounded Black Hollow. Her mouth opened in appreciation. "It's beautiful!"

"I agree. Your mountains are pretty but so are uninterrupted sunsets and sunrises. In the Hollow you don't see the sun until it's well into the sky."

"I love my mountains," she said defensively.

"Of course you do. I love my home, too. But there are other places that are pretty as well. Other places that would make good homes."

She frowned at him. "Don't start that again."

"Me?" he asked innocently. "I'm not starting anything."

Clouds had gathered to the north and west, however, and a wind was sweeping them closer. Megan knew the weather wouldn't hold much longer. Snow could be falling before morning with the clouds moving in so fast. "We have to find a place to stay for the night. It's getting dark."

Caleb nodded. He narrowed his eyes and gazed around. "Look. Isn't that a house?"

"Where?" Megan tried to make herself taller on the mule. "I think I do see something."

They rode toward it. Soon it became obvious it was another of the abandoned houses they had been seeing all afternoon. This one was no more than a shack, but its walls and roof seemed sound. There was even a shed for the animals.

Caleb dismounted as they approached and motioned for her to be quiet. He went to the nearest window and looked in. "Good. No one is here. You go inside while I put the animals in out of the cold." He untied the sacks and tossed them to her.

Megan went to the only door and opened it cautiously. It seemed strange to walk into someone else's house, even if it was abandoned. She was familiar with every cabin in the Hollow and had rarely been in a house she hadn't known from birth.

This was no cabin. It was made of planks that had been milled. The cuts were too uniform for them to have been cut by hand. Even though it had only one room, it had once been nice by Black Hollow standards. There had even been paper on the walls. Megan could still make out the stripes and ginger-colored medallions.

There was no furniture. Whoever left had had no intention of returning. The house looked as if it had been empty for a long time. A layer of dust covered everything. Megan looked for a broom but nothing had been left behind.

Caleb came with the bedrolls under his arm. "I'll go out and find firewood before it's too dark to see."

"I'll help you."

Together they gathered enough wood to last them through the night. Darkness was coming quickly now. In the Hollow it would have been dark for more than an hour. Megan felt as if she had ridden the mule for a week at least.

Caleb built a fire and soon some of the damp chill was gone from the room. Megan spread out the bedrolls, leaving a space between them. He watched her in amusement. She could already tell she hadn't brought enough cover. The house was so drafty she would feel a breeze on her back no matter how close she sat by the fire.

"We should be there by this time tomorrow if nothing slows us down." Caleb took out the food and cut them each some meat. "You could have Seth released by the next day. Assuming no one asks too many questions and the guards don't care much one way or another."

"Do you think anyone will see the smoke and come to this house?"

"I doubt it. We have to risk it. I'd feel better, though, if you'd give me the gun. If someone does come in, I'm a better shot."

"I can shoot a man."

"I remember. But I'm trained to do it."

That silenced her. She thought of Caleb as a gentle lover and a scholar who had read many more books than she had. It was at odds to remember he was also a soldier and that he, too, had lost some of the civilization he so valued. "If anyone comes in, I'll give you the gun then," she compromised.

"Megan, I'm not going to escape and leave you alone out here. What sort of man do you think I am?"

"I want you to be able to tell your superior officers that I had the gun and that you didn't. I don't want to get you into trouble."

He sighed and ate a slice of dried apple.

The fire crackled merrily and Megan felt a bit cheered by it. Outside she could hear the wind making the bare trees creak and rub together. "It's a good thing we found this place. We would be really cold out there."

He nodded. "It's not easy sleeping outside when it's this cold. We had tents, of course, but there were nights we just couldn't get to them for one reason or another. The wagons carrying them bogged down or went to the wrong place or we walked into a battle without expecting to. We had to sleep on the ground those nights and I can tell you it gets awfully cold. By morning it's as if all the cold has seeped into your bones, and it's hard to move."

"It's a wonder you didn't freeze. A woman froze at the Hollow one winter when I was a girl. She was simple-minded and a widow and lived alone. We think she just let the fire go out and froze in her sleep. It was a terrible thing to see."

"As a child you shouldn't have been allowed to see her at all." He looked almost shocked.

"In the Hollow the adults believe the children become stronger by not being babied." She looked away. "I don't agree."

"If you ask me, you agree with hardly anything the Hollow believes. You don't belong there."

"They are my people. My family loves me and I love them."

"You're a stubborn woman. You know that?"

She smiled and nodded. "You aren't the first to notice." She tossed another broken branch onto the fire. "I think that's one reason Mama and Papa were so glad when Seth asked me to marry him. They weren't sure anyone else would. I've always been outspoken."

"I don't consider that to be a fault."

"You're unusual."

"Not for my family."

"Tell me again about the Christmas tree," she said to change the subject.

"We leave it outside until Christmas Eve so it will be less likely to catch on fire. We put a sheet under it to hide the bucket of dirt the tree stands in. Mama puts candles on the boughs. We have candle holders that were made especially for that purpose. On the very top Papa hangs the star. It's the same one we've used ever since we started having a Christmas tree. Felicity hangs the ornaments she and Mama made."

"Candles on a tree and it in the house. Imagine!"

"Then we pile the presents under it and open them the next morning. Felicity is like a little monkey with all her jokes and antics. She couldn't keep a secret if her life depended on it so we all know what she has for us long before Christmas, but she forgets she's told us so it's still new for her." He laughed softly.

"On Christmas Day the candles are lit while we sing carols. We keep several buckets of water close by just in case, but we've never had a fire. The whole room smells like a forest beneath the scent of the candles and spiced cider."

"I've never had spiced cider."

He leaned closer to her. For a long moment their eyes met. He could see the firelight dancing in her dark eyes, as well as the longing. For reasons he couldn't imagine, she was firm in her decision not to go north with him, even though she loved hearing about his life there. The only possible reason was that she didn't love him after all. He must have been wrong about what she was feeling during their night of loving.

Caleb knew all too well that he loved her. Knowing he would soon be away from her was an agony to him. He had already decided to go back with her to the cabin, even if Seth would be with them. He didn't trust Seth to protect her and she might not be able to remember the route they had taken. There was no point in telling her or she would argue about that, too. Caleb wasn't looking forward to seeing her with the man she was supposed to marry.

Once she was alone with her people, would she relent and marry Seth just to keep peace? He wasn't sure. Megan was stubborn to a fault, but it would take a lot of strength to stand up to the entire settlement.

What would happen to her if she insisted on being left alone? That didn't bear thinking about too closely. Her cabin was too far removed from the others for them to offer protection. It might be a long time before men remembered they couldn't take any woman they found unguarded just because the war was over. He had seen too many pillaging troops to believe peace would happen overnight.

He knew these thoughts would give him nightmares for a long time.

Gently he kissed her lips and felt them part beneath his. Megan's kisses were like summer wine. She was made for a man who would love her and care for her and give her freedom to pursue whatever she pleased. She was made for him. Caleb had known a great number of women and Megan was the only one he wanted to spend the rest of his life with. It might take that long for him to understand her, because she was kissing him as if she loved him, body and soul.

He laced his finger into her hair and felt it loosen to his touch. His heart was racing and he knew he was only torturing himself. Making love with her would just make the parting more difficult. Loving her only once had nearly cost him his soul.

''We should get some sleep,'' he forced himself to say.

She nodded, her face bent forward so he couldn't see what she was feeling. He held her for another few minutes. He had to remember everything about her so his nights wouldn't be entirely empty forever. He knew in his heart that no other woman would ever take her place.

He released her and pulled the bedding together. "You'll freeze before morning the way you have it placed." He lay down and drew her down beside him so she was nearest the fire. His body heat met hers and he drew the covers over them.

Megan's head rested on his shoulder. Her eyes were dark and unreadable. Was that pain he saw there? Caleb kissed her again, more gently. Whatever she was feeling and deciding, she had to do it herself. She knew he loved her and wanted to marry her. He wasn't going to make it more difficult for them both by badgering her over it. Not when he was of more than half a mind to ride on past Corbin and take her to Pollard's Crossing whether she wanted to go or not.

He hardly slept that night. He preferred to spend the hours watching Megan sleep and hearing the soft measure of her breath.

Chapter Thirteen

"Do you know how much farther it is to Corbin?" Megan asked.

"We'll be there in about an hour." Caleb had been brusque all day. She knew he was angry over being traded for Seth.

"At least it didn't snow here. We're making good time."

"I suppose it could be classified as 'good.'"

"Caleb, there's no reason for you to be so angry with me. This should be your happiest day. Soon you'll be able to see your family again, even if just for a visit."

"No, soon I'll be back in battle again."

"Not with your leg, surely!"

"Obviously I can still ride a horse. It's not as if I'm expected to fight and march on foot. I won't see my family until the war is over."

"You've said that could be any day now." She didn't like the idea of sending him back into danger. "Are you certain you'll be sent back to your regiment?"

"I'm positive."

"I could keep you prisoner," she offered.

"Don't you think Seth will notice I'm living in the back room? He's likely to shoot me himself. Especially if he ever finds out we've made love."

He rarely alluded to that night. At times Megan wondered if he wished it had never happened. Certainly he hadn't tried to seduce her since. Of course, he hadn't been the sole seducer that night, as she recalled. "I'm not going to tell Seth or anyone else."

"That's a relief. With your proclivity for taking risks I wasn't sure about that. Some women feel they have to unburden their consciences before they can be happy."

"I'm not some women and I don't feel guilty about making love with you."

He finally looked at her. "You don't?"

"No. Do you?" she challenged.

"Not for a single second."

She nudged the mule into a faster gait to keep up with the horse. If he didn't feel guilty about it, why hadn't he tried to make love with her again? This proved he didn't love her. He didn't even love her enough to feel guilty about having taken her to bed. She tried to harden her heart against him but it was impossible.

"There's a town not far from here. I think we should stay there tonight."

"I'm not sure a town would be a good idea. I was thinking maybe we could find a farmer who would let us sleep in his barn."

"I don't know about you, but I'd like a decent bed if one is to be had. A hayloft would be a good second choice, though."

"Is your leg hurting badly?"

"I'm all right."

She knew he was lying. "I didn't bring any money. I had planned to avoid people."

"I have the money I was carrying when you found me."

"That just doesn't seem right, taking your money at a time like this. I mean, I'm getting ready to trade you. It's almost like robbing you."

"No, it's a kindness to let me sleep on a mattress. Once I go back to my regiment, I'll be sleeping on the ground or on a cot at best. This may be the last mattress I sleep on until the war is over."

"In that case, it's all right for us to stop in the town," she conceded. "Besides, I can send a telegram to the prison from there. I was going to find a boy and send him with a message, but this is better. I can be certain that the prison received the telegram."

"How are you going to do that without money?" he asked curiously.

She frowned in thought. "I forgot telegrams aren't free. I never sent one before. Maybe I could sell my extra dress."

"You're not doing any such thing. I'll pay for the telegram, too."

"I can't let you do that."

"If you're dead set on doing this, I'm going to see that you do it the safest way possible."

They soon rode into the town. It was larger than Raintree and the houses were more prosperous. Megan didn't see a single cabin. All the houses and stores were made of red brick. Even the streets were brick. She thought it would be hot there in the summer.

Caleb rode to a two-story house with a sign out front that advertised rooms for rent, and he dismounted. He came to help her off the mule and she was glad of the assistance. As soon as her feet touched the ground pain shot through her feet and legs. "If I ever get back home, I never want to see a mule again," she muttered.

Caleb laughed softly. She noticed he was limping badly as he preceded her up the walk.

The woman of the house took his word for it that they were man and wife and, since he was now wearing his officer's uniform, they were treated with respect.

"You could have asked for separate rooms," Megan hissed as they led their animals around the house to the barn.

"How would I have explained you? As my captor? That didn't strike me as a good idea." He grinned at her. "This way you can keep a close eye on me and be certain I don't escape at the last minute."

"Maybe that's a good idea."

He shook his head and his grin broadened as if he found her answer amusing.

They put the horse and mule in separate stalls and poured them each a measure of feed. The ricks were already filled with hay. Megan was glad. She was too tired to climb into the loft and fork some down.

They went up to the room and Megan tried to act as if she and Caleb did this sort of thing all the time. The room was clean, if small. There were white cotton curtains at the windows and a white counterpane on the bed. The floor gleamed with wax. "She's a good housekeeper," Megan concluded. "I've heard some inns are like pigsties."

"That's why I picked a boardinghouse. Inns are cheaper and they attract a lower clientele. I can be fairly certain that you'll be safe here."

Megan put down the sack of clothes. She wanted to lie on the bed and not move until morning. Then she noticed there was only one bed. "We can't sleep in the same bed."

"We've done it before. We slept together last night," he said reasonably.

"That was different. We were freezing last night. This room has a coal heater." She went to it and noticed the landlady had already put a fire in it. "I've never slept in a room with a real heater. When I was a child, I sometimes slept by the fireplace if I was sick, but Papa says it makes a child stronger and healthier to sleep in the cold."

"You've never told me a single thing about your father that makes me like him in the least." Caleb went to the window and looked out. "You can see the street from here."

"Papa loves me. That's why he wanted to do whatever would make me strong and healthy."

"My father loves me, too, but he didn't raise me to be a Spartan. All our bedrooms had fireplaces or coal heaters. Even the servants' rooms."

"Servants? What servants?"

He paused. "My parents' house was built to accommodate servants."

She nodded. "I suppose some are. Rooms like that can be shut away if they aren't needed, I guess. I can't imagine a house with that many extra rooms, but I've read books that say some are built large."

She pondered the idea that his parents lived in a house large enough to house servants. When he had been so adamant that he wasn't offering her a position if she went north with him, she had formed the opinion that his parents' house was of a modest size, like a log cabin, only made of clapboards. Now it seemed she had been wrong in that conclusion. "This is the largest house I've ever been in," she said, hoping he would elaborate. "I wonder if it was built to be a boardinghouse or if the owners had a lot of children. It's a good thing it was built so large or the lady who owns it wouldn't have any extra rooms to rent out. Does your mother rent out her extra rooms?"

"Not that I know of." He kept his back to her.

Megan had the strong impression that he was keeping something from her, but she couldn't figure out what it could be. Maybe he had been stretching the truth about the servants' rooms and was embarrassed over it. She had heard Seth take liberties with the truth before, and she knew that being caught in a falsehood would bother a man like Caleb. She smiled. It was sweet of him to be still trying to impress her in hopes of convincing her to go north with him.

"We'll have a hot meal tonight," he said. "That comes with the room."

"I wonder if I should go down and help her cook it," Megan said uncertainly. "It would be the polite thing to do."

"No, it's not necessary."

Megan sat on the edge of the bed so he could have the only chair. "I'm not used to sleeping in a strange house and having a meal cooked for me while I don't lift a finger."

He sat opposite her. "Some live like this every day."

She laughed. "I think you and I have read too many books," she said tactfully. She knew all too well how much work was involved in taking care of a house and cooking meals. Even with a houseful of daughters, a woman would have a lot of work to do.

Caleb seemed to be amused but he didn't argue.

"I guess I had better go find the telegraph office. I want to be sure the prison gets my message."

"Let's go."

They walked down the street to town. There were many Union soldiers on the streets and Megan was extremely nervous. Couldn't they tell she was Confederate and somehow intuit that Caleb was her prisoner? Not that he looked or acted like a prisoner by any means. He took her elbow when she had to step from a boardwalk to the street and he opened the door for her when they reached the telegraph office. Megan wasn't used to such attentions.

"Yes, ma'am?" the telegraph operator said.

"I want to send a message to the prison at Corbin."

He picked up his pen, dipped it in the well and waited.

"I have Captain Caleb Morgan and I want to trade him for your prisoner, Private Seth Brennan."

The operator looked up at her sharply and his eyes narrowed.

"Write it just as she said it," Caleb said calmly.

"Also say that I'll wait for them in a clearing by the river. There must be one there somewhere."

Caleb said, "Tell them the clearing near the south bend. They'll know how to find that. Say it's the place with the large oak."

Megan wasn't aware that he was that familiar with the area around the prison. "Tell them the exchange will take place tomorrow morning, early." She waited until he wrote it down.

"I don't understand," the man said. "Is this here man a prisoner of some kind?"

"You don't have to understand it. Just send it." Caleb reached in his pocket and brought out the money.

They waited until the operator had tapped the message into the machine. Megan could imagine it speeding along the black wires and thought it must be magic for it to be received and understood. "Now what?" she asked Caleb.

"Now we wait until tomorrow morning and ride to the oak."

The operator was still watching them suspiciously but Caleb nodded a goodbye to him and opened the door for Megan to leave.

"There's no telling what that man must have thought," she muttered as they went back to the boardinghouse. "I never considered having to tell someone the message. Suppose someone tries to take you away from me?"

"I'll refuse to go. If I have to be away from you, it might as well be the way you intended."

Supper at the boardinghouse was better than Megan had expected, though the cook had seasoned the meat in a way Megan had never tasted and the potatoes were cooked almost into a gravy. There were two other paying guests, both elderly men. The landlady treated them as if they were long-term renters. Megan found this surprising. In her experience, when people were too old or too infirm to live alone, they went to live with family. Could it be that neither of the men had any family?

After the meal the two men went into the parlor for a game of checkers, but Megan and Caleb went up to their room.

"It's embarrassing that they know we're in here together," she whispered as he closed the door.

"They all think we're married."

"But we know that we're not!"

"If you tell her that, I'll have to go sleep with one of the old men and you won't know if I slip away in the night or not."

She frowned at him. "You're just making it more difficult for me."

"Message or no message, we can ride out of here tomorrow and be in Ohio in a matter of days. We might even be able to go by train and get there even sooner."

"And what about Seth? What would that do to him, having his hopes raised and then dashed if I don't show up?" She frowned at him. "Besides, I haven't lost a thing in Ohio so there's no reason for me to go there."

"In that case, I suggest we go to bed. Both of us need the sleep and we should get up early in the morning to get to the clearing in time." He began unbuttoning his shirt.

Megan turned her back. "I think I'll just sit up for a while."

"Why?"

She knew he wouldn't rest until she gave him the answer so she said, "I didn't think to bring a nightgown. I expected to be sleeping outside on the ground every night and I thought my clothes would be warmer."

"You can sleep in your chemise."

She looked at him over her shoulder. He had stripped to the waist and was bending to take off his shoes. She hastily turned away again. "I would be next thing to naked. I can sleep in my dress."

He sighed and straightened, then came to her. Turning her to face him, he said, "Your modesty is arriving a bit late. I've already seen you. And quite a bit more."

"A gentleman wouldn't mention that."

"Take off your dress and get in bed. If you don't, I'll do it for you. You need a good night's rest and you can't get one in all those clothes."

Megan moved away from him and started unbuttoning her blouse. She knew he was right but that didn't matter. Her resolve not to touch him again was already weak. How could she sleep beside him and not make love with him?

She heard him move to the bed and pause to blow out the light. She relaxed a bit. Darkness was better. Quickly she removed her skirt, blouse, stockings and shoes. She felt bare. Even in the hottest part of the summer she wore cotton nightgowns that reached from wrist to neck to floor. The sheets were cold against her skin as she slipped into bed.

She stared up at the dark ceiling. She could hear him breathing beside her. Her body felt rigid from the effort of not touching his. Had he removed all his clothing, too? The thought was too tempting and she held her breath until her heart calmed again.

"Megan?" he said. His voice was deep and soft in the darkness.

"Yes?"

"What if I say we'll get Seth tomorrow, I'll talk to the officer in charge and explain that I'm not staying in Corbin. We can take Seth back to Black Hollow and you can leave with me then?"

"I'd have to say no, so don't ask me."

"Even if Seth is home safe?"

"My family is still in the Hollow. You're asking me to give up everyone who loves me. It's not as if I can go with you and come back for a visit later. If I leave, it's forever. I've never met your parents or seen Pollard's Crossing. What if I hated it there?"

"We could move somewhere else."

"And you could come to hate me. No, that would never do. I'd have to pretend to be happy and before long we'd stop speaking and eventually you'd find someone else and there I'd be."

"I didn't realize I was such a rascal until you explained it."

"It's not you. That's the way it is. No man can be expected to stick to a marriage if he doesn't have love to keep him happy. It's human nature to find someone who loves you and to want to be with that person more than any other. I don't want to find myself in that position. I'm going back to the Hollow."

He was silent for so long she thought he had gone to sleep. "I guess I was hoping for more than you're willing to give. I thought . . . It doesn't matter. Go to sleep."

She turned her face on the pillow to look at his dim profile. "You thought what?"

"Never mind. Obviously I was wrong. Good night." He rolled to his side and put his back to her.

Megan rolled to the other side. It hurt her to see his indifference. Even though she would have refused, she had thought he might offer to make love with her. Or at least kiss her. Instead, he had rolled over and was going to sleep.

Below she could hear the laughter of the elderly men at their game of checkers and occasionally the higher laugh of the landlady. The house had its distinctive pops and cracks as it settled for the night, but instead of being comforting like the night sounds she was familiar with, they were disturbing.

The window was a dark square set in the darker wall. She could see a half-moon through the trees. The moon's light, combined with the streetlights, drowned out the stars. Somewhere down the street a dog barked sleepily.

Moving as slowly as she could, she reached out her foot until it barely touched Caleb's leg. Comforted by his presence, she was able to go to sleep.

Caleb felt her touch and it seemed to set fire to his nerves. Had she moved in her sleep? She had been still for a long time. Sleep was nowhere near overtaking him. All he could think of was her lying next to him in her thin chemise. She didn't know it, but she had been silhouetted against the window as she undressed and it had been torture to watch and know he couldn't touch her.

Not for the first time, he cursed Seth and the Hollow in general. Couldn't she see that these people treated her poorly? It was all well and good to love one's parents, but hers seemed to give her nothing in return. Even the Christmas gifts she had worked so hard on had been poorly received, and her father had actually refused to keep his! Caleb would treat her so much better if only she would give him the chance.

He listened to the dog bark once more, then fall silent. He could hear her breathing but he couldn't tell if she was asleep. If she wasn't, would she have let her body touch his? Megan was an enigma that Caleb doubted he would ever understand.

Not that he would have much longer to try.

"Megan?" Bridget called as she opened the door to the cabin. Silence greeted her.

She went to the end of the porch and looked at the smokehouse and other outbuildings that stood beyond the clothesline. Megan was nowhere to be seen. On closer inspection, Bridget saw the door was missing from the smokehouse. Had soldiers forced their way inside? She had to find Megan!

Bridget went into the house and called her sister again. From the kitchen window she could see the barn. Its doors were closed so she knew Megan wouldn't be out there. It was possible she had gone into the woods to get a portion of her hidden cache of meat or for some other plausible reason.

But something about the cabin didn't feel right. Suddenly Bridget realized what was wrong. There was no fire in the hearth.

She went to the ashes and held her hand over them. They were already cold so the fire hadn't gone out recently. Even the bricks were cold. Fear began rising in her. No woman ever let her fire go out during the winter. Certainly Megan wouldn't have. She hurried to the bedroom and looked inside.

The bed was neatly made and most of Megan's things stood where they should be. All her clothes weren't on the pegs but that could simply mean she hadn't done her washing on the appointed day. Bridget went to the pitcher and basin on the wash stand and felt inside. They were not only empty, but dry inside. She knew Megan took a sponge bath in the morning and again at night every single day. The pitcher and basin should have been damp.

She was becoming more alarmed by the minute. Especially when she opened the door to the back room and saw a makeshift bed. Someone, presumably Megan, had put kegs under the door of the smokehouse and had put a mattress and bedding on top. What would possess her to do such a thing? No one was living here but Megan.

Bridget's heart was hammering as she went back into the main room. There were no signs of a struggle. So where was she?

She went to the table and finally noticed a bit of paper under the container of pickled peppers. She picked it up. Megan's handwriting leaped up at her.

I've captured a Yankee captain, and I've gone to Corbin to trade him for Seth. I took Papa's horse and mule and I'll be home as soon as I can. Don't worry about me—

                                            Megan

Bridget ran from the cabin, slamming the door behind her. She didn't stop running until she reached the settlement. "Mama!" she cried out as she dashed into the house. "Megan is gone!"

"What?" Jane looked up from the tablecloth she was mending. "What's this about our Megan?"

"She's gone to Corbin to get Seth!" Bridget shoved the note at Jane.

Jane took it and read it twice. "Where did you get this?"

"In Megan's cabin. It was on her table. The fire has been out long enough for the ashes and bricks to be cold. She's not there!"

"Go get your father!"

Bridget ran out, calling for Samuel as she went. Her heart seemed to have leaped into her throat. How had Megan done such a thing? How would she even know the way to Corbin?

She found Samuel in the barn. "Papa, come quick. There's trouble!"

"Yankees?" he asked, automatically rising.

"No, it's Megan!" She turned and ran back to the house.

Jane was rereading the note. She looked up when Bridget and Samuel entered the cabin. "Samuel, you'd better read this."

He took it from her and read it slowly. Samuel had never been one to take to reading and writing so it took him a while to decipher it. "Megan captured a Yankee? She's gone to trade him for Seth? What's she mean by this?"

"I don't know," Bridget said as she wrung her hands together and shifted from one foot to the other. "I went up to ask her something and she wasn't there. I looked everywhere and I found this note. She must have been gone at least a day. The cabin is cold."

Samuel made a growling sound. "How in tarnation could that girl capture a Yankee? And why didn't she come to me about this?"

"I don't know, Papa." Bridget looked at her mother as if Jane might be able to supply the answer.

"I'm going to look for her." Samuel took his rifle from the mantel and strode out.

"Mama? Should I call the other men and tell them?" Bridget asked. "What should we do?"

"I reckon there's not much we can do. Maybe your papa can overtake them." Jane patted the chair beside her. "Sit down, Bridget. We're not going to start worrying until we know more about what's going on."

Bridget sat down and automatically picked up her sewing. "I just can't believe she would do something like this. I'd be too afraid to capture a Yankee and to go all the way to Corbin! What if the Yankee hurts her?"

"I don't know!" Jane's voice was short, a sure sign she was worrying as much as Bridget was. "Your papa will take care of it." She jabbed the needle into the cloth.

Bridget's movements were slow as her mind whirled. Even for Megan this was terribly daring and dangerous.

"She should have come to the men," Jane said angrily after a few tense minutes. "She should never have taken it upon herself to head off on her own. She doesn't know the way to Kentucky, let alone to Corbin! And how can she hope to get there with some strange man as her prisoner?"

Bridget shook her head, her eyes wide. "I'm real scared for her, Mama."

"Don't be!" Jane stabbed the cloth again. "It's the worst possible luck to think she may not be safe. We have to trust in the Lord to look after her." After a pause, Jane added, "What can be taking Samuel so long?"

"He's only been gone a few minutes, Mama."

Jane put down her sewing and started to pace. "There haven't been any Yankee patrols around here lately. Not that I've heard of."

"I haven't heard of any, either. I guess she found a man wandering around lost." She didn't want to mention the extra bed that had been made in the cabin. That implied the man had spent at least one night there. Which also meant Megan would have had time to come to the men of the settlement for help. It wasn't as if she captured him and started immediately for Kentucky.

Several hours later Samuel came back. His face was drawn with worry as he put his rifle back in place on the mantel. "I couldn't find her," he said. "It's true she took the horse and mule. They aren't where I keep them."

Jane went to him. "Should we sound the warning bell?"

"I went to the Brennans' cabin and talked to them and to Brother Grady. They're all of the opinion that we should wait and see if she shows up."

"Wait and see!" Jane exclaimed. "That's our daughter they're talking about! We can't just wait and see if she comes back alive!"

"Be quiet!" Samuel snapped. He sighed and put his arm awkwardly around Jane's shoulders. "She's going to be fine, Jane. Brother Grady is calling a special prayer service for her tonight. We'll pray her to safety."

Jane's eyes filled with tears. "Can't you and the other men go after her? Or look for her a bit longer?"

Samuel didn't meet her eyes. "I said the exact same thing to Brother Grady and he told me this is a test of our faith. He quoted Scripture about children lost in the wilderness and things like that and he said if we believe strong enough, she will be delivered back to us."

"But that's not good enough!" Jane burst out.

Bridget stared at her. She had never seen her father put his arm around her mother and she had certainly never heard Jane argue with him.

Jane braced her body defiantly. "Our Megan is out there with some strange Yankee! You men have to do something about it! If Brother Grady is too afraid to go after her—"

"Jane! You're forgetting yourself!" Samuel took his arm away and glared at his wife. "I won't mention to Brother

Grady what you just said about him because I figure you're real upset over all this and don't know what you're saying."

She looked as if she were about to dispute this. Samuel held up his hand for silence. Jane clamped her mouth shut and turned her back on Samuel. She stalked to her chair and jerked up the tablecloth she was mending. Her needle plunged in and out of the material as if furies were after it.

Bridget stared from one parent to the other. What was happening in the cabin was almost more amazing than what Megan had done.

Samuel looked at his wife as if he wanted to go to her and agree that she was right, but Jane refused to see the expression on his face. After a while, he turned and left the cabin. His shoulders were bent as if he were carrying a great weight on his back.

Jane glared after him.

Bridget dared to reach over and pat her mother's arm. "She will be all right, Mama. Brother Grady said so."

"Just finish your mending, Bridget," Jane said in a clipped voice. "And don't talk to me right now."

Bridget did as she was told. Slowly she threaded her needle in and out of the cloth as she thought about all that had transpired. She had never thought she would ever see her mother angry at her father or that Jane would dispute Brother Grady in anything. But then, Bridget had never thought the day would come when Megan would leave Black Hollow. Amazing things were happening and they gave Bridget a great deal to muse over.

Chapter Fourteen

Megan's nerves were on end the next morning as they approached the appointed clearing. They had arrived earlier than the soldiers in order to gain the advantage. They hid their animals in a thicket at the edge of the woods and went on foot to the chosen spot.

As the sun rose they passed through the last arm of the woods. "Is that it? Is that the oak?" she asked as she caught sight of the clearing.

"That's it. You can see why I knew any soldiers in the area would know how to find this place."

The oak was magnificent, with arms that stretched out and swept down to the ground. It filled almost the entire clearing, and the space under the branches seemed as large as a cathedral. It was the largest tree Megan had ever seen.

"When do you think they will be here?" she asked. A bird was singing an early-morning song and the woods seemed too peaceful to be in a place of war.

"Soon, I would imagine. They'll want to get here early for the same reason we did. If they get here first, they can position soldiers around us."

Megan looked at him. "Why would they want to do that?"

"Why would they want to give up a prisoner when it's not necessary? They'll want to capture you, as well."

"No gentleman would do a thing like that. I'm a woman!"

"This is war and you've taken a Union prisoner. That makes you a Confederate and it's only a matter of circumstance that you're also a woman. That's what I've been trying to tell you."

"I think you're worrying over nothing." All the same, she looked about uneasily. Unless the woods here were full of small animals, someone was moving around in the trees to either side of them.

Caleb nodded as if she had spoken. "I hear them. Point the gun at me."

"I don't want to aim—"

"Just do it without arguing. If they think you might really kill me, they aren't as likely to shoot you on sight. Incidentally, I'm going back with you. Otherwise, they'll simply shoot you and Seth if they can't take you prisoner easily."

Fear joined the uneasiness in her middle. This was far more dangerous than Megan had expected. For the first time she realized what she was doing was extremely foolhardy. These weren't just men she was about to deal with, they were the enemy and they might want to kill her! She pointed the gun at Caleb.

"You did load it, didn't you?" he whispered.

"Of course. I'm not a complete fool."

His eyes darted toward a clump of saplings beyond the clearing. "Someone is coming." He looked around at the woods on either side.

Megan leaned forward eagerly. Two Union soldiers, one of them wearing a captain's insignia, were coming into the clearing. With them was a man dressed in rags of Confederate gray. His hair was as dark as it should be, but was longer than Seth usually wore his. Still, it was understandable that he wouldn't have had a way of getting a haircut. He didn't raise his face but he was the right height.

"Is that Seth?" Caleb whispered.

"I think so."

"You're not sure?"

She shook her head. Would months in prison account for the fact that he was stockier than before? Surely he would have lost weight in prison, not gained. And there was something about the way he carried himself that wasn't familiar. Inspiration struck her. She pursed her lips and gave a melodious bird whistle.

The Confederate soldier didn't seem to notice it.

With a frown, Megan tried again. This was a signal she and Seth had used since childhood and no amount of time in prison would make him forget it. When he still didn't look in her direction, she said, "That's not Seth!"

"What? Are you positive?" Caleb looked from the man to her and back again.

"Seth would answer me. I'm telling you, it's not Seth!"

The Union soldier in charge called across the clearing. "We've brought Seth Brennan. Are you unharmed, Captain Morgan?"

"Yes," Caleb called in return.

"Show me Seth's face," Megan shouted. She had to be positive.

The man in rags lifted his face a few inches. The resemblance was strong but she shook her head. "That's not Seth Brennan!"

"Sure it is, ma'am," the captain returned. "I'm positive this is the man you want to trade for."

"It's a trick!" Caleb said as he grabbed for her gun.

Megan was quicker. She raised it and fired. The soldier grabbed his right arm and stumbled. The man posing as Seth yanked a pistol from his waist and aimed it at her as guns popped all around them.

Megan heard the mosquito sound of a bullet singing past her ear as Caleb grabbed the pistol and yanked her into the cover of the trees. "Run!" he shouted.

She could hear bodies crashing through underbrush all around her and panic gave her added speed. With Caleb's hand firmly on the small of her back and pushing her forward, she dashed through the trees, holding her skirts as close to her as possible.

"Get to the horses!" he said.

"No! We can't outrun them. This way!" She grabbed his arm and pulled him off at an angle.

"We're going in the wrong direction!"

"Hush!" She frantically searched the woods for the bushes she had seen on the way in. They had to be nearby!

Suddenly she spotted them and she yanked Caleb in that direction. They tore through the bushes and Megan saw the cave she had spotted earlier. It wouldn't be an adequate place for defense, but it offered a good hiding place. She hoped no bear had decided to winter in there.

As soon as they were inside, Megan pulled Caleb down beside her. Moments later two soldiers ran past, pistols drawn. They signaled and split in two directions to search for them. Megan and Caleb sat in the semidarkness and tried to not even breathe.

Before long, the man who had pretended to be Seth also ran by. He no longer looked at all like the man he had pretended to be. Megan felt her heart rise in her throat. They had tried to trick her. She and Caleb had almost been killed! The soldiers had opened fire on Caleb as well as her. Had they thought she was also pulling a switch on them?

An hour later the woods were quiet. Megan risked a whisper. "Do you think it's safe to leave yet?"

"Not yet. The soldiers at the prison are likely bored and willing to search longer than this. I just hope they don't find our horse and mule. It's a long walk back."

"Is this why you insisted on hiding them and walking in?"

"I thought there might be difficulties. Riding a horse through woods as thick as this would be slower than running on foot. Besides, we would make a larger target." He looked at her. "How did you know this cave was here?"

"I noticed it as we passed by earlier. I'm used to living in the woods. I was pretty sure these bushes must be hiding a cave by the way they were growing." She glanced over her shoulder. "I just wish it were a larger one." She could see the back wall only a few feet away.

"It's large enough." He eased into a more comfortable position and patted the ground beside him. "You might as well get comfortable. We can't go anywhere for a while."

She sat beside him and leaned against the cold rock wall. Her stomach rumbled. They hadn't taken the time to eat before coming to the clearing and their food was still tied to the saddle. "I don't see why they didn't just give me Seth and let me leave. What harm could that possibly do?"

"It's the idea of it. Turning prisoners loose goes against the orders the commanding officer would have received. I'm not important enough to the army for the officer to risk an official reprimand." He grinned at her. "You should have captured General Grant instead."

"I'll do that next time," she grumbled.

"You wouldn't like him. His cigars are rank and he's not much better."

"You know General Grant?" she asked. "You never told me that."

"I didn't know it would impress you."

"I'm not impressed," she said. "I just never knew anyone who actually knows a real general."

"They aren't much different from anyone else. Except that most of them have a bad attitude toward anyone who isn't also a general."

"There's a lot about you I don't know," she said. "I know about your hometown and your family, but you seldom talk about yourself. Why is that?"

He shrugged. "My life has been rather mundane. So far, aside from the war, you're my biggest adventure."

She laughed, putting her hand over her mouth to muffle the sound. ''Me? An adventure?''

''You're the only thing I'll want to talk about when I'm an old man and sitting by the fire. I classify that as an adventure.''

Megan rather liked the thought of that.

They heard the sound of men coming through the woods and they fell silent. Megan was amazed they couldn't hear her heart pounding in her throat. Quietly, Caleb raised the pistol and checked the bullets left in the cylinder, then pointed it at the mouth of the cave. Megan tried not to breathe. She could see the dark blue of the uniforms and one soldier's face. If he looked in their direction, he would see them.

With his other hand, Caleb slowly pushed her head forward so her dark hair would hide the white of her skin. Megan stayed there, curled into a ball and more frightened than she had ever been in her life. She heard the small click as Caleb cocked the pistol. If they were seen, he fully intended to kill the men.

After what seemed to be a lifetime, the men moved away. By their conversation, Megan knew they were giving up. The soldiers thought she and Caleb were far away by now.

''I want you to promise me something,'' Caleb whispered. ''Promise me you won't try to free Seth again.''

''I promise. Why didn't you tell me it would be this dangerous?''

He couldn't suppress an exasperated sound. Megan smiled.

They waited another hour and heard nothing. Cautiously Caleb moved out of the mouth of the cave and crouched in the bushes. ''I think they've all given up,'' he said.

Megan came out to join him.

''Let's just hope they didn't find our horse and mule.''

She nodded. If the horse and mule didn't return safely, her father would be really upset. But, of course, the horse would have to go north with Caleb. Megan would have to weather the storm with her family alone. But then, she thought, when had she ever done otherwise?

They moved as silently as possible through the woods. Megan saw the distinctive blaze on the horse's face through the trees and pointed. Caleb glanced around to be certain they weren't walking into a trap, then pressed the small of her back to signal her to go to the animals.

When they were there, Caleb tossed Megan onto the mule and he mounted the horse. In a canter, they put as much distance as possible between themselves and the woods before the animals needed a rest.

They slowed to a walk and Megan said, "I guess we'll have to say goodbye at the next town."

"No, we won't."

"I'm not going north."

"Neither am I just yet. I'll see you safely home first."

"But that's two days' ride from here! Your leg—"

"My leg was well enough to come this far. I'll take you back and then leave. I'm afraid the horse will have to come with me, however, at least as far as the nearest train station. I'll send you payment for him as soon as I get back to my regiment."

"You should go home. Not back to the fighting."

"I have no choice in the matter until this war is over." He looked as if he hated the thought of going back to the bloodshed and horror she knew he must have faced. "Home," he said softly. "At times I wonder if home is still there. It feels more like heaven to me now."

She reached out and touched his arm. "It will be over soon. You've said so yourself."

He smiled. "I hope I know what I'm talking about."

The trip back to Megan's cabin was uneventful. As before, they avoided the places where they were likely to encounter soldiers of either side and as soon as they were into Confederate territory, Caleb traded his uniform for Owen's homespun.

The cabin looked wonderful to her. She kicked the mule into a reluctant gallop and as soon as they were in the barnyard, she slid off his back. In the joy of being in her own yard again, she didn't even mind the pains in her legs and feet from having ridden so many hours.

They tied the animals to the porch rail and went inside. Megan looked around. Nothing was changed. "Maybe no one even knows I've been gone," she said hopefully. "It feels as if we've been gone forever, but it's only been a few days."

Caleb went to the table. "Didn't you leave a note here?"

"Yes." She hurried closer. "It's gone! They've been here."

Their eyes met.

"I have to go down to the settlement before someone comes back up here. Go into the back room and stay there until I return."

"Be careful, Megan."

She tried to smile. "They're my family, Caleb. They won't hurt me." She wished she were entirely sure of that herself.

She mounted the horse and led the mule down the road that wound into the settlement. As soon as she was sighted, there was an outcry. Naturally, she thought, Bridget or whoever had noticed she was gone would have told all the others. She forced herself to smile and wave.

Jane came running to meet her, Bridget close behind. "What on earth has gotten into you?" her mother demanded. "Are you all right?"

"You've had us worried sick!" Bridget seconded. "Why would you try such a thing?"

"I had to try to get Seth released. Yes, Mama, I'm all right."

Samuel came running up and heard the exchange. "Where's this Yankee you said you had?"

"He escaped. I wasn't able to get Seth," she added needlessly. The Brennans had joined them, and she knew they would have as many questions as her family.

"How did you come up with a fool idea like that? Samuel demanded. "I've a good mind to take my razor strap to you!"

"I'm sorry, Papa. But I had to try."

"Where did you get a Yankee in the first place?"

This was one of the lies she had rehearsed in her mind. "I happened upon him in the road out front of my cabin. He was lost."

"See, Mama?" Bridget said. "I said I thought she found one that was lost."

Megan nodded. "I held a gun on him and tied him up. Then I went after the horse and mule and we rode north."

"There's no way you could have gotten all the way to a prison in Kentucky," Jane said. "Sometimes I wonder about your mind, child."

"I got there," Megan said with a proud tilt of her head. "I even had the men bring Seth out to meet me. But it wasn't Seth. They were trying to trick me. In the excitement, my prisoner escaped."

Brother Grady came puffing into the group. "A woman taking such a thing on herself? Unnatural! It goes against all we believe in here!"

"I'm sorry, Brother Grady. I saw the opportunity and I had to try." She lowered her eyes and tried to look contrite. Something had happened to her on the long trek that altered her feelings about the settlement. She was no longer seeing the people in the same light she once had. Everyone was more angry with her for taking a risk than relieved that she was safely home again.

"What would we have done without the horse and mule?" Samuel demanded. "You stole them from all of us.

You know the rules. If we have only one mule, he belongs to us all until we can get more."

"I brought them home again," she said a bit too sharply. "I didn't steal them! I only used them to try to get Seth back." She looked at Sarah Ann Brennan. "Surely you don't blame me!"

Sarah Ann's eyes filled with tears. She was still breathing hard from having hurried. She opened her mouth to speak, but Aaron silenced her with a stern frown. "We can't condone stealing or a woman trying to put herself in a man's place," he said sternly. "You should have come after your pa or me and we would have gone. Likely we could have gotten Seth, too!"

"No, you couldn't! I told you, they didn't bring him out. It was a trick. I was lucky to escape with my life!"

"You should have been safe at home, not traipsing all over the country." Samuel scowled at her and took the reins from her hands. "Don't you ever think of doing something like this again. Do you hear me? You're not too big to whip!"

"Yes, Papa." She wasn't able to keep the sarcasm out of her voice. "And thank you for saying how glad you are to have me back all in one piece."

Samuel took a step forward as if he would strike her for being rude to him in front of most of the settlement. Jane reached her first. She grabbed Megan's arm and shook it angrily. "Hush! Think what you're saying and where you are!"

Megan lowered her eyes. "I'm sorry, Papa."

Samuel was somewhat mollified. "We were worried sick about you," he said gruffly. "We're glad to have you back."

"Come in and warm yourself," Jane said. "I've put on some stew for dinner and it's likely done by now."

Megan shook her head. "I just want to go home, Mama. Thank you anyway."

"I'll go with you," Bridget said. "You shouldn't be alone up there."

"No. I'm not afraid." Megan smiled faintly. "I just rode all the way to Corbin, Kentucky with a Yankee prisoner in tow. I'm not afraid to stay in my cabin alone. I'm welcoming the quiet."

She knew everyone was watching her and not understanding her refusal of Bridget's company, but Megan was too tired to care. She only wanted to be home and away from everyone but Caleb.

The mountain seemed steeper than usual as she walked home. Her muscles were aching and she felt as if she hadn't slept in days. When she came in sight of her cabin, she was surprised and glad to see the thin finger of smoke drifting from the chimney. As usual Caleb hadn't followed her orders about staying hidden and he had started a fire. She found herself smiling.

When she came in, he was kneeling by the fireplace. "How did it go?" he asked.

"Not too badly." She sank gratefully into the rocker and leaned her head back on the headrest. "Everyone is angry with me. Brother Grady thinks I'm an unnatural woman. Bridget probably thinks I've lost my mind for not wanting her to come stay with me tonight and Mama is wondering why I don't want any of her stew. Other than that, I'd say it went well. Except for being accused of stealing the animals," she added.

Caleb pulled off her shoes and began rubbing her feet. He was wise enough not to make any comments about her reception in the village.

Megan turned her head to gaze into the fire. It was comforting to see warmth and a hearth that was all her own. "I told them you escaped."

"I put in some meat to boil, along with potatoes. We'll eat late, but at least it's not jerky and dried apples."

"Thank you for doing that for me." She couldn't imagine a settlement man starting the fire and supper for his wife. Chores were clearly defined and a man didn't do women's work unless he was unable to find a wife and had no female kin.

"You look more exhausted than you did before you went to the settlement. What are you thinking?" he asked.

"I saw them in a different way today. It frightened me."

"Different in what way?"

"I don't know." She couldn't tell Caleb. He already disliked everything he had ever heard about the settlement. He wouldn't be so calm if he knew her father had threatened to whip her in front of everyone and that no one had spoken up in her defense. Megan knew Samuel had meant every word he said. "I don't think I'm hungry. I may just go to bed."

"Maybe that would be a good idea."

She dragged herself out of the rocker and went to her room. When the door was closed behind her, Megan leaned her head back against the wood and let the tears come. Her homecoming wasn't at all what she had expected it to be.

Slowly she undressed and pulled the white cotton gown over her head. She loosened her hair and brushed it until it was smooth. The entire settlement had been worried about her, but shouldn't relief that she was safe have outweighed their anger? Why did they act as if she had done something wrong in trying to free Seth? She knew the answer in her heart. It was because she wasn't a man. Her going after him like that had indirectly shamed all the men in the settlement for not having done it themselves.

She opened the door enough to let heat in and hurried into bed. The sheets were like ice and she curled into a ball for warmth. In the next room she could hear Caleb moving about, doing the small things a person did after a long day. The sounds reminded her of when she had been a small child and she had lain in bed and listened to what her mother referred to as putting the house to bed for the night. The sounds were deeply comforting.

The tears came again. Megan was so tired she didn't try to stop them. No one would know anyway. Caleb would be leaving soon, perhaps as early as the next morning. There was nothing to keep him here any longer. He would go back to his regiment and perhaps engage in more battles like the one in the clearing. But this time if he was injured, she wouldn't be there to take care of him. The tears flowed faster. She would never know if he survived the war or not.

No, she thought, that wasn't true. Somewhere deep inside, she would know if Caleb were alive or dead. Their souls were too intertwined for her not to know. She thought back to the day she had the premonition of death. Nothing had come of it and that was odd. She had never known that feeling to prove untrue. But even if she was losing that uncanny ability, she would know if Caleb was hurt. He was a part of her soul.

Secretly she was glad Seth hadn't come back with her. At least she was safe from refusing him until the war was over. No one need know her intentions until then. She thought again of the angry faces she had seen and knew that her family and Seth's would be even more angry when they learned she wouldn't marry Seth and that she would stay in the cabin alone. Assuming her father would let her. Megan was no longer certain of that. Would her independence be considered worse than her taking the horse and mule? She had a feeling that she would be in for a battle of wills.

She looked at the doorway as Caleb came to it. "Are you asleep?" he whispered.

"No."

He came into the room and she smelled the stew he brought with him. Caleb lit the lamp and sat on the side of her bed. "You should eat something." He dipped the spoon in the bowl and held it to her lips.

Megan tasted the stew and her stomach rumbled hungrily. Until now she hadn't realized how hungry she was. She tried to take the bowl from him but he shook his head. As if she were a sick child, he fed her.

Megan watched every move he made. No one had ever coddled her like this and she wanted to remember every minute of it.

"What are you thinking?" he asked.

"I was memorizing you."

Their eyes met. Megan sat straighter and put her arms around him. Caleb put the bowl on the table and held her, neither of them speaking. She felt his warm strength and the steady beat of his heart. She kissed the pulse in his throat and laid her face against his skin.

"How can I ever bear to leave you?" he asked softly.

"You can because you have to do it. You have no choice. None of us do, really. I'm learning that."

"There is always a choice," he said. "Always."

"But sometimes the price is too much." She was thinking about him being labeled as a deserter if he didn't go back to his regiment. From all she had seen, she knew he hadn't lied about the North winning the war and that it would be over soon. He would have to be dutifully mustered out or he would never be able to hold his head up again when the war was mentioned. Duty and loyalty were as important to him as they were to her.

Caleb held her tightly and buried his face in the luxuriant masses of her hair. He no longer cared about anything as much as he cared about her. If she said the word, he would never leave her and never regret the decision. Instead, she was sending him away. "Megan," he whispered, as if her name were another word for love. There was no argument he could use, apparently, that would change her mind. She was determined to stay and equally determined that he should go. Even though he knew she was right about his leaving, he hated the thought.

"Hush," she whispered, her breath soft in his ear.

Caleb kissed her and felt the too familiar torment of his spiraling emotions. Beneath the fabric of her gown he could feel the luscious curves and yielding flesh that haunted his memories and his dreams. He ran his hands over her, enjoying the feel of her against him, her breasts rounded against his chest. She hadn't braided her hair and it flowed down her back to the bed. Beneath it, her back was warm. He gathered her hair in his hands and felt the silken softness of it.

Gently he laid her down on the bed and matched his length to hers. She held him tightly as if she were afraid he would leave her. Nothing was further from his mind.

She began unbuttoning his shirt and he kissed the warm hollow where her neck met her shoulder. The pulse beat there so quickly he knew she was as hungry for him as he was for her. There was a bittersweetness in knowing this could be the last time he would kiss her, hold her. Make love with her. Caleb groaned at the thought.

Megan kissed him as her small hands slipped beneath his shirt. As she stroked his back and sides, Caleb thought he wouldn't be able to control himself. His desire for her was quickly growing into a need. When she ran her fingers into the waistband of his trousers, he stood and shucked off his clothing as he gazed down at her.

In the lamplight her skin was golden, her hair pooling beneath her like a fiery aura. Her eyes were so dark they had become black, edged with the lace of her eyelashes. Her lips were slightly parted and moist from his kisses and he could see the even row of her white teeth beneath.

Slowly Megan stood and began unbuttoning her gown.

Caleb rolled onto the bed and watched as she exposed inch after inch of skin. He knew she was enjoying tantalizing him and he loved it. Megan was no woman to pretend she disliked lovemaking. Instead, she reveled in it.

When the gown was completely unbuttoned, she let it drop to the floor with his clothes. She stood before him in naked beauty. Her hair had drifted over one shoulder, hiding her breast. She brushed it aside and came to the bed.

Caleb opened his arms and she lay beside him. Her skin was cool and he warmed it with his own. Slowly he began kissing her, exploring every inch of her body, tasting the softness of her skin, running his tongue over the curves of her breast and hip. Her hands were on him, touching him with a wonder as great as the first time they had made love. He promised himself that he would love her in such a way that he would never fade from her memory.

He ran his tongue over her breast and flicked the nipple. Then he took it in his mouth and suckled it until she arched toward him. He rolled her beneath him and she opened her legs for his entrance. Caleb kissed her until the room began to spin. Megan looped her leg around his, drawing him into her.

When they became one, Caleb thought for a minute he wouldn't be able to hold back. He fought against his body's instincts as she kissed him and stroked his back and buttocks. She murmured soft words to him that had no meaning in his state of arousal.

Slowly he began to move, and the pleasure tore through him. Megan rolled her head on the pillow and cried out softly with desire. He kissed her, knotting his hands in her hair to bring her face to his. There was a wildness in them both because they each knew this could be the last night they would have together.

He loved her. Megan was the woman he had been created to love and he ached from wanting her. Her body was so soft and so hot beneath him. Her breath was sweet in his mouth. Her hair made a cloud of fire beneath them.

As he moved, Megan's breath came faster. She was so responsive! He could marvel at it even as his own body cried out for satisfaction in hers. Suddenly she made a sound of pure ecstasy and held him tightly. He felt the rhythmic pulsations that meant she had reached the first of her plateaus. Caleb was determined that she reach many this night.

Floating on the ocean of their shared passion, Caleb loved her. Because he believed she didn't want to hear him ask her again to leave with him, he used his body instead of words to tell her of his great love. Of how he never wanted to be apart from her. Time after time he brought her to the brink and tipped her into the tumult of desire. She loved him in return with the unleashed passion that was so intimately Megan.

When at last he could hold back no longer, Caleb moved with her and didn't check his body's desires. Together they climbed one final mountain and spun off into sheer pleasure and ecstasy. He held her close as his fulfillment ripped through him, blinding him to everything but her. Megan reached her peak at the same time and she cried out as their souls entwined together.

Caleb lay beside her and held her gently as the world formed again around them. She was the center of his universe and his sole reason for living.

Their eyes met and he could read the wonder in hers and knew his must look the same. More than anything he wanted to tell her he loved her, but he knew if he did he might not be able to leave her. He wasn't entirely certain that he could leave, even if he didn't tell her.

Gently he brushed the hair back from her face and traced the loved lines of her features. She smiled at him and touched his face as if she, too, were memorizing and treasuring every inch of him. He wanted to remember the way her hair grew into a peak at her forehead and how her ears lay flat against her head. How her long eyelashes were like black lace and the way her smile made a tiny crease near the corner of her mouth. "You're so beautiful," he whispered.

"I want tonight to never end. I want us to go on forever just like this."

"We can. All you have to do is go north with me."

She put her fingers on his lips to quiet his words. "Tonight there is only us. No one else in the world exists."

"You're my world." It was as close to a declaration of love as he thought she would want to hear. "I'll never understand you," he said, almost to himself.

"I know," she agreed.

Caleb kissed her and felt his passion begin to respond to hers. Their kiss deepened and he began stroking her body as hungrily as if they had not already made love. The night lay long before them.

Chapter Fifteen

Megan propped herself on one elbow and gazed at Caleb. He still lay asleep, his breath moving his deep chest at regular intervals. They had made love all night, dozing to wake and make love again. Never had she felt so happy and so thoroughly satisfied. But even as she looked at him, her body responded.

Why couldn't she go with him? It made no sense to deprive herself of him just because he didn't love her at the moment. Didn't love sometimes grow between a couple after they were wed? Their temperaments were well matched and they liked each other. Other marriages had thrived on less. As for his falling in love with another woman, that might never happen.

Megan touched his hair, taking care not to waken him. She had so much to decide. If she went with him, she would never see her friends or family again. She was positive that her father would never forgive her. She would be as dead to them as Owen was. Whatever her mother and sister felt, they wouldn't go against Samuel. Only Megan and Owen had the rebellious streak.

She tried to imagine herself living with Caleb in the town with white picket fences and clipped lawns. As a bachelor, he must still live with his parents, she thought. She didn't know how he earned his money, but she reasoned it would be a while before he could save enough for them to have a home of their own. That meant she would have to live with his parents as well, and she wasn't at all certain that they would take gracefully to him having a Rebel bride. She could picture the two of them living with her own parents and it wasn't a pretty thought.

She didn't doubt for a minute that his parents loved him, but that was entirely different. Parents wanted their children to marry people of their own kind. Since they lived in town and she had been in the mountains all her life, they wouldn't have much in common. Other than the inn on their journey, Megan had never slept in anything but a log cabin. Pollard's Crossing probably didn't have many of those. A house made of cut timber must be terribly expensive, she thought. It could take many years for them to afford that.

For a brief moment she considered asking him to stay with her. His regiment would never know where to find him so there would be no repercussions. But she knew it would never work. Caleb wouldn't lie about having fought for the North and even if he did, his accent would give him away the first time he opened his mouth. Her father or one of her kin was likely to shoot him "by accident." With no sheriff or courts, mountain justice was apt to be abrupt and final.

Megan leaned forward and kissed his shoulder. He smiled in his sleep and her heart warmed. If only he loved her, she would go with him to the ends of the earth. But even though they had made love all night and although he had taken her to realms of pleasure she had never dreamed existed, he had never once said he loved her.

She had almost told him. Now she was sorry that she hadn't. Last night had been a perfect opportunity. But she had been afraid he would stop what he was doing so she had kept quiet. Leaning close to him, she whispered so softly he would never be able to hear, "I love you."

Caleb slept on but he reflexively reached for her. Megan let him draw her closer and laid her head on his shoulder.

In the window the sky was slowly turning a pearly gray. She should already be up but she couldn't bring herself to pull away. A bird was singing in the tree closest to the cabin, even though it was winter and no bird should care if it was dawn or not. Megan listened to the notes and thought it was like her own personal miracle. The bird was singing the love she couldn't express.

She noticed Caleb's breathing had altered and she looked up to find he was awake and watching her. They smiled at the same time.

"We slept late," she said, tracing her finger over the muscles of his chest.

"We hardly slept at all." He drew her on top of him and wrapped her hair in a skein about his hand. "You're beautiful in the morning, too."

Warmth filled her. "I'll go make you some breakfast."

"Is there a rush?"

"I should be up and about in case Mama or Bridget comes up the mountain. Since I've been gone, they may come to check on me."

"We wouldn't want them to find us like this." He made no move to release her.

Megan didn't want to be released. "By now I should have your meal on the table and beans in to soak for dinner."

"You've become hopelessly lazy after your travels. The sun must have been up minutes."

She laughed and bent to kiss his chest. "I don't want last night to end," she confessed. "When I get up and get dressed, it will be over."

"I know."

Their eyes met and Megan tried to will her feelings into him. Surely she had enough love for both of them.

"If you keep looking at me like that, I may not be able to leave."

"And then Papa would shoot you."

"I wouldn't like that."

"Nor would I." A sadness crept over her. He really did have to leave. To keep him from seeing her unhappiness at the thought, she rolled out of bed and began dressing.

"I like to watch you."

She smiled. "I used to be shy. I thought I'd never want to dress or undress in front of any man." She glanced back at him. "In the village, it's discouraged, even between husbands and wives."

"I thoroughly dislike the settlement. Doesn't anyone there ever enjoy life?"

"Of course they do. But in other ways."

"You didn't lump yourself in with them that time," he observed. "You said 'they' not 'we.'"

She didn't reply. Would it be so bad to live in a house with strangers if she could see Caleb every day? She knew she had to decide quickly. "I'll fix your breakfast."

Megan made the porridge Caleb liked and laced it with some of her precious cinnamon. Since this was his last breakfast here, she wanted it to be special.

They ate in silence, as if each was afraid to use up the words that lay before his departure. She washed up the dishes as he went in the back room and put on his uniform. When he came out, he looked larger and almost like a stranger, she was so accustomed to seeing him in Owen's clothes. Slowly she dried her hands on her apron, then removed it and hung it on a peg. "I guess I had better go get the horse."

"I won't need the saddle. You keep that."

She nodded. She was afraid to speak. This was the beginning of his goodbye.

Samuel had been awake since well before daylight. This wasn't unusual for him. With winter making the days so short, he had to rise early to get everything done. Besides, Brother Grady said a person who spent unnecessary hours in bed was going to hell. Samuel did everything possible to avoid that.

Jane sighed when he shook her awake. She hardly ever complained. He was fortunate in that. She and Bridget were as biddable as any two women he had ever seen. It was a good thing, too, since his two older children had been rebellious from the cradle.

"Get up and start the coffee," he said. "It will be morning soon."

Jane rolled unprotestingly out of bed. Samuel pulled on his trousers and sat on the bed to put on his shoes and socks. He had been troubled ever since Megan had come back with her fantastic story about the Yankee. In the earliest morning hours he had put his finger on the flaw in her tale. How did a person hold a gun on a man while she tied him up? It wasn't possible.

He was frowning as he reached for his shirt. Had Megan been lying? What could she gain by that? He had no answer. But one thing Brother Grady preached constantly was that it was a man's obligation to his family to be sure they stayed on the narrow path and didn't stray onto the one bound for hell. He wanted to get some answers from Megan and he wanted them fast. She was so headstrong, once she put her mind to a thing she was hard to dissuade.

Jane had the coffee in the pot by the time he slicked back his hair and came into the main room. He glanced up at the loft. Bridget was still asleep. There was no movement up there at all.

When the children had grown as tall as his waist, Samuel had put up a partition to separate Owen's cot from the girls', and when the girls became a bit older he had built steep stairs to take the place of the ladder. Now Bridget had the warmest and most comfortable place to sleep in the entire cabin. That bothered Samuel because he knew privation honed a soul to righteousness, but he couldn't see a way around it. His cabin was too small to put her anywhere else.

Jane tossed a double handful of oats into the boiling water and left it to cook while she went to dress. She was quiet in the morning and Samuel liked that, too. He didn't like a lot of conversation before breakfast. Even as a small child, Megan had talked incessantly whether anyone answered her or not. Seth would be getting a handful when it came to managing her.

Bridget had always been his favorite. Not only was she obedient, she reminded him of Jane at that age. Jane had been the prettiest girl Samuel had ever seen and he had proposed to her after he had known her only a few days. She and Bridget fit into Black Hollow life perfectly. Not Owen. Samuel refused to think about him. Owen was dead for all practical purposes.

Megan was just like Owen. Samuel was counting on Seth being able to bring her in line. Sometimes a husband could accomplish what a father couldn't.

He poured himself a cup of the chicory coffee and went to get his rifle from over the mantel. "I'm going out for a bit, Jane. I'll eat when I get back."

"All right, Samuel," she called from the tiny bedroom.

He stepped out into the cold air and looked around. It was still dark but he could tell by the feel of the air and earth that dawn wasn't far away. Samuel had lived so many years close to the earth that he could judge such things.

Instead of going up the road, he circled through the woods and up the hill to Megan's cabin. He wanted to see her without being seen. At times that was the only way to know what was going on.

He knew the woods around her cabin as well as he knew the land around his own. There was a large oak stump from a tree he had cut to make one of the foundation logs of her cabin. It was close enough to her clearing for him to see the cabin and still be concealed by the woods. He easily found the stump and sat down. From time to time he sipped the coffee to keep warm.

Within half an hour he saw the door open. Megan stepped out, wrapped in her heavy shawl against the cold. Her head was down as if she were in deep thought and she never looked in his direction. Samuel was about to conclude that he had been wrong when the cabin door opened again.

A Union officer stepped out onto the porch and called to Megan. She paused but didn't turn to look back at him. The soldier came off the porch and went to her. Samuel was so surprised he almost forgot he was holding a cup of hot coffee in his hands. This was much more than he had expected.

The man went to Megan and put his arms around her. She leaned back against him and closed her eyes. The man said something to her but he spoke so softly Samuel couldn't hear him. Then, before Samuel's amazed eyes, the man turned Megan around and kissed her with greater tenderness than most men would show a well-loved wife.

Samuel jumped to his feet and tossed the coffee cup aside. He came out of the woods, the rifle aimed squarely at the soldier. "Get away from her," he growled.

"Papa!" Megan exclaimed. Instead of backing away, she held to the man.

She stared at him in terror. Of all the times for her father to be there! For months she had feared this would happen, but today, when Caleb would be leaving within an hour, it *had* happened.

Samuel came toward them. She knew by the expression on his face that he would shoot Caleb if she moved an inch from him. "Papa, this is Captain Caleb Morgan. He helped me try to free Seth," she said quickly. To Caleb she added, "This is my father."

"I figured as much," Caleb said. His voice was cold and tense, the way it had been in the barn when the men had attacked her. She knew he had his pistol and that he was as dangerous as Samuel.

"Get away from him, Megan," Samuel commanded. "Do as I say!"

"No, Papa! I'm not going to let you shoot him!" She felt Caleb's hand go to the gun he wore at his waist. "Don't hurt him, Caleb!"

Samuel's gun barrel didn't waver. "You been living here all along, Yankee?"

"I was wounded. She took care of me. When I was able to travel, we went to the prison at Corbin and tried to free Seth."

"Now why in tarnation would I believe you?" Samuel said. "You're still here and you look fit to me." He glanced at his daughter. "You left out this part in your story, didn't you? Did you think we're all blind and crazy and wouldn't never suspect nothing?"

Megan had no intention of ever letting anyone know how long Caleb had been living in her cabin. "He wasn't here all that long. You saw how he limps. He's not fully healed yet."

"It won't matter in a couple of minutes. Get away from him!"

Megan stepped away, but she came straight toward Samuel, keeping her body between the two men. "Put down your rifle, Papa. Let me talk to you."

"Ain't nothing to say." Samuel's black eyes flicked at her again. "You been living in sin with this man? Is that it?"

"Papa . . ."

"He's the enemy and you let him touch you?" He struck at her and Megan fell. He finally saw that Caleb had drawn his gun and that it was pointed straight at his heart. Samuel blinked. It was a standoff.

Megan scrambled to her feet. She could see by Caleb's expression that the only reason he hadn't shot Samuel was from fear of a stray bullet hitting her. "Wait! Both of you!" She stood between them, glancing from one to the other. "Papa, Caleb is leaving. I was on my way to get the horse for him."

"You was giving him my horse!" Samuel was so angry she could see him shake.

"He can't walk all the way to a train station! His leg isn't that strong yet!"

"I don't care if he has to crawl! You shouldn't never have offered him the horse!" Samuel's voice dropped to a gravelly growl. "Besides, I'm going to shoot him before he walks a step."

"No, you're not!" Megan glared at her father. "Because I love him." She heard Caleb draw in a sharp breath behind her but she didn't dare look away from Samuel.

"You're promised to Seth Brennan!"

"I'm leaving with Caleb, Papa." Megan knew at that moment she couldn't have let him go. Whether he loved her yet or not, she would have gone with him anywhere.

"Like hell you are!"

"Come on, Megan," Caleb said in that cold, dangerous voice. "Let's go. We can walk to Raintree and find a horse there."

"You ain't taking my girl!" Samuel looked as if he would shoot at him whether Megan was in the way or not.

"Both of you! Put down the guns before someone gets hurt!" she pleaded. Neither listened, nor had she really thought they would. She walked to Samuel, more wary this time of staying out of his reach. "Papa, let us go."

"No!"

"You let Owen go. Now it's my time."

"Owen was a man. You're nothing but a girl and no girl of mine is traipsing off with no Yankee! I'll shoot both of you first!"

With a sickening feeling in the pit of her stomach, Megan knew he meant it. She turned back to Caleb. Tears welled in her eyes, making him seem to waver. "I can't go with you."

"I won't leave without you," he said firmly.

"He means it. He'll kill us both." She saw the uncertainty in his eyes. "Please, Caleb. Leave. I'll be all right."

"He's pointing a gun at you! I'm not leaving you with a man who's just threatened to kill you!"

"He's my papa. He won't shoot me. Go, Caleb. You have to leave. What would I do if he shot you?" The tears were rolling down her cheeks and her voice broke. "I couldn't bear to live if he killed you." She looked back at Samuel. "Promise me you'll let him go if I stay here."

Samuel looked as if he were considering. Finally he gave a single curt nod.

Megan moved closer until the rifle was inches from her stomach. "Papa, if you're lying about this, I'll never forgive you and I'll never be seen in the settlement again. You know I mean what I'm saying."

For a long time Samuel was silent. Then he said, "Get out my sight, Yankee."

Caleb took a step toward Megan. "Will you be all right?" he asked.

She nodded. In a voice that trembled, she said, "I love you, Caleb. I'll always love you."

"I love you, Megan. And I'll be back for you."

"You come back this way, Yankee, and I'll shoot you and feed you to the dogs." Samuel's voice was cold and steady.

Caleb gave Megan another long look, then he turned and started walking up the road toward Raintree.

Megan felt as if her heart were breaking. She knew she might never see him again, in spite of his promise to return. Even if he did, the chances of her being free to leave with him then would be no better than they were now. A sob shook her and she wrapped her arms about her body.

He had said he loved her! If she had known that, they would be safely in Pollard's Crossing by now. She would never have returned to Black Hollow if she had known that. But at least Caleb was leaving with the knowledge that she loved him in return.

She heard a sound and turned to see Samuel aiming the rifle at Caleb's back. With a cry, Megan threw herself at him, jamming the rifle barrel into the dirt. She glared at her father. "You promised! I'll never speak to you again for lying about this! You were going to shoot him in the back! As soon as I can, I'm leaving Black Hollow and I'll never return."

"I'll see you dead first," Samuel promised her solemnly. Megan knew he meant it.

He grabbed her arm and yanked her around toward the settlement. "Come on. You ain't living up here alone ever again!"

Megan cried silently but she knew Samuel couldn't shoot Caleb as long as he was gripping her arm. She struggled just enough that he couldn't turn her loose. She also walked with reluctance to give Caleb a longer head start in case Samuel sent the men after him.

When they reached the cabin, Samuel shoved her inside so hard she tripped and fell. Pain shot through her and she glared up at her father as Jane and Bridget screamed. Jane hurried to her.

"What's going on? Samuel, what on earth are you doing to our Megan?"

"She was consorting with the enemy." He shoved his rifle onto the mantel and spit into the fire as if the word made a sour taste in his mouth. "She was up there with a Yankee living in her cabin all this time."

Bridget helped her to her feet. "Megan? Is this true?" To their father, she said, "It can't be true, Papa. I've been up there off and on ever since she moved in."

"Then you're a blind fool. He was there. She up and told me he went with her to Corbin to get Seth. No wonder they couldn't get him! That Yankee had a nice safe place to wait out the war and a woman to do whatever he wanted of her!"

Jane put her arm around Megan. "No, Samuel! Our Megan wouldn't do that. She's always been a good girl."

"No, she ain't! She's as damned fool headstrong as her brother was. I curse them both!"

"Samuel!" Jane stared at him in shock. He wasn't a man to use words lightly.

"If she was a man, I'd have shot her on the spot! Or I'd have sent her packing! I'd have shot Owen for less."

Megan didn't point out that if she was a man she wouldn't have been in that position. It frightened her that he was mentioning Owen's name. He hadn't said it since Owen left.

"Megan?" Jane said. "What happened?"

"After the battle in the clearing, I found Caleb wounded and doctored him. I was going to trade him for Seth. But somehow I fell in love with him instead."

"There! You see? She's admitted it to you! She's as guilty as sin!" Samuel looked as if he would like to beat her within an inch of her life. He even took the razor strap off the wall and came toward her.

"No!" Jane put her arms around her. "You're not going to beat her, Samuel. She's a grown woman now. She's under your protection!"

Megan glared at him. She had never heard her mother speak against anything her father did.

"If you hurt her, I'll speak against you in church!" Jane added.

This made Megan look at her mother in amazement. Before, Jane would never have even hinted at such a thing.

"I mean it, Samuel. I'll really do it. I told you when Owen left that I couldn't ever stand to lose another child. You're not going to hurt our Megan!"

Bridget didn't speak, but she came closer and put her arms around Megan as well.

Samuel glared at the three of them. For a terrible moment Megan thought they were all about to get a beating. Then he threw down the strap and stormed out. She felt her mother relax and knew Jane had had the same thought.

"He can't do this to me," Megan said through clenched teeth. "Caleb and I love each other!"

"Hush!" Jane glared at her. "You don't know what you're talking about!"

"If you knew him, you'd like him, Mama. He's kind and gentle and—"

"He's the enemy!" Jane stepped away. "Is it true that the two of you were living up there in your cabin? In sin?"

Megan slowly shook her head. What had happened between Caleb and herself had been right, not wrong. "It wasn't a sin, Mama."

Jane nodded as if she were relieved to have that much to hang on to, even if they were splitting hairs with words. "If anyone asks, I'll tell them that. That he never touched you." Before Megan could speak, she gave her a silencing look. "Don't you say one word. Now help me get this house clean."

Megan got the broom and started sweeping the already spotless floor. Jane was proud of her wood floor—not every cabin in the settlement had one—and she never let dirt settle on it. Megan's thoughts were in a turmoil. Caleb loved her! She would never see him again!

"Did you really fall in love?" Bridget asked when their mother went out to put the washtub on the fire. "With a Yankee?"

"He's a man, Bridget. Not our enemy. He reminds me of Owen in a way. You'd like him." She stopped sweeping and hugged the broom handle to her. "He's tall and handsome, and best of all, he talks to me. Really talks! Like you and I do. And he smiles often and you'd love to hear him laugh." Her voice trailed off. "Bridget, what will I do if I never see him again?"

"You'll marry Seth and make him a good wife."

"I'm not going to marry Seth. Caleb will come back for me. He said he would."

Bridget stared at her. "You'll go away with him? You'd have to, you know. He would never be accepted here."

"I know." She took Bridget's hand to emphasize the importance of what she was about to say. "He's from a place called Pollard's Crossing, Ohio. Remember it in case he comes for me and I have to leave without telling you goodbye. We don't know where Owen is, but this way you'll always know where I live."

"You won't run away with him. You can't." Bridget pulled away and started to lift the basket of dirty clothes.

Megan caught her arm. "Yes, I will. I don't know when he'll come for me, but I know he will if he stays alive until the war is over." Her voice trembled at the prospect of his not surviving that long. "And when he does, I'll go with him."

Bridget lowered her voice to a whisper in case their mother was closer than they thought. "I would do the same for my Patrick. I'd go anywhere just to be with him."

Megan smiled to see someone understood.

That Sunday Megan was spoken against in church. Brother Grady himself called her to come down front. At first Megan refused to move. Then her father leaned past Jane and she knew she would walk willingly or be taken there by force.

With all the dignity she could summon, Megan rose and walked down the aisle to the front of the church. She kept her chin high and refused to look at all repentant. Embarrassment blazed in her cheeks from being singled out, but she kept quiet.

"We all know what Megan Llewellyn has done," Brother Grady said in a sorrowing voice. "She has trafficked with Satan and shared her cabin with the enemy."

A murmur ran through the church even though Megan was positive everyone there already had heard about Caleb.

She faced them and refused to let any emotion show on her face.

"We must pray for her, my brethren and sisters. We must pray for her immortal soul." Brother Grady looked at the Brennans. "I wouldn't blame you good people if you didn't allow her to marry your son, Seth. I wouldn't blame you at all. But we have to forgive even the vilest of sinners and sometimes a sinner can be brought about through duty. Seth is a good man and may be able to do that job right well."

Megan's eyes met Sarah Ann's and the older woman looked away. Aaron stood up. "I believe she ought to marry him. Me and Samuel have already been dividing up the land and figuring what goes to who. I don't reckon she ought to be allowed to mess that up. When Seth comes home, he'll marry her."

"You're a saint if there ever was one," the preacher intoned. "Not many would overlook a transgression of this magnitude."

Samuel stood up. "I've punished her. She's felt my razor strap on her back. She won't stray again." He sat back down.

Megan met his eyes unflinching. He had beaten her when he came back home that day. She still had bruises on her back. This had determined her as nothing else could have to leave the settlement. Once the war was over and traveling was safer, she was leaving, even if Caleb didn't come back after her. She could somehow find her way to Pollard's Crossing and go to his parents. They might give her shelter until she found a way to support herself.

Brother Grady nodded. "That's as it should be, Brother Samuel. It's our duty to tend to our womenfolk. Now, Sister Megan, what do you have to say for yourself?"

The eyes of all the congregation swung back to her. This was the time she was supposed to apologize publicly and to beg their forgiveness and to request prayers for her soul. For a long time Megan was silent. Then she said, "Caleb and I did nothing I'm sorry for. I love him and he loves me. When Seth comes home, I will not marry him." She thought this was as good a time as any for her father to hear her plans.

A louder murmur swept through the congregation. Brother Grady looked at her as if he thought she had lost her mind. "You don't mean that. You're promised to Seth."

"I'm breaking that promise." She kept her head high and her gaze unwavering. She might be afraid, but no one had to know it. Her eyes met Bridget's. "I'm moving back to my cabin. I'll live there alone."

"You ain't going to do no such thing!" Samuel burst out, leaping to his feet. "No girl of mine is going to live up there doing God knows what!"

Brother Grady silenced him with a frown. "Control yourself, Brother Samuel. You're forgetting where you are."

Samuel mumbled an apology but he continued glaring at Megan.

"I can't marry Seth if I love someone else," she said to Sarah Ann. "It wouldn't be fair to him."

Sarah Ann nodded slightly and touched her eyes with her handkerchief. Aaron only frowned and crossed his arms over his chest.

"Well, I can see Brother Samuel and Brother Aaron have their chores cut out for them," Brother Grady said. "I urge them not to let anger lead them entirely. Let us pray."

Megan refused to bow her head. Her angry eyes stayed locked with Samuel's. She knew she had taken a big chance. He might beat her half to death when he got her home and Jane wouldn't be able to stop him. But at least she no longer had to pretend that she would marry Seth.

The prayer seemed to go on forever. Megan's feet and legs ached from standing in one spot. She could see the others in the congregation were also shifting silently. At last Brother Grady had brought down all the divine guidance and hellfire he could summon and he ended the prayer and the service.

Everyone stared at Megan, but no one came up to her to speak to her. Megan was glad. She had said all she had to say and didn't want to argue with anyone.

By the time she worked her way to the door and was out of the church, her family were well on their way home. She could see them ahead, walking stoically as if they were leaving a funeral and not a mere Sunday service. No one spoke to Megan at all. The few who met her eyes turned away as if they were ashamed to have been caught looking in her direction. Megan was secretly relieved. Being shunned was the least of her worries.

When she arrived at her parents' home, she expected the latch to be drawn against her. Instead, the door was ajar so she walked in. "Mama, I'm sorry I embarrassed you. I had to do what I did. I'm going back to my cabin now." She ignored her father. She had said she would never speak to him again and she intended to keep that promise. Even when he was whipping her, she had never spoken to him.

Bridget glanced at her parents, then back at Megan. "I could come up and live with you. That way you wouldn't be alone."

Jane looked at Samuel. He turned away and crossed his arms stubbornly. "Get that woman out of my house, Jane," he said.

Jane turned to Bridget. "I reckon it would be a good idea for a few days, anyway. Just until things calm down. Megan, you did a bad thing. I doubt the settlement will forget it anytime soon."

"I did what I had to do," Megan said firmly. "If Bridget wants to come stay with me for a while, I would welcome the company."

"Bridget, you know folks may speak against you for siding with her," Jane said.

"She's my sister, Mama. I'm afraid for her to be up there all alone with the whole settlement mad at her. Someone might try to hurt her." Bridget's eyes were earnest. "Please, Mama?"

Jane looked at her husband's back. "It would be a good thing for all of us to have a little distance between us right now. You can go. But Megan," she added, "don't do anything to put Bridget in the position you're in. Come to church on meeting days and behave yourself."

"Yes, Mama."

Megan waited until Bridget gathered up her clothing and shoved it into a tow sack. Bridget had no more belongings than Megan and it didn't take long. In all that time, Samuel never relaxed his stance.

They were silent as they left the cabin. No one called to them as they crossed the bridge and went up the road. Megan's heart felt heavy in her chest. "You shouldn't be siding with me, Bridget," she said as they reached the cabin. "People will be angry with you, too."

"I don't care. Megan, once Patrick is back home, can we live here with you? There's that extra bedroom and I don't want us to stay with Mama and Papa. It's embarrassing. Do you know what I mean?"

"I understand. Of course you're both welcome." Megan stopped and looked at her cabin. She hadn't been back since Caleb left. Her father had been keeping her under close surveillance. Had Caleb come back and been unable to find her? No, she thought, he would have ridden straight into the settlement and found her come hell or high water.

Bridget went up the steps. "It's hard to believe you had him here and I never knew. I've *been* here and I never saw him."

Megan sighed and followed her inside. "It's hard for me to believe at times, too. But he was here."

"For as long as you said? That battle in the clearing was way before Christmas. He was here that long?"

She nodded. "At first he was hurt so bad I thought he would die and I didn't want to risk Papa and the men trying to move him. Then—" she paused "—we fell in love."

Bridget watched her, her blue eyes round with amazement.

Megan pushed open the door to the room Caleb had used. "You can have this room. There's a bed."

Bridget looked at the makeshift bed, then at Megan's bedroom. "I saw that bed the day I came up here looking for you. Megan, if you didn't sleep together..."

"We made love. And I don't regret it." She sat down on the bed and buried her face in her hands. All of a sudden she felt tired to the bone. "Bridget, I tried to fight what I felt for him. I knew none of our people would understand, but I fell in love anyway. I did everything Brother Grady and Papa accused me of. And I would do it again." She looked up at Bridget with defiance.

"You're not a bad person." Bridget smiled and came to sit on the bed beside Megan as they had when they were girls. "To tell you the truth, just between the two of us, Patrick and I didn't wait until we were married either."

Megan smiled sadly and sighed. "I don't blame you. You and Patrick have always been in love." She paused and drew in a deep breath. "I miss Caleb so much." She touched the pillow that had cushioned his head. Loneliness swept over her. "Being here, I can feel him all around me."

"Is he really coming back for you?" Bridget's voice sounded full of awe at so great a love. "Even though Papa almost shot him?"

"Yes. He's coming back." Megan wouldn't let her mind dwell on the fact he could be in danger with his regiment. Surely no one would send him back into battle with a bad leg. She was determined to believe that. "He'll be back."

Chapter Sixteen

The winter seemed to drag on forever. More and more often Megan and Bridget saw soldiers from both sides pass by the cabin. By now all of them had the hollow-eyed stare of men in shock and suffering from privation and exhaustion. It became rare to see a Confederate soldier in a whole uniform. Even the butternut replacements for the original gray were becoming worn out from the men having to live outside year around. Most soldiers had only one uniform so they were filthy as well as tattered.

Megan's precious supply of horse meat was starting to dwindle as spring finally approached. Spring came late to the mountains every year but this time winter seemed especially reluctant to relax its hold. Megan hoped their food would last until crops could grow and berries ripen.

The snows became less regular and finally stopped altogether, except for those on the very top of the mountain. The trees grew knobby with leaf buds. A violet appeared in the woods, then another. Spring finally arrived.

It took months before anyone in the settlement other than Bridget and Jane spoke to Megan. She didn't care. Her heart was too heavy for her to want to have contact with others. If it hadn't been for Bridget's presence, she would probably have struck out for Pollard's Crossing in spite of the war and whether she knew the way or not. But she knew Bridget would be blamed for not watching her more closely and she didn't want that.

True to her word, Megan never spoke to her father. But since he never spoke to her either, she knew he probably hadn't noticed. Jane and Bridget tried everything they could to make peace between them, but Megan had inherited Samuel's stubbornness and she held as firm as he did.

When the frosts were over, Megan and Bridget worked the garden and planted the seeds carefully hoarded from the year before. Megan looked forward to the added burden of work that came with the warmer months. When she was busy she had less time to think and less time to long for Caleb.

She thought about him almost constantly. Had he gone back into battle or had the army sent him home to finish healing? When she saw the lines of hungry men passing the cabin, she prayed that he was faring better than they were.

In early April Megan was surprised to find Samuel coming across her yard. "Bridget," she called into the cabin. "Papa's coming."

Bridget came out, the broom still in her hand. Megan held her ground. This was her cabin, her land. She wasn't going to leave her porch just because Samuel was there. He never looked at her.

"Bridget, I've got news. General Lee has surrendered to Grant at Appomattox. The war is over." His face was stiff as if he had privately thought all along the South would win somehow.

"Thank God!" Bridget said, clasping her hands together.

"You'd do well to keep words like that to yourself," he said. "This means the South has lost."

"But now Patrick will be coming home!" Bridget went down the steps and hugged her father. She looked back at Megan. "Isn't that wonderful news, Megan?"

"Yes. I thought it would never end."

Samuel fixed her with a cold glare. To Bridget he said, "Your mama is expecting you for dinner. Afterwards there's a prayer meeting at the church."

"Take the lantern in case Brother Grady runs late," Megan advised. She no longer attended the church. Being shunned had its advantages. She did all her praying in the woods behind the house and felt more in tune with God there than she ever had in Brother Grady's church. She also knew that Samuel was angry over her doing this. She was supposed to be contrite and beg forgiveness, not revel in her aloneness.

"Megan, you've got to come with me. This is a special occasion," Bridget pleaded.

"You know I'm not welcome at Mama's house. She will understand."

"We don't need her, Bridget," Samuel said. "Why don't you come along now? I know Jane's got her hands full since this came about on wash day."

Bridget cast an imploring eye at Megan. Megan shook her head. She went back inside.

She was rarely alone in the cabin these days and she missed that. Bridget was a good companion but with her in constant attendance, the cabin had lost all traces of Caleb. Megan went to the door of the back room and looked at the bed where he had slept. Bridget had made the room her own. Her dresses were hung on pegs with her nightgown and sunbonnets. Bridget's hairbrush and comb were on the bedside table and a pink coverlet was on the bed. But in Megan's mind she could still see Caleb lying on the bed, dwarfing it by his size.

She had never known she could miss anyone so much.

She had frequently thought about the day he had left. When it came down to it, if her father hadn't appeared, would she have gone with him? In her heart she believed she would have. But at the time she hadn't known he loved her. That made such a difference.

If she had gone with him, he would have taken her to his parents' house and left her there while he rejoined his regiment. That could have been worse than being here. In the Hollow she at least knew she had Bridget and their mother, and she was living in a way that was familiar to her. She had to smile. Living hand to mouth had little to recommend it.

She heard the door close and saw Bridget come in to put the broom away before leaving.

"I'll stay here if you want me to."

"No, Mama needs you and there's the church service. You don't want the settlement to think I'm being a bad influence on you."

"Please come with me. Megan, you can't spend the rest of your life up here, not speaking to anyone but Mama and me."

"I know." She knotted her hands together.

"God forbid, but what if Caleb was killed or never comes after you?"

Megan felt the cold grip that was familiar from having thoughts like this. "I don't know. I've thought I might try to find Pollard's Crossing on my own."

"You'd go all the way to Ohio? What if his people don't want you?"

"Would I be any worse off? No one in the settlement speaks to me, as you well know. I've seen small boys snicker when I walk by. Once they even threw rocks at my house. No one will ever forget I lived here with a Yankee. At least I might be welcome at the Morgans' house. Maybe."

"You're a Confederate. They're Northern. They could also hate you."

"I know." She went to the rocker and sat down. She leaned her head on the tall back and closed her eyes. "How did my life ever get so tangled up?"

"You've always had a talent for it."

Megan smiled wryly. "You'd better run on. Mama will be expecting you."

"Are you certain you'll be all right here alone?"

"Of course I will be. I like being alone. If you mean will I head north before you come back, no. I'll give Caleb more time to find me. I'm not even positive where Ohio is, much less which part of the state Pollard's Crossing is in." She got to her feet. "Besides, I have wash to do, too."

"I won't be late." Bridget hurried out.

Megan went to the tub where their soiled clothes were soaking. Washing really took three days. One to soak the clothes, one to actually wash and dry them, and one to sprinkle them and iron them. It was one of the most laborious chores of keeping a house.

She started wringing the clothes and put them in a basket to carry them out to the washtub. At least the day was clear. Last wash day she had dodged raindrops to finish and had ended up drying the clothes inside by the fire. Did Caleb have clean clothes and a fire? She tried not to think.

Caleb had been among the troops at Appomattox. When he was on horseback his limp was no hindrance and he fought fiercely in order to end the war as soon as possible. He wrote his family about Megan and told them of his intention of going after her once the war was over. He also wrote Megan, but he had no confidence any of the letters reached her since they had to cross at some point from Union hands to Confederate.

Like the others, Caleb found Appomattox to be both a relief and almost an anticlimax. Everyone knew the South had been outlasted but not outfought. There was no honor in fighting men who hadn't eaten in two days, sometimes longer. The South had been fighting in desperation that day. Like Caleb, they knew the war was over but they couldn't bear to give in to the inevitable.

After the battle, Caleb rode across the battlefield, helping the survivors find all the dead and wounded. The worst sounds were those of the horses. A wounded horse screamed until it was put out of its misery. The soldiers lay as quietly as possible and were harder to locate. At intervals he heard pistol shots, which meant more animals were being dispatched. In his gut he was so sick of war that he could understand how a man could kill barehanded.

At least now he would be mustered out and sent home. With the surrender of the general in chief of the Confederacy, the other Southern troops would soon surrender. It was only a matter of waiting until word reached them and the last battles were fought. For Caleb the war was over.

When he was mustered out with the others who weren't career army, he was glad to ride away. He had been issued a horse that was of fairly good quality. If it hadn't been for its brand it wouldn't be unlike others he had owned before the war. Caleb decided to keep it on general principles. It had taken him safely through the last months of war and deserved retirement from the army.

He didn't ride north, however, but almost due west. He had made a promise to Megan and he intended to carry it out.

Corbin, Kentucky had been intended as a temporary prison, but since it had opened so late in the war, it was still in operation. He recognized the countryside and thought again how lucky he and Megan had been to get out of there alive. He made a detour through the clearing and past the cave, now invisible behind the thick leaves of the bushes. He still didn't know how they had escaped.

At the prison he tied his horse with the others and went in search of the commanding officer. The man was named Captain Rockwell and he didn't remember Caleb's name from the attempt to free Seth.

"I've come about a prisoner," Caleb said. "His name is Private Seth Brennan and I'm to escort him to Tennessee."

Rockwell had heard about Lee's surrender to Grant, and was obviously more interested in being mustered out himself to care if Caleb wanted every prisoner there. "Brennan. The name's not familiar. What does he look like?"

"He's not tall. I think he has dark hair." He described the man chosen to substitute for Seth since Megan had thought at first it was he.

"Half the prisoners here have dark hair and a lot of them are average height. Would you know him if you saw him?"

"No."

Rockwell called a sergeant over. "You've been here longer than I have. Is there a prisoner named Private Seth Brennan?"

The sergeant frowned as he tried to remember. "The name is familiar." He shook his head. "I can't recall. You're welcome to go into the yard and look for him."

Caleb followed the man into the stockade.

Early in May Patrick returned to Black Hollow. At first he looked like another of the ragged men whom Megan had grown accustomed to seeing. Then she recognized him. "Bridget!" she called. "Bridget, come quick!"

Bridget ran outside and gave a strangled cry. She jumped off the porch and ran into Patrick's arms. They stood there in the road holding each other and crying. Megan stayed back, giving them time to be alone.

Wiping her eyes, Bridget led him into the cabin. Megan had already ladled him a bowl of stew and had the biscuits left from breakfast ready for him. Patrick was thinner than she had ever seen him and it seemed strange for him to be in a uniform. His arms, formerly heavy with muscles from doing the settlement's blacksmithing, were smaller and his clothing hung on him.

"I'm so glad to see you!" Bridget said in a sob. "Patrick, I've missed you so much!"

He attacked the bowl of food as if he hadn't eaten in days. But he couldn't keep his eyes from Bridget. "I've missed you something awful."

"Have you been to the settlement?" Megan asked. "Do your parents know you're home?"

He nodded. "That's how I knew to come here. They said Bridget is living here now."

"You're welcome to stay here, too. It will be more private than living with either of your parents." Megan wondered if anyone had told him why Bridget was living with her.

His eyes met hers. "I hear there's been some excitement around here."

Megan sighed. He knew. "Whatever they told you, it wasn't that way."

"I'd like to hear it from you," he said.

"I found a wounded Yankee and nursed him back to health. My plan was to trade him for Seth. Seth is in the prison at Corbin, you know?" She waited until Patrick nodded. "I tried to make the trade, but we were set up. We were almost killed. Somehow between finding Caleb and him getting well, we fell in love."

She looked him squarely in the eye. "I love Caleb, not Seth, and I've told everyone that I don't intend to marry Seth when he comes home. I'm still being shunned and Bridget moved in with me to keep people from talking about me any more than they already are. Papa and I aren't speaking and probably never will."

"I see."

"I never met Caleb," Bridget said as she reached out to touch Patrick, as if she still couldn't believe he was here. "But he sounds like a nice person. Even if he was the enemy," she added quickly.

"So if you can't abide being my friend," Megan said, "I understand. The only people in the settlement who talk to me these days are Bridget and Mama. But if you want to live here, you're welcome."

Patrick looked at Bridget. He finally smiled. "I reckon we'll stay here, if there's room."

"There's plenty of room!" Bridget said with relief. "I was so afraid of us living with Mama and Papa. Not that they wouldn't welcome us, but there's so little privacy in the loft." She stopped abruptly and blushed.

Megan got another bowl of stew for Patrick. She was happy for Bridget, but seeing Patrick made her miss Caleb even more.

"Who is this Yankee?" he asked when he took the re-filled bowl.

"Caleb Morgan is his name. He's a captain. His home-town is Pollard's Crossing, Ohio. Do you know where that is?"

Patrick shook his head. "I never heard of it. But I never got as far north as Ohio."

"He says he's coming back for her," Bridget said. She laced her fingers with Patrick's free hand. "They're in love."

"What does Seth say about all this?"

"I couldn't bring myself to write him about it. Not with him in a Yankee prison. I'll have to tell him when I see him. Assuming someone from the settlement doesn't beat me to it. Mr. Brennan is really upset with me. They may have already written him."

"I'll help you tell him. Seth can have a pretty bad tem-per." Patrick smiled at Bridget even as he talked to Megan.

"Why are you being so kind about this?" Megan asked. "I don't understand."

"I know what it's like to love somebody. I wish he weren't a Yankee, but I reckon you do, too."

"You won't hate him because he's the enemy?"

"You know me better than that, Megan."

She smiled. "I've always held you in high regard, Pat-rick."

Bridget was smiling and blushing as if she were almost too excited to restrain herself.

Megan picked up a basket. "I'm going to leave the two of you alone. I'm going to gather poke salad for supper."

She left the cabin and went into the woods. She had no reason to gather greens but she knew Bridget and Patrick wanted to be alone. Although they had been married more than a year, they were still newlyweds in every way that counted. Patrick had left for the army when they had been married only a few days. And he had been gone for so long.

The woods were alive with spring. Megan saw a deer and fawn in the clearing where the wolves had treed her the winter before. It cheered her to see them and it helped erase her memory of that awful day when she had thought the wolves would get her if she didn't freeze first. She hoped never to pass a winter with such privation again. But at least she had had Caleb.

She had hoped he would have come for her by now. Perhaps, she told herself, he had been far away, even in another state. It would take time to travel so far. He might not even have a horse. Or he might be wounded again.

Megan went to the creek and sat on a flat rock by the water. She had come here often as a child. By leaning over she could see fish swimming lazily in the golden water and her own wavery reflection. She had called this her wishing rock because it seemed like a place fairies might come. "Send Caleb back to me," she whispered to the water. Immediately she felt foolish to have done such a childish thing.

Patrick's broad-mindedness had surprised her. He and Seth were friends and she had expected to have some opposition from him. The war had changed him and apparently had changed his attitudes as well. She wondered what he had been told about her in the settlement and if that had colored his reasons for accepting her. Or maybe it was because he knew she and Bridget were close friends as well as sisters. Megan was just grateful it had worked out this way.

She stayed in the woods most of the afternoon. When she returned with poke salad in her basket, she made plenty of noise as she came across the yard. Bridget was by the sink when she came in the door, and by the sparkle in her sister's eyes Megan knew she had stayed away long enough. "I found some greens. It's so nice to have fresh food for a change."

"I'm just glad to have food at all," Patrick said as he came into the room. He smiled at Bridget and winked. "I've missed being here."

"We've missed you, too," Megan said.

"I'll go down to the settlement after a while and get the rest of my things. I may as well get moved in."

"I'll walk down with you," Bridget said. "I don't want you out of my sight for a long time yet."

Megan poured water over the greens to clean them. "How was Seth captured, Patrick? Weren't you in the same regiment?"

"Yes, but he was at the wrong place at the wrong time. He wasn't wounded. At least not as far as I could tell. Somehow he got separated from the rest of us and the Yankees found him."

"How did that happen? Aren't you all supposed to stay together?"

"Yes." Patrick thought for a minute. "If you were still planning to marry him, I would never tell you this, and I'd appreciate it if you never let his parents know. Seth was trying to desert."

"He was?" Her hands stilled in her chore. "He was a deserter?"

"He couldn't abide the army. You know how he is about following orders. Seth always wants to do things his own way and that's not how an army is run. He and the captain were always at odds. One day he told me he was getting out and asked me to go with him. I refused. I didn't like being there, but I couldn't turn tail and run out on the others. I told him I wouldn't let on which way he went, but I couldn't go with him."

"Then you didn't see him captured? It didn't happen in battle?"

"No, he was picked up by a Yankee patrol. We got word of it through headquarters. I guess they send out the names of prisoners or something. Anyway, that's what happened."

"We assumed it was in battle," Bridget said. "I hope the Brennans never find out."

"They won't unless Seth tells them. He can't be proud of what he did."

"He wrote them to tell them he was in prison at Corbin but he never mentioned how he came to be there." Megan jabbed at the poke salad greens. "Isn't that just like him? He can be so exasperating!"

"I reckon that's one word for it."

"He never wrote me at all," Megan continued. "He sent a letter to his parents twice and didn't even include a note for me either time!"

"He's always been a trifle odd," Patrick said with a shake of his head. "I just hope he doesn't expect me to verify he was captured honorably in battle. I don't think I can bear to do it."

"And you shouldn't," Bridget said. "He did wrong and you don't have to lie for him!"

"I just wanted you to know, Megan. Since everyone is so upset over you not marrying him, I wanted you to see that I agree with you."

"You could be ostracized for staying under the same roof with me," Megan had to tell him. "I'm still being shunned."

"Papa wouldn't let you stay here alone," Bridget told her. "You know he wouldn't. If we don't live here, you'll have to go back home."

Megan looked at Patrick. "I'm afraid you've come home to a difficult situation. I'm sorry."

"I like this cabin and I'd be honored to share it with you." Patrick put his arm around Bridget and kissed her forehead. "This will work out just fine."

"Maybe by next year there will be a baby," Bridget said with another of her blushes. "We'll soon have to build on to it."

Megan nodded. She knew eventually the cabin would no longer be hers, but theirs. She would be the old-maid sister who lived with them. The idea wasn't pleasant but it was better than going back to her parents. "I'll start dinner."

That night she discovered the cabin wasn't as soundproof as she would have liked. Even with her head under her pillow, she could hear the sounds from the back room. Megan knew it was a good thing they were here and not at their parents' house, but she didn't want to hear them any more than her parents would have.

Finally the cabin was quiet and Megan cautiously uncovered her head. The darkness lay soft and silent in the room and she heard the quiet sounds of the cabin settling for the night. A low snore told her Patrick was finally asleep. She sat up in bed and hugged her knees to her chest. Was it going to be like this every night? Until now she hadn't given any thought to the way sounds carried from one room to another. And she couldn't tell Bridget. Her sister would be thoroughly embarrassed. Certainly Megan couldn't discuss it with Patrick.

She went to the window and looked out. She couldn't see anything but darkness and a scattering of stars. Caleb was somewhere out there, under the same stars, perhaps even looking up at them at that moment. Why hadn't he come for her?

Perhaps he wouldn't come back at all.

Megan lit the lamp and picked up her copy of *The Mysteries of Udolpho*. Opening it to the first page, she began to read.

Chapter Seventeen

Megan and Bridget had started piecing a quilt made of tiny hexagons no larger than an inch across. Both were veteran quilters and enjoyed sitting by the fire and piecing the top from old dresses and flour sacks.

"Do you think we'll get it quilted by summer?" Bridget asked. "It's taking longer than we expected."

"We're almost through with the top. We could ask Mama to come up and have a quilting bee."

"With just the three of us?"

Megan nodded. "I don't think any of the other women would come. Do you?"

"I suppose not."

Although Bridget never admitted it, Megan knew she missed the social aspects of the settlement. Since Bridget had come to live with her, some of the people there were shunning her as well. They had become more friendly since Patrick's return, but none of the women would have considered coming to a quilting bee at Megan's house or at Jane's if they knew Megan would be there. As much as Megan enjoyed privacy, she also liked company occasionally and she missed women's conversation.

"Addy Johnson is going to have a baby," Bridget said. "Mama told me so at church last Sunday. Matthew is proud as a peacock."

"I'm happy for them." Megan drew her thread through the fabric.

"Maybe we won't be far behind them," Patrick said.

Megan looked at Bridget, who was smiling and ducking her head. "You, too?"

"I think so. Don't tell Mama yet. I want to be positive first."

"I hope you're right. You'll be good parents." It was true. Patrick and Bridget both had more patience than anyone else Megan knew. "I wonder what it will be like to have children about," she said almost to herself.

"We don't know yet that there will be one. You know what Mama says about tempting fate. We shouldn't even talk about it until we know for certain."

"I've been thinking that we could add a loft above the kitchen," Patrick said thoughtfully. "I could build stairs on the wall by our room."

"I think we should just add a room off the service porch," Bridget put in. "Remember how hard it was to climb those steep stairs, Megan?"

"The ladder was worse."

"I remember! It was a pure wonder we didn't fall and break our legs. No, I'd rather have another room."

Megan didn't give her opinion. More and more the cabin was becoming Bridget and Patrick's. She supposed that was only natural since they were the married couple and the ones who would bring children to the place. Still, Megan missed the days when the cabin had been her sole property. "We'll have to sew baby gowns and bonnets."

"Now see, Patrick?" Bridget said. "I told you not to tell her until I was positive. It's the worst possible luck to make baby things before one is on the way."

"I'll wait until you tell me you're certain," Megan conceded. "But I hope you're right." She knew Bridget must be almost positive or she wouldn't have told even Patrick. Their mother had known a woman in Ireland who bragged about carrying a child before it was true and she had been sterile for the rest of her life. That story and others like it had been part of Megan and Bridget's earliest upbringing.

She tried not to think that more than enough time had passed for Caleb to return for her. Patrick had been home long enough to begin a baby.

"I could ask some of our friends to come up for a quilting bee," Bridget said to change the subject. "Maybe they're just waiting for an invitation."

"You can ask them if you like." She looked up at the ceiling. "Patrick, can you hang some hooks up there? I could borrow Mama's quilting frame."

"I'll build you a frame and hang the hooks."

Bridget smiled at him. "Thank you, Patrick."

He smiled back at her.

Megan felt more lonely than when she had lived there alone.

Eventually the thousands of tiny pieces were sewn together and Megan was proud of their efforts. The pattern was one called "Grandmother's Flower Garden" or as their mother referred to it, a honeycomb quilt. It made a bright splash of color in the cabin.

"Do you think it's too bright?" Bridget asked. "It didn't seem so brilliant when we were cutting out the pieces."

"I like bright colors."

"But Brother Grady says somber ones are best."

"Bother Brother Grady!"

Bridget looked shocked. "Megan! What would Mama say?"

Megan frowned. "Bridget, don't you ever want to think for yourself? I can't see a single thing wrong in making a brightly colored quilt or in wearing dresses that aren't dull and faded. This is a beautiful quilt and one we can be proud of."

"It really did turn out pretty, didn't it?"

"I'm sorry I say things that upset you, but sometimes I feel as if I'm smothering here. Now that I'm seldom in the settlement and never talk to the other women I'm starting to see everything in a different way. Take me, for instance. Do you think I'll be shunned for the rest of my life? Is that fair?"

"Well, as far as the settlement is concerned, Caleb was the enemy," Bridget said doubtfully,

"I love him. Why should I be punished forever because I fell in love with a man who isn't from Black Hollow?"

"You shouldn't have slept with him, Megan. That's the worst part of it, as near as I can tell."

"You slept with Patrick before you were married. You told me so yourself."

"But I know it was wrong."

"I'll bet a lot of girls in the settlement have done the same thing. Haven't you noticed it seldom takes nine months for the first babies to arrive? They can't all be born early!"

"I don't know anything about that and we shouldn't be talking about it."

Megan sighed. Most of her efforts to teach Bridget to think for herself had failed. "Well, at least the quilt top is finished." She watched Bridget turn away. "What's wrong?"

"I asked my friends and they can't come up for the quilting bee. Most of them said they were too busy with their own houses but a few told me their husbands won't let them."

"We don't need them. We'll quilt it ourselves." Megan tried to hide how much this information hurt her.

"I was hoping this would get everyone on speaking terms again."

"So was I," Megan admitted. "But it didn't so we aren't going to worry about it. There's one thing I do want you to do for me, though."

"Of course. I'll do anything you ask."

"Start mixing with our friends again. Go down to the settlement and visit them. Just because they won't come around me doesn't mean you should be ostracized, as well."

"Maybe I'll go visiting some now that the weather's warmer."

Megan knew Bridget was so loyal she would become a recluse if she thought that would make Megan's life easier. "You're a good sister, Bridget. I never lose sight of that."

Bridget hugged her. "Let's go see how Patrick is coming along with that quilting frame."

By the next day the frame was installed on the ceiling hooks. A pulley system raised the quilt up out of the way during the day and lowered it when it could be worked on. Patrick was as proud of his first addition to the house as if he had personally invented quilting frames.

On the appointed day Jane came to the cabin, carrying her basket of sewing threads and precious needles. To Megan's surprise, Samuel was with her.

Samuel and Patrick situated themselves on the porch to whittle and mend one of the straight-backed chairs. Samuel never spoke to Megan and looked straight through her as if she wasn't there. Megan did the same to him but it hurt her. She had never been his favorite and he had always been strict and stern, but she had always believed he loved her. Now he was making it clear that he didn't.

The women lowered the quilting frame and stretched the quilt top, batting and muslin backing over it.

"You sure made a bright one," Jane commented. "I hope we don't go blind working on it."

Megan laughed. "It's not that bad, Mama."

Jane smiled at her. "I can see you found a use for those yellow flour sacks nobody else wanted to buy. But where did you find the red?"

"That's the petticoat that I bought with egg money that year."

"I remember now. Your papa was scandalized. We couldn't even hang it out on the line to dry for all the comments from the neighbors."

Megan nodded. "I guess I've always been scandalous. Even when I don't intend to be."

Jane glanced at the men outside the window. "You should try to tone it down a little. Just for a while. I don't know if Samuel will ever find it in him to talk to you again. Maybe if you tried to act a bit more contrite it would help."

"But I'm not contrite, Mama. Not at all."

"That doesn't mean you can't appear to be." Jane gave her daughter a look of exasperation. "We all have to pretend at one time or another. That's the way folks get along together."

"I'll consider it." Megan didn't want to flatly refuse her mother's request, but she knew she would never forgive her father for trying to shoot Caleb in the back. To keep her resolve firm, she still had a vivid recollection of the beating Samuel had given her. She didn't even want him sitting on her porch.

Bridget brought chairs to the quilting frame. "Mama, I have some good news." She smiled at them both. "I was going to wait, but I just can't hold back any longer. Patrick and I are going to have a baby."

Jane's face lit up. "A baby! You're sure?"

"Yes." Bridget nodded, her blue eyes sparkling. "I'm sure enough to talk about it."

Megan smiled. She hadn't thought Bridget would be able to keep a secret of this magnitude.

"Now you know it's bad luck to say it's true if it's not. You recall what happened to the woman I knew in Ireland."

"I remember. We're really excited. Patrick is going to build a dogtrot room off the service porch. He says that's the easiest way to add to the house."

"There's no need to rush into that. It will sleep in your room for quite a while. And it won't hurt it to have a cot in here. You girls never had a room of your own and it didn't bother you a bit."

"It would have been nice if we had though," Megan said as she started quilting. "Owen could have had the loft to himself."

Jane darted a quick look at the window. "Hush! You know you're never to talk about him. What if your papa was to hear?"

"Don't you miss him? I know I do." Megan frowned at the cloth. "I miss him a great deal."

"So do I," Bridget agreed. She, too, looked at the window to be certain her father was still out of hearing range.

Jane shut her lips firmly. "I was told never to talk about him and I'm not going to. Obedience is the foundation of a good marriage. You girls would do well to remember that."

"I think love makes a better foundation," Megan said.

"I'm so happy Patrick is home," Bridget said to draw them to a safer subject. "At times I thought that awful war would go on forever!"

"It seemed as if it did." Jane was more than willing to talk about something less forbidden.

Megan jabbed her needle in the fabric and stabbed her finger beneath. She was tired of talking only about safe subjects and of seeing Bridget and their mother constantly striving not to mention anything that could be considered wrong by Samuel or Brother Grady.

The conversation drifted to news about the people in the settlement—who was having a baby and who was sick and who was planning to marry. Birth, marriage, death. The constant triangle. Megan stirred up the next waves by saying, "I'm thinking about writing a book."

Both the other women stopped sewing and stared at her. Jane found her voice first. "You'll do no such a thing!"

"I like to make up stories in my head, and I could draw pictures to illustrate it. It will be a children's book. About a rabbit," she added.

"You can't be serious!" Bridget's mouth dropped open. "Write a book?"

"You don't have the least idea how to go about such a thing! No woman in the settlement would even consider it."

"Well, I'm already ostracized. How much more could they do to me? I might as well do as I please." Megan had known they wouldn't encourage her to write a book, but she had thought they would be more understanding than this.

"They could do quite a bit more! You're still living here, aren't you?" Jane was visibly upset. "No one has driven you away. If you have to write something, write a religious pamphlet. Not a book!"

"No one will allow you to do it," Bridget said with conviction. "Megan, why do you have to be so controversial?"

"I don't consider writing to be controversial. A lot of women outside Black Hollow write."

"Name one!" Bridget challenged.

Megan frowned at her. "Mrs. Radcliffe, for instance. *The Mysteries of Udolpho* is my favorite book. And there's Jane Austen."

"I never heard of either person," Jane said firmly. "Forget about it."

Megan knew at that minute she was going to write her book and somehow find a way to get it published. "Maybe when I get older I'll be considered eccentric," she said in an attempt to cheer them.

"You aren't older and you should behave yourself."

Megan gazed out the window, trying to fight down her rebellion. Her mother came to visit so seldom and she didn't want to argue. It was only that she felt as if she were caged in a box lately. She had been encouraged to think when

Caleb was there and she found it impossible to revert to mindless obedience.

She was looking out the window when a buggy drove into view.

For someone to pass the cabin was no longer unusual. Men frequently rode past on horseback or in farm wagons. Since the army had extended the road to the town down the mountain, travelers often used it. Not many buggies frequented the area, however, and this one was richly appointed. There was something about the man driving the buggy that was familiar.

Slowly she started to stand. She knew the way he held his head, the carriage of his shoulders. He was too far away for her to see his features and he wore clothes she had never seen before, but she knew him.

Without a word of explanation, she ran from the room, across the porch and down the steps. He let the horse glide into a fast trot and met her where the road bordered the yard. Caleb jumped from the buggy and embraced her.

Megan held to him tightly, breathing in the essence of him and molding her body to his. "Caleb! You came back!"

"Did you ever doubt it?" He released her enough to tilt her head up to his. For a moment they looked into each other's eyes, then he kissed her.

She felt as if her world had spun into fantasy. Was he really here? Holding her and kissing her right on the open road? With her family staring on in shock?

She ran her hands over his back and arms. "You're all right? You haven't been wounded again?"

"No. I'm perfectly well."

She struck at his arm, then embraced him again. "Then why did it take so long for you to come back to me? Do you have any idea how I've worried about you? I pictured you dead or shot to pieces or sick!"

"You didn't get my letters?"

"Of course I didn't. Would I have worried about you if I had?" She looked up at him. "You wrote me letters?"

"Reams of them." He looked past her to the cabin. "Does your papa have his rifle with him?"

She laughed. "Not today." She kept her arm about him. "Come on. You should meet my family. They've heard enough about you."

They walked across the yard, his horse leading behind him. Megan discovered she was crying and brushed at the tears as more took their place. "Mama, this is Caleb Morgan. My Yankee," she added as a way of definitely identifying him.

Caleb took Jane's hand and held it briefly. "Ma'am. I'm pleased to meet you." He looked at the woman beside her. "And you would be Bridget. I would have recognized you anywhere."

"I'm Patrick Cassidy," the young man said. "Megan talks about you often. This is Samuel Llewellyn."

Caleb gave Samuel an unflinching look. "We've already met." He didn't offer Samuel his hand, nor did Samuel look as if he would have touched it.

"What are you doing here?" Samuel demanded. "I told you if you came back, I'd shoot you."

"I came back for Megan." Caleb looked at her. "I promised her I would."

Megan smiled up at him and hugged him closer.

"There's something I have to tell you," Caleb said to the others. "I'm afraid it's not good news. Seth won't be coming back."

"What do you mean?" Patrick seemed to be reluctant to be too friendly toward Caleb. Not long before they would have been expected to shoot each other.

"I went to the prison at Corbin as soon as I was mustered out," Caleb said to Megan. "I promised you I'd bring Seth home and I hadn't forgotten. He's dead, Megan."

"Dead?" she exclaimed. "Seth died?"

"There was an outbreak of measles. Prisons are a breeding ground for diseases of all sorts. Seth and quite a few others died, along with some of the guards. He was dead before we ever went to Corbin. They couldn't have produced him if they had wanted to."

"Seth is dead," Megan repeated. "When did it happen?"

He handed her some papers. "These are the records. It wasn't easy finding them. The commander who was at Corbin when Seth was there has been transferred and the new one doesn't believe in keeping records on prisoners." He gave her time to read the date. "It was about the time his letter arrived in the settlement, as near as I can tell. Remember? The time you became so uneasy?"

Megan nodded. "I remember! I went to everyone I knew well in the settlement to see if they were healthy. It was Seth!"

"Seth died in prison," Patrick said in a stunned voice. "I never considered that would happen." He put his arm around Bridget, who was crying quietly.

Jane lifted her chin stoically. "I'll break the news to Sarah Ann and Aaron. They'll take it best from me."

Samuel muttered a swear word and spit. He continued to glare at Caleb. "You've said what you came to say. Now leave!"

"I'm going with you," Megan said quickly. "I'm not going to be away from you again."

He smiled down at her. "All the way down to Tennessee I was hoping you'd say that. Otherwise I would have had to stay here."

Megan smiled up at him. "It won't take me long to get my things."

"Wait. I have more news. I also found Owen."

Jane took a step forward and was stopped by Samuel's frown.

"Where is he?" Megan asked as much for her mother and sister as for herself.

"He's in Cat Springs, Ohio, just as you guessed. He's well and sends his love. We'll pass through there and you can see him for yourself."

"Tell him we send our love back to him," Jane said, ignoring her husband. "Tell him to write to me." She met Samuel's frown with one of her own. "It's been too long since I heard from my son."

"If a letter from Owen or Megan comes, I'll burn it before you ever lay eyes on it." Samuel stood and started walking away. His anger showed in the set of his shoulders and his stiff strides.

"He'll be all right," Jane said in a tired voice. "He's been mad at me before." To Caleb she said, "You're sure our Owen is well? Is he happy?"

"He looked happy to me. He said to tell you he's courting a girl and that he's going to ask her to marry him. I believe he said her name is Eliza."

"Eliza," Jane repeated and smiled. "It's a good name. I'll try to write to him. His papa won't like it, but I'll try."

Megan hurried up the steps and into the cabin. The others might think Samuel was simply leaving in anger, but she wasn't so sure he hadn't gone after the other men in the settlement to drive Caleb away.

She grabbed a tow sack and started tossing her things in. There weren't many. At the last minute she took the quilt off her bed. It was one her mother had pieced for her and it had special memories. She ran back to the door, then paused to look at the interior of the cabin once more. At one time she had expected to spend the rest of her life here. Now she would probably never see it again. Megan closed the door behind her.

Caleb smiled when she stepped out onto the porch. He and Patrick had been exchanging awkward conversation. Bridget had started smiling again.

Megan handed her things to Caleb to put in the buggy and turned to hug her family goodbye.

"He's a right nice man," Jane said. Her blue eyes were moist with tears she was trying to fight back. "I reckon he will take real good care of you."

"I like him, too," Bridget whispered. "I can see why you love him."

Megan hugged them each close, breathing in their aroma of homemade soap and starch for the last time. "I'll miss you both more than words can say."

"I know. I'll write to you." Bridget glanced at Caleb as if to see if he would object. He smiled at her.

Jane nodded. "I'll understand if you don't write us, Megan. Your papa isn't a forgiving man. We likely won't be able to answer. You know how hard it is for me to get to town without him along, too. And I never know if letters from the post office in Raintree ever get where they're supposed to be going."

Megan knew what she meant. Letters rarely came from Jane's family. She and Bridget had speculated from time to time as to whether or not their father was destroying them. Samuel didn't like to think there was a world beyond Black Hollow and he didn't want his family to have ties with outsiders. "I'll write. Whether you get them or not, I'll send letters to you often. I know how Papa is. If I don't hear from you, I'll understand."

As she was going down the steps, she saw Samuel and several of the men from the settlement approaching. She moved to Caleb and took his hand. All the men had rifles.

"Leave," Jane said urgently. "Leave now!"

Caleb handed Megan into the buggy, then climbed in himself. His movements weren't hurried.

"I'll miss you!" Bridget called to her. "Write to us!"

Patrick watched the men as if he were wondering how to handle what could turn into a lynching in his front yard. "We'll think about you, Megan," he said. "Be going, now."

Samuel went up the steps to Jane and took her none too gently by the arm. "Get home! You've been gone long enough."

Jane tried to pull away. "I'm telling our Megan goodbye."

"Your Megan is dead!" Samuel pointed the gun at Megan. When Jane continued to struggle, his attention was drawn to her.

Megan put her hand on Caleb's leg for reassurance. She wasn't at all certain what her father was going to do. "Drive away, Caleb," she whispered. "Hurry!"

Caleb reached beneath the buggy seat and brought out a rifle and pointed it at the older man. "Samuel, you ran me away once and it's not going to happen again. Nobody but a coward would hurt a woman. Not that I think you're above it, but it's not going to happen in my presence. Turn her loose."

For a long moment Megan held her breath. Then Samuel shoved Jane at Bridget and lifted the rifle to shoot Caleb. Patrick jumped at him and yanked the gun away.

"No one is getting shot in my yard!" Patrick said angrily. "If you were so eager to shoot Yankees, why didn't you join up with Seth and me?"

Bridget stared at him with her mouth open. For a son-in-law to talk back to his wife's father was unheard of in the settlement. Patrick didn't back down. He glared at the other men. "That goes for you, too. Pa, if you shoot either one of them, I'm taking Bridget and following them straight to Ohio and you'll never see me again!"

Cassidy glanced at his cronies and lowered his rifle. They did the same.

Caleb smiled at Patrick. "Thank you." He tipped his hat to the ladies and reined the horse around. As if they were out for a leisurely Sunday drive, he drove up the road at a trot.

Megan still gripped his leg. She expected at any moment to hear a gunshot. There were arguing voices behind for a while but they gradually faded in the distance.

"You can stop cutting off the circulation in my leg now," Caleb said with a laugh. "We're out of range."

She loosened her grip. "I'm sorry."

He laughed and put his arm around her. "I think it went rather well. Don't you?"

For a moment Megan only stared at him. Then she started to laugh.

They drove to the town past Raintree where they could board the train. Megan felt underdressed in her plain housedress. When she had put it on that morning, she had never dreamed she would leave home in it. She drew her lightweight shawl around her to hide its plainness.

Caleb drove them to a boardinghouse not far from the railroad station. Megan watched him pay for their room and didn't object when he introduced them as husband and wife. It was enough to simply look at him again.

A boy took their belongings up to the room, Megan and Caleb following close behind. When they were alone, Caleb took her in his arms. "I've missed you like life itself."

She held him close. "I'll never be apart from you again."

They kissed and Caleb gazed down into her eyes. "Did you mean what you said the day I left? That you love me?"

"Of course I did. How can you even ask?" She smiled. "You said you love me, too. I wish I had known that sooner."

"You knew it. You must have."

"I'm not a mind reader, Caleb. You never said it."

"I thought you didn't want me to. I've loved you almost since the beginning."

"We wasted so much time! We could have lost each other forever. If Papa hadn't chased you away that day, I might never have said it aloud. I was waiting to see how you felt."

"I wouldn't have left without telling you. That's why I followed you into the yard. I was about to say I loved you when he stepped out of the woods."

"Caleb," she whispered, "I was so afraid you'd never come back. That you were wounded again or killed. Or that you decided you didn't love me once you were away from me."

"No, Megan. Time only made me love you more."

"I had already told everyone I wouldn't marry Seth. That's one reason I was being shunned. Of course my living with you had already earned me that honor." She looked up at him and traced the line of his lips with her fingers. "What will your parents say about me?"

"I've written them about you. I also told them that if you didn't come with me, I would stay in Black Hollow until you changed your mind."

"You know you'd never be welcomed there. What were you thinking of?"

"I was counting on that. I was pretty sure you'd come to Pollard's Crossing if it would keep me from being shot. I just didn't expect it to happen within minutes of my arrival."

"I had already told Bridget and Patrick that I would be leaving with you when you came for me. They understood. I think Mama does, too. I never fit in the settlement. Not really."

"There's one other thing we have to do."

"What's that?" She felt as light as a thistle in his arms. She would have agreed to anything.

"I want you to marry me."

"I love you, Caleb. I fully intend to marry you."

"Put on your prettiest dress. I'll go arrange for a preacher." He paused at the door. "Oh, there's one other thing. Something you don't know. I'm rich."

She stared at him. "Rich? How rich?"

He grinned. "You'll never have to mend clothes again." He closed the door behind him.

For a moment Megan stood there digesting what he had said. Never once in all the months she had known him had she considered he might not be as poor as all the other people she knew. Rich? She wasn't even positive what that meant.

With a smile she started changing into her Sunday best dress. He had probably been exaggerating.

They were married within the hour in a chapel not far from the boardinghouse. The ceremony was different from all the ones Megan had seen in the settlement. This preacher smiled often and didn't sermonize about hell a single time. When he pronounced them husband and wife, Caleb kissed her. She blushed to be doing this in church, but she kissed him back.

Whatever the future might bring, rich or poor, whether his family liked her or not, she knew she could face it with him. Hand in hand, they left the church.

Epilogue

"Felicity, will you hand me that piece of black velvet?" In the ten years since Megan had come to Pollard's Crossing, she and her sister-in-law had grown very close.

"This is going to be a beautiful quilt. I can't wait to see Mama's face on Christmas morning." Felicity leaned close to the mix of velvets and satins to place her careful stitches in the crazy quilt.

Megan smiled. "We've worked hard on it, haven't we?" She paused in her stitching. "I remember I was working on a quilt the day Caleb came back for me." She laughed and shook her head. "I wonder if Bridget and Mama ever finished quilting it. I'll bet they never used it if they did. It was bright enough to light up a room!"

"I love bright colors," the little girl in the small rocker said. "I'm going to make my baby doll a quilt and it's going to be as bright as I can make it."

Megan smiled at her daughter. "I'll help you, Katie. You decide what pattern you want it to be." At three years, Katie was almost old enough to learn to sew and this would be a good way for her to start.

Her older sister, Amelia, was eight years old and already accomplished at sewing. She gave the younger girl a smile that was a replica of Megan's. "I'll help you, too. But you're not to get angry if your thread snarls."

Katie gave her a superior smile. "Mine won't."

Megan and Felicity exchanged an amused glance. Katie wasn't known for her patience.

Felicity said, "Have you seen Abigail lately?"

Katie nodded her curly head. "Papa is reading to her in the library. She wanted to hear Mama's new book." She stopped rocking and said, "I think I'll go hear it again, too." She trotted from the room, her footsteps muffled by the Oriental rug.

"She's growing so fast," Megan said. "So is your Abigail. She may be a year younger, but she's almost as tall as Katie. They're as close as sisters."

"Better," Amelia said in her most adult voice. "They never disagree."

Felicity laughed. "That's because Abigail never crosses her. You wouldn't argue with her either if you let her have her way all the time."

Amelia wrinkled her nose. She and Katie seldom had a real argument but Amelia was fond of bossing her younger sister about.

"My William and your Thomas have big plans. They want to ride their ponies to the bandstand when we go down to hear the music tomorrow." Felicity tied a knot in her thread and cut it free.

"All the way to the bandstand? I'm not sure they're old enough for that." Megan frowned slightly as she considered. "That's several blocks away. They're only five."

"Caleb and Will have discussed it. They will send us in the buggy and walk with the boys. That way William and Thomas will feel they're on their own without being in any danger."

"It's so handy for us to live next door." Megan put the black velvet in place and trimmed a corner to make the design prettier. "Will is a nice man. I know Caleb considers him to be a brother."

"I like Owen and Eliza, too. It's a pity they don't have children yet."

"They're still young." Megan put her needle into the cloth. Owen and his wife had moved to Pollard's Crossing the year before. Megan loved seeing him so often, but she, too, was concerned that they might never have a baby. She looked over at her youngest, Priscilla, in her crib. The baby was sleeping and sucking her thumb. "I've been so lucky."

"Caleb is a wonderful person. I'd like him even if he weren't my brother."

"I remember how frightened I was to meet all of you. I was so afraid you'd all hate me."

"Nonsense. Caleb loved you so we knew we would love you, too. And we were right. Mama and Papa think of you as a daughter. You know they do."

Megan nodded. "You can't imagine how amazed I was when I saw where you lived. I had never seen such a big house in my life. I thought several families must live in it at first, like a boardinghouse. Up until then, I had never known anyone who didn't live in a log cabin or a dogtrot house."

"I remember. You kept looking around and saying 'yes, ma'am' to the servants."

"They intimidated me. Especially Jarvis. I had never seen a butler in my life and never dreamed they existed outside of books." She looked around the room with its jade wallpaper and gold curtains and beautiful furniture and paintings. "Then Caleb brought me here to show me his own house. He even said that if I didn't like it, we could buy a different one." Her voice was soft with the recollection. "I thought it was like a palace."

"I guess it would be, compared to a log cabin." Felicity tried to understand, but she had grown up in her parents' elegant house and had been around servants since her birth.

"You can't possibly realize the difference. When Caleb told me about the white picket fences and clipped lawns and ladies who sat on their verandas and sipped lemonade in the summer, I thought he was telling me a story. Now I have a house like that and I sit on my veranda and I, too, have lemonade.''

"And it wasn't easy for you to learn to sit there, was it?" Caleb said from the doorway.

"I thought you were reading to the girls," Megan said. After ten years and five children, her heart still raced when she saw him unexpectedly.

"They ran out of patience." He sat beside her. "Remember how you used to be determined to help Maggie clean the house?"

Megan laughed. "She finally threatened to quit if I didn't leave everything alone."

"She meant it, too. Maggie had the house running just the way she wanted it and she had her own status to think of. She couldn't ever admit that her mistress was as good at scrubbing floors as she herself was."

Felicity laughed. "I remember, Megan. You used to fidget on the porch swing because you knew the wash was being done and you weren't helping."

Caleb reached out and rubbed the back of Megan's neck. "It was fun teaching you to relax and enjoy life."

Megan gave him a smile that promised more as soon as the children were in bed for the night. "Felicity was just telling me the boys are riding their ponies to the bandstand tomorrow."

"Will and I are going to walk with them. Mama and Papa have decided to go, too, so you can all ride in one carriage this way."

"Mama Abby is feeling well enough to go out? I'm glad. I've been so worried about her lately."

"So has Papa," Felicity admitted. "He told me privately that he was afraid the doctor was mistaken and that there is something really wrong with her."

Megan didn't tell either that she had again had the eerie sensation of knowing death was near someone she knew. She had been afraid it was her mother-in-law, but the feeling had gone away several days ago and hadn't returned. "I think I'll go over there before dinner and take her some of those orange cookies. She loves them and it will give me a chance to invite them to ride with us."

"She would like that." Caleb looked up as their butler came into the room and waited to be noticed. "Yes, Franklin?"

"A letter has come, sir. For Mrs. Morgan."

Megan held out her hand. "Thank you, Franklin." Even after all these years the butler was able to intimidate her slightly. She took the letter and looked at it. "I think it's from Bridget!" Her eyes met Caleb's and her hand shook as she opened it.

Quickly she read Bridget's cramped hand. It was one of the few she had received since she left Black Hollow. There had been no letters at all in the past five years, though she still wrote regularly. "It's Papa," she said. "He passed away."

Felicity dropped her sewing and came to sit closer in commiseration. "I'm so sorry! What was wrong? Does it say?"

"Bridget thinks it was his heart. She says his color wasn't good for quite a while and that he had been having chest pains off and on." She looked at Caleb. Even though Samuel had threatened to shoot him every time he had seen Caleb, her husband had never spoken against him. "Bridget says Mama is taking it pretty well. But she's asking for me."

Caleb waited for her to make the decision.

"I have to go to her."

"Of course you do," Felicity said. "Caleb understands. Don't you, Caleb?"

"I expected you to say that. I would have suggested it if you hadn't."

"It's such a long trip!" Megan looked at the baby again. She had never allowed a nanny to be established in the house. She insisted on raising her own children. They had never been away from her.

"I'm going with you. We can leave as early as tomorrow."

She took his hand. "Thank you, Caleb. I knew you'd say that. But the children!"

"I'll be glad to keep them. It would be a pleasure to me," Felicity said. "They'll be next door and can run back and forth. It won't be so strange for them, that way."

"Or we could take them with us," Caleb suggested. "Personally, I think that would be best."

"We could take them to Black Hollow? We could do that?" Megan stared at him.

"Of course we could. The train goes almost to Raintree and we can hire a carriage from there. I'm not sure a mere buggy would accommodate us now that there are so many of us." He kissed her hand. "You always wonder what Bridget's children are like and your family must feel the same about ours."

"We could stay in a real log cabin?" Amelia asked in excitement.

Megan had almost forgotten the girl was in the room. "Yes. That's all there is to sleep in there."

"A whole town of log cabins?" Her eyes, so like Caleb's, were wide.

"They need to meet the rest of their family," Caleb said. "This could be the best time to do that."

She nodded. She knew what he meant. The journey was so long and the reception in the Hollow so uncertain, they might never go there again. "I believe you're right. We can't go tomorrow, though. There are clothes to wash and iron if we're to pack properly. The funeral is long past, of course. There's no real rush. And I have to put together our mourning clothes."

"I have a black dress you can wear," Felicity offered. "We'll need to shorten it and take it up a bit in the waist, but that won't take long. As young as the children are, I think black armbands such as Caleb will wear are perfectly acceptable."

Because she was almost afraid to think what their reception might be, Megan found herself worrying over details. "Bridget does say Mama asked for me to come. But what about my cousins and the others in the settlement? They could make the visit very uncomfortable, especially for our children."

"Why is that, Mama?"

Megan didn't know how to answer her.

Caleb thought for a minute. "Amelia, run over to Uncle Owen's house and tell him about the letter. Ask him if he can take time off work to go with us."

"Owen, too?" Megan stared at Caleb. "You really must have been good at military strategies!"

"It's time to bury hatchets."

Amelia skipped from the room, excited over the prospect of a trip. By the time she reached the front door, she was singing.

"Amelia doesn't understand mourning," Felicity said. "We haven't had a death in the family since they've been born. She never meant to be frivolous at a time like this."

"I know." Megan went to the window and watched her eldest daughter cross the sleepy street. "I was remembering Papa. He was so many contradictions, in a way. He loved all his children, but he was able to turn his back on two of us for the rest of his life. I could never do that to my children." She felt a tear rise in her eye and she brushed it away.

Caleb came to stand behind her and put his arms around her. "You don't have to go if you don't want to."

"No. This is something I want to do. Like you said, my family has never seen our children. All my life Mama said she wanted to live to see her grandchildren. I was thinking how fleeting life can be. This could be the only opportunity they'll have to meet. And Mama and Bridget will be glad to see Owen, too, I think, and to meet his wife."

The baby woke and made a whimpering sound. Megan went to her and picked her up. "The children will win my cousins over if there's still hard feelings. Who wouldn't love this one?" She rubbed her nose against the baby's and little Priscilla cooed happily and patted at her mother's cheeks.

Megan smiled at Caleb. "I'll be ready to go by day after tomorrow."

"I'll be looking forward to seeing our cabin again." He grinned at her.

Megan glanced at Felicity. This was as close as they ever came to admitting they shared more than a roof in that cabin. But the memories came over her and she smiled. "So will I."

* * * * *

Weddings by DeWilde

Since the turn of the century the elegant and fashionable DeWilde stores have helped brides around the world turn the fantasy of their "Special Day" into reality. But now the store and three generations of family are torn apart by the divorce of Grace and Jeffrey DeWilde. As family members face new challenges and loves—and a long-secret mystery—the lives of Grace and Jeffrey intermingle with store employees, friends and relatives in this fast-paced, glamorous, internationally set series. For weddings and romance, glamour and fun-filled entertainment, enter the world of DeWilde...

Twelve remarkable books, coming to you once a month, beginning in April 1996

Weddings by DeWilde begins with
Shattered Vows
by Jasmine Cresswell

Here's a preview!

"SPEND THE NIGHT with me, Lianne."

No softening lies, no beguiling promises, just the curt offer of a night of sex. She closed her eyes, shutting out temptation. She had never expected to feel this sort of relentless drive for sexual fulfillment, so she had no mechanisms in place for coping with it. "No." The one-word denial was all she could manage to articulate.

His grip on her arms tightened as if he might refuse to accept her answer. Shockingly, she wished for a split second that he would ignore her rejection and simply bundle her into the car and drive her straight to his flat, refusing to take no for an answer. All the pleasures of mindless sex, with none of the responsibility. For a couple of seconds he neither moved nor spoke. Then he released her, turning abruptly to open the door on the passenger side of his Jaguar. "I'll drive you home," he said, his voice hard and flat. "Get in."

The traffic was heavy, and the rain started again as an annoying drizzle that distorted depth perception made driving difficult, but Lianne didn't fool herself that the silence inside the car was caused by the driving conditions. The air around them crackled and sparked with their thwarted desire. Her body was still on fire. Why didn't Gabe say something? she thought, feeling aggrieved.

Perhaps because he was finding it as difficult as she was to think of something appropriate to say. He was thirty years old, long past the stage of needing to bed a woman just so he could record another sexual conquest in his little black book. He'd spent five months dating Julia, which suggested he was a man who valued friendship as an element in his relationships with women. Since he didn't seem to like her very much, he was probably as embarrassed as she was by the stupid, inexplicable intensity of their physical response to each other.

"Maybe we should just set aside a weekend to have wild, uninterrupted sex," she said, thinking aloud. "Maybe that way we'd get whatever it is we feel for each other out of our systems and be able to move on with the rest of our lives."

His mouth quirked into a rueful smile. "Isn't that supposed to be my line?"

"Why? Because you're the man? Are you sexist enough to believe that women don't have sexual urges? I'm just as aware of what's going on between us as you are, Gabe. Am I supposed to pretend I haven't noticed that we practically ignite whenever we touch? And that we have nothing much in common except mutual lust—and a good friend we betrayed?"

HARLEQUIN®

Don't miss these Harlequin favorites by some of our most
distinguished authors!
And now, you can receive a discount by ordering two or more titles!

HT #25645	THREE GROOMS AND A WIFE by JoAnn Ross	$3.25 U.S./$3.75 CAN. ☐
HT #25648	JESSIE'S LAWMAN by Kristine Rolofson	$3.25 U.S./$3.75 CAN. ☐
HP #11725	THE WRONG KIND OF WIFE by Roberta Leigh	$3.25 U.S./$3.75 CAN. ☐
HP #11755	TIGER EYES by Robyn Donald	$3.25 U.S./$3.75 CAN. ☐
HR #03362	THE BABY BUSINESS by Rebecca Winters	$2.99 U.S./$3.50 CAN. ☐
HR #03375	THE BABY CAPER by Emma Goldrick	$2.99 U.S./$3.50 CAN. ☐
HS #70638	THE SECRET YEARS by Margot Dalton	$3.75 U.S./$4.25 CAN. ☐
HS #70655	PEACEKEEPER by Marisa Carroll	$3.75 U.S./$4.25 CAN. ☐
HI #22280	MIDNIGHT RIDER by Laura Pender	$2.99 U.S./$3.50 CAN. ☐
HI #22235	BEAUTY VS THE BEAST by M.J. Rogers	$3.50 U.S./$3.99 CAN. ☐
HAR #16531	TEDDY BEAR HEIR by Elda Minger	$3.50 U.S./$3.99 CAN. ☐
HAR #16596	COUNTERFEIT HUSBAND by Linda Randall Wisdom	$3.50 U.S./$3.99 CAN. ☐
HH #28795	PIECES OF SKY by Marianne Willman	$3.99 U.S./$4.50 CAN. ☐
HH #28855	SWEET SURRENDER by Julie Tetel	$4.50 U.S./$4.99 CAN. ☐

(limited quantities available on certain titles)

	AMOUNT	$
DEDUCT:	10% DISCOUNT FOR 2+ BOOKS	$
ADD:	POSTAGE & HANDLING	$
	($1.00 for one book, 50¢ for each additional)	
	APPLICABLE TAXES**	$_____
	TOTAL PAYABLE	$_____
	(check or money order—please do not send cash)	

To order, complete this form and send it, along with a check or money order for the
total above, payable to Harlequin Books, to: **In the U.S.:** 3010 Walden Avenue,
P.O. Box 9047, Buffalo, NY 14269-9047; **In Canada:** P.O. Box 613, Fort Erie, Ontario,
L2A 5X3.

Name: _____

Address: _____ City: _____

State/Prov.: _____ Zip/Postal Code: _____

**New York residents remit applicable sales taxes.
Canadian residents remit applicable GST and provincial taxes.

HBACK-AJ3

This May, keep an eye out for
something heavenly from

SPARHAWK'S Angel

by Miranda Jarrett

"Delightful...5★s"
—*Affaire de Coeur*

Available wherever Harlequin books are sold.

BIGB96-3

BRIDE'S BAY RESORT

UNLOCK THE DOOR TO GREAT ROMANCE AT BRIDE'S BAY RESORT

Join Harlequin's new across-the-lines series, set in an exclusive hotel on an island off the coast of South Carolina.

Seven of your favorite authors will bring you exciting stories about fascinating heroes and heroines discovering love at Bride's Bay Resort.

Look for these fabulous stories coming to a store near you beginning in January 1996.

Harlequin American Romance #613 in January
Matchmaking Baby by Cathy Gillen Thacker

Harlequin Presents #1794 in February
Indiscretions by Robyn Donald

Harlequin Intrigue #362 in March
Love and Lies by Dawn Stewardson

Harlequin Romance #3404 in April
Make Believe Engagement by Day Leclaire

Harlequin Temptation #588 in May
Stranger in the Night by Roseanne Williams

Harlequin Superromance #695 in June
Married to a Stranger by Connie Bennett

Harlequin Historicals #324 in July
Dulcie's Gift by Ruth Langan

Visit Bride's Bay Resort each month wherever Harlequin books are sold.

HARLEQUIN ®

BBAYG

Bestselling authors

ELAINE COFFMAN
RUTH LANGAN

and

MARY McBRIDE

Together in one fabulous collection!

OUTLAW Brides

Available in June wherever Harlequin
books are sold.

HARLEQUIN ®

LET BESTSELLING AUTHOR

ERICA SPINDLER

TEMPT YOU WITH

FORBIDDEN FRUIT

Beautiful and headstrong, Glory St. Germaine was born into one of New Orleans's finest families. But good *and* evil run through three generations of Glory's family. Her mother, Hope, and grandmother, Lily, are trapped by shame, secrets and circumstances. And Victor Santos, in love with Glory, is trapped by his own past. Can Victor and Glory find a way to put the past behind them? Or will their love remain forbidden fruit?

Available this April at your favorite retail outlet.

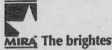

MIRA The brightest star in women's fiction   MESFF